The HAMLET EXPERIMENT

DAVID SHIFRIN

Comfort PUBLISHING

The Hamlet Experiment

For information, address Comfort Publishing, PO Box 6265, Concord, NC 28027. The views expressed in this book are not necessarily those of the publisher.

This book is a work of fiction. Any resemblence to anyone living or dead is purely coincidental.

First printing

Book cover design
by Colin L. Kernes

ISBN: 9781935361503
Published by Comfort Publishing, LLC
www.comfortpublishing.com
Printed in the United States of America

PROLOGUE

A frigid nor'easter wind whipped and snapped two oversized flags standing guard before the majestic Boston courthouse. One of the flags bore the stars and stripes, the other the blue and gold crest of the Commonwealth of Massachusetts.

Behind them stood the granite sentinel of justice, its sloping semicircular facade and soaring white pillars supporting the overcast vault of a January sky. In spite of the cold, the courtyard and expansive marble steps teemed with would-be spectators, clamoring for admittance to the crowded courtroom.

Inside the building ,full fledged bedlam prevailed because of the first case on the morning docket: "Commonwealth v Sanderson."

Dr. Nancy Sanderson's alleged crime had been sensationalized in glaring headlines for the past six months, and now that the trial was about to begin, reporters, ethicists, columnists, and bloggers from much of the civilized world waited impatiently for the sordid details to emerge.

Franklin Burke, Boston's District Attorney, was ready and anxious to make his opening statement. Known for his family money and grandiose political ambitions, Burke had come fully equipped to take advantage of this trial's national exposure. Photographers clicked away frenetically as he arrived in a chauffeur driven Lincoln Town Car, emerging with a mid winter tan and celebrity smile. His courtroom entrance was equally well scripted: perfectly tailored Hugo Boss suit, elegant necktie with matching pocket square, and entourage of assistant DA's following like a flock of solicitous ducklings.The presiding judge banged his gavel, indicating that the trial had finally begun. As Burke approached the jury box he adjusted his snow-white shirt cuffs and clasped his manicured fingers.

"Ladies and gentlemen of the jury," he began in Bostonian diction, "surely you have heard about this case, and as you know, pre-trial publicity can prejudice a potential juror, but you were chosen because you swore that you would be able to maintain objectivity despite the damning evidence you may have read in the papers or seen on television. On the other hand, you are obligated to equally consider both sides here, so if the evidence shows beyond a reasonable doubt that this suspect did commit this crime, you are compelled to find her guilty as charged. And I'm going to tell you right now," he said, his voice rising, "that this woman is guilty of murder. I'm not talking about any kind of accidental result of what she did, or what might have been, or some kind of trumped up manslaughter defense. I want you to carefully the information as it is presented to you, without regard to the fact that the accused is a doctor, or a brilliant researcher, or that she is young and attractive, or anything else that might muddy your decision. Because I'll say it again, there is no doubt that this doctor is guilty. Guilty of murder! And it is my job as a representative of the people of Massachusetts to convince you of her guilt. So by all means, keep an open mind. Listen to the evidence. Consider everything. But when the evidence makes it clear that she acted wantonly, and that she recklessly toyed with a man in the prime of his life by conducting an unconscionable experiment, by committing a crime against nature with no more remorse than if she had swatted a fly, I am sure you will do your civic duty and find this defendant guilty of this horrific crime."

Burke paused, steepled his fingers and then nodded to the jury box. "Thank you, ladies and gentlemen. Thank you for your attention, and on behalf of your fellow citizens, I thank you for giving so generously of your time and careful consideration."

As Burke returned to his station the courtroom spectators shuffled and sighed, but before they could collect themselves the defense attorney intentionally created a commotion by noisily pushing back his chair."Guilty!?" he boomed while moving to center stage. "Guilty, you say? Why, this little lady's no more guilty than you or me!" This was the moment many had waited for: a performance by the flamboyant Charlie Cross, the country's most notorious defense lawyer. Known as "The Cowboy," Cross's cornpone drawl, snakeskin boots, string tie, and gray ponytail made him stand out like a sore thumb among the eastern establishment. Early in his career he had been belittled and scoffed at, but after a long line of experienced prosecutors suffered the humiliation of a crushing defeat at Cross's hands, he was taken quite seriously. Even in highbrow Boston, the threat of Charlie Cross had his opponents diving for cover. To their relief, he had recently announced his retirement, but this was his last case and he wanted it to be remembered as the trial of the century. Nancy Sanderson's indictment for murder fit his scheme perfectly, and she readily accepted his offer to defend her.

On the day before the trial he had called a press conference.

"Never lost a murder trial,boys," he crowed, thumbing his red suspenders and ignoring the female reporters,

"And this sure as hell ain't gonna be my first. Y'all can call me Charlie," he said with a wry smile, "'cause I consider y'all my friends, even though I don't exactly fit in around here. But there's a good reason for what they say about me," he chortled, wagging his index finger: " 'Don't cross Cross!' Then, after waiting for their laughter to subside, "Now, don't forget. Y'all just stay close by, 'cause believe me, boys, I'm gonna be givin' you plenty to write about!" But that was yesterday. Now, standing before the jurors, Cross reverted to his humble country lawyer image.

"Looka here, folks. We all know a fella died, and of course that was unfortunate, but to accuse Dr. Sanderson of murdering him? Now that just ain't right. Sure, there was an unusual procedure here, but the patient was fully informed about his risks, and he went along with it all the way. Not only that, he actually pushed Dr. Sanderson to do it. Pretty much begged her, in fact." Cross turned up his palms and took on a puzzled expression. "So now, you tell me. Does that make her guilty of murder? Your district attorney has asked you to keep an open mind and consider the facts objectively. Well now, I surely agree with that." He paused briefly. "Ya know," he mused, "jurors have a tough row to hoe 'cause y'all don't have the luxury of lettin' your emotions get in the way. So all I'm askin' is that you consider the facts, cause I'm gonna tell 'em to you straight." He raised an index finger. "Do y'all remember Harry Truman?" he asked. "He could be a feisty sort, so when he was President, the reporters used to say, 'Give 'em hell, Harry!' And ol' Harry gave 'em a good answer "I don't give him hell," he said. "I just tell 'em the truth and they think it's hell!'"

And that's what you'll her from me, folks-the truth!" He paused with a slight bow and a sweeping right arm.

"I thank you for listening, and God bless you."

To the surprise of those who had predicted that Cross would strike out with a Boston jury, there were smiles and gestures of approval throughout the courtroom. Clearly, his folksy style had scored a connection. As he took his seat, an immediate buzz began to grow among the spectators. But one individual remained quiet and apart. Sitting in the back of the courtroom, Dr. Joshua Cantor stared into mid space, his calm exterior belying a tormented mind. Cantor was more than just a casual courtroom spectator.

He had, in fact, been an integral player in the events leading to this day. A torrent of images and memories overwhelmed him; his pulse raced in concert with his thoughts.

He closed his eyes and reflected on how all of this had evolved. Just six months ago, life had been, well, normal. How could all of this have happened so suddenly?

How could something so noble as medical research to assist childless couples have spiraled into deceit, death, and the spectacle that the worldwide media had dubbed "The Hamlet Experiment?"

ONE

Josh Cantor stopped to grab a deep breath. His shoulders sagged, and only partly because of sleep deprivation. Lately, his joy in delivering babies was tempered by the heavy void in his personal life. Trudging down the hall after performing an emergency cesarean, he opened the door to the family waiting room where he was about to tell a new father that his wife and baby girl were doing fine, and that he could see them both as soon as they arrived in the recovery room. Yes, today had been a good day, but as he hurried to get to his office he couldn't help thinking about what he and his wife were going through, and he prayed for the strength to carry their burden.

TWO

Sarah Moore was late, and it frightened her. On her apartment's western wall, sympathetic shadows danced in response to her frenetic figure-eight pacing. As she stopped to attack the miniature buttons on her portable phone the shadows froze, then came alive again as her pacing resumed. Several rings passed without a response.

"C'mon, c'mon," she pleaded.

Then, at last, an answer. "Cambridge Computerworks. Hold, please." Synthesizer chimes repeated a mindless ditty until she was reconnected. When Sarah finally got the chance to speak, her cultured diction cracked with emotion. "Hello, Alice. This is Sarah. May I speak with Michael, please?"

The distress in her voice caught the attention of the busy receptionist, who punched the hold button and then hit Michael Wilson's intercom.

"Call on line two, Mike. It's Sarah."

Michael was absorbed in a project that was scheduled for completion by noon. Instinctively, he reached for the receiver, then looked back to the computer screen which glared its demand for his attention. Conflict creased his forehead as he struggled to hold his train of thought. He spoke while continuing to focus on the screen.

"Alice, I'm running kind of late right now. How about asking her if she'd mind using the voice mail and I'll call her back just as soon as I can?"

The receptionist returned to Sarah and shifted to her professional cheer.

"He's running late, Sarah. He asked it you'd mind leaving a message."

As she listened to the reply, her face took on a knowing smile. Then she connected back to Michael.

"You might want to take this call right now, Romeo," she smirked. "She says to tell you <u>she's</u> late, too." Michael's heart skipped a beat. He pushed his office door shut and picked up on the blinking extension, trying to sound lighthearted. "Hi, Sookie, what's goin' on?" Her silence froze him.

His mouth went dry.

She eked out a plaintive whimper.

He turned off the distracting screen and strained to listen.

"What'd you say, Hon? I didn't hear you." He winced as she broke into tears.

"I said I'm late, Michael, I'm late!"

THREE

Wearing a lab coat over his blue scrub suit, Josh slipped into his office through a side door while his receptionist offered coffee to a waiting room milling with restless patients. Neatly arranged on his otherwise disheveled desk were three messages, the day's appointment list, and his standard on-the-fly breakfast of orange juice and darkly toasted bagel.

"Thank you, Bridget," he said aloud as he plopped down in his chair. He paused to take stock of his day, lingering over his wife Aviva's picture and wishing there were children's faces next to hers.

Each time this happened he was struck by the irony of being a childless infertility specialist. Not that they hadn't tried. Aviva had become pregnant several times, each one ending in heartbreaking miscarriage. There had been four of them. Or maybe five, the last one ending so early they barely had a chance to get excited. It didn't even seem like a real pregnancy, just an equivocal pregnancy test that turned cruelly negative within a day after she had experienced a tiny bit of spotting. That one was particularly hard on her. Not so much a disappointment as a slap in the face.

Sometimes Josh wondered if he was masochistic, forcing himself to endure this ritual day after day. And there was more, an aggravation that virtually rubbed salt in the wound. In his desk drawer he kept two miniature sterling silver picture frames, a well-meaning gift from his favorite aunt who had doted on him since childhood and always told him he'd have beautiful children. He was superstitious about this gift, wanting to believe that something given with such a happy heart would surely come to good one day. But lately he had begun to worry that the tarnish on the frames was an omen.

There were other articles on his desk as well, including several mementos from appreciative patients, those who had managed to have children through his medical intervention. Somehow he was able to separate the symbolism of these gifts from his personal situation, happy for his patients even though it was something he wished for himself.

For Aviva it was more difficult. She had immersed herself in her own career but Josh couldn't ignore the lines of torment that had begun to shadow her formerly cheerful face. He often fantasized about what he'd give to restore that easy smile.

Still, in all, Josh Cantor found a strong measure of fulfillment in his world of private practice and part-time clinical instruction at the Boston Lying-In Hospital. This was what he had always dreamed of and he was more than satisfied with his lot, no matter how hassled or stressful things were at that particular moment. Even after the long night he looked forward to seeing his patients.

Returning to the business at hand, he reviewed his messages, all written in Bridget's hand. The first two were routine. The last one caught him by surprise.

"Dr. Nancy Sanderson called. Said she knew you. Message on voice mail."

Josh's world stopped for a millisecond. Reading the words again, slowly, he leaned back in his chair and looked at the telephone where a tiny yellow light flashed for his attention. He lifted the receiver, punched in his privacy code, and played the recorded message.

"Hey, Josh. It's Nancy. Just calling to say hi and let you know I'll be coming back to the Lying In next month. Recently landed a big research grant, by the way. Speak to you soon. Bye now."

There was a definite lilt in her voice, and more than a hint of smugness.

He grunted and shook his head. It was just like Nancy to drop a bombshell and not leave her number. She would call back on her terms. Their personal relationship was ancient history and they hadn't spoken for years, but she was still pushing his buttons. A smile came to his face as he wondered at his reaction. After shaking it off he turned back to his phone and keyed the first number on his speed-dial list.

"Hi, Viv. It's me."

Aviva Cantor was relieved to hear from her husband.

"Joshua! What happened last night? I thought you were coming home after that delivery."

"So did I, but her labor got complicated. You know: anxious husband, medico-legal stuff ... you know the rest. It got kind of late so I didn't want to wake you. After all that she didn't deliver until this morning."

"Baby all right?"

"Baby's fine, mother too. Tired doctor, though. I was up and down a dozen times last night. Then in the middle of all that, I had to take a patient to the OR for a miscarriage."

"I'm sorry, Joshua. No sleep at all?"

"Couple hours, but I'm okay. How about you, Hon?"

"Doing okay," she answered bravely. "Been at my desk since seven. I woke up early and when you weren't here I decided to get breakfast at the office. Turned out good, actually. Got a lot of work done with no one else around."

Her voice trailed off, followed by a short silence and then a change in tone. "Josh, can I ask you about something?"

Josh knew what was coming. It was requiring increasingly little provocation to reawaken this topic and she was grasping at straws. He steeled himself and brightened his voice, already wishing he hadn't mentioned the miscarriage case.

"Sure, Hon. What is it?"

"You know that new medication we were talking about? The fertility drug in the newspaper article?"

"You mean for you, Viv?"

"Well, you know. I was just thinking maybe ..."

"I wish I could encourage you, honey," he answered gently, "but that really doesn't apply to us. That stuff is used to help people get pregnant. That's not our problem. We're getting pregnant just fine. We just need to figure out how to hold onto them. Something else will come along, though. If you don't give up, then I won't either."

Josh tried to sound reassuring despite his own doubts. They were both over thirty-five, after all. It was getting late. Even some fertile couples began having problems with pregnancy at this age. But he reminded himself not to mention the word adoption again. Nor could Aviva accept the idea of a surrogate to carry their baby.

The idea that someone might not take care of herself while pregnant with their child, or worse, change her mind and claim the baby as her own, was her worst nightmare.

As an only child of Holocaust survivors, Aviva had repeatedly heard the stories of murdered relatives, and now she dreamed of reclaiming them. In her heart of hearts she cherished the hope that the children she bore would carry the essence of those martyred souls. Her voice came back on the phone.

"No, Joshua," she said resolutely. "I won't give up."

It was well past noon when Bridget Walsh poked her head through his door. Bridget was a large woman, on the far side of middle age and possessing a strong motherly instinct when it came to her employer who was nearly twenty-five years her junior. She addressed him in her twinkling brogue.

"How're ya doin', Doctor?"

"I'm fine, Bridget, but I thought we agreed you'd call me Josh," he teased her.

Dimples surfaced through the blush in Bridget's cheeks.

"You know I can't bring myself to do that, Doctor. It's just not the way I was brought up."

She composed herself as her expression changed to concern.

"Tsk, tsk," she clucked, tilting her head. "You look so tired, Doctor. It was another hard night for you, wasn't it?" she observed.

Josh was familiar with Bridget's overtures. He looked at her expectantly.

"You know I hate to bother you, Doctor, but I do have a favor to ask of you."

"Anything for you, darlin'," he teased her again, mimicking her brogue. "Just name it."

"Well, there's one more patient in the waiting room and I'm hopin' you might be willing to see her today. Just a young girl, she is, and she didn't have an appoint- ment, but she called in a panic earlier this mornin', scared to death she might be pregnant, and I couldn't help feelin' sorry for the poor thing." Bridget wrung her hands while conjuring up her next sentence. "She's here with a young black gentleman.... He's nicely dressed and all... but she's not wearin' any ring on her finger, if you get my meaning, Doctor." Josh tried not to smile at her morality struggle. "Sure, Bridget. Why don't you ask them in and we'll see what we can do."Bridget breathed a sigh of relief. "Thank you, Doctor. I'll get them right away."

A handsome couple walked into his consultation room, both of their faces masks of concern. Josh introduced himself and extended his hand.

The young woman tossed back her shoulder length hair and attempted a smile. "I'm Sarah Moore," she offered nervously, "and this is my fiancé, Michael."

Josh noticed a subtle upward tilt to her chin, and that her sculpted jaw barely moved as she spoke. "Finishing school," he thought.

Her partner shook his hand with a self-assured grip. "Michael Wilson. I want to thank you for seeing us today, Doctor."

Michael was, in fact, grateful that Dr. Cantor would work Sarah into his schedule. Having heard his name from a friend, they just decided to take a chance on being seen today. And not only did they not have an appointment, Cantor was an infertility specialist and they didn't have that kind of a problem.

When Michael saw him, however, he began to have misgivings. This doctor was young; wholesome to be sure - well-scrubbed look and ready smile - but at the same time somehow artfully neglected, mop of unruly hair framing a boyish face. Plus, the consultation room was too laid-back to suit him. Up-to-date telephone system but otherwise conventional fixtures without a computer terminal in sight, and too-comfortable furnishings that reminded him more of somebody's study than a medical office. As a software designer, Michael would have been reassured by a high-tech environment. This place looked more like a mom-and-pop operation.

On the other hand, the diploma wall was impressive: Amherst College, M.D. from U. Penn, then an ob/gyn residency followed by an infertility fellowship at the prestigious Boston Lying-In, where Dr. Cantor currently held a clinical teaching position. In addition, there was a plaque indicating a two year stint in the Navy at the Bethesda Naval Hospital with a discharge rank of lieutenant commander. Calculating the years represented by each of these certificates, he figured the doctor to be well into his thirties, but he looked younger and Michael continued to feel the stirrings of doubt.

Sarah had no such misgivings. She liked the office's informal ambiance and soon warmed to Dr. Cantor's easy manner. As they settled into their chairs Josh turned to her.

"My receptionist tells me you think you might be pregnant, Sarah."

She brushed back the hair from her forehead. "Yes, I think so, but my pregnancy test was difficult to read. I couldn't tell for certain if it was positive."

"How about your menstrual history?"

"I've been irregular since my teens, so I wasn't concerned until I skipped a second period."

"All right, but let's back up for a minute. Tell me if a pregnancy is a good or bad thing for you right now."

They spoke simultaneously.

"A good thing," he answered.

"A bad thing," she said.

Josh watched as Michael turned to her in surprise. "I thought we were going ahead with it! You never told me you felt this way." Sarah reached for his hand, her eyes pleading. "I'm sorry, Michael. I didn't have the heart, but I don't think this is the right time for us to have a baby."

Despite the gentle delivery of Sarah's disclosure, Michael was jolted into stiff silence, prompting Josh to intervene.

"Well, you two don't have to decide this right now, but we should do an internal exam so you'll have the right information to act on."

"Would it be all right for Michael to come into the examination room with me?" Sarah requested.

"Of course," Josh answered. "The nurse will help you change."

Sarah's examination was as inconclusive as her home pregnancy test. Josh asked her and Michael back into his consultation room and considered how to approach them. Without frightening Sarah unduly, he needed to be honest with her, and he would have to be forthright with Michael. Composing his thoughts, he leaned forward, resting both forearms on the edge of his weathered oak desk.

"Sarah, your uterus is barely enlarged. I think you're probably pregnant but you must be quite early. I can't even tell you at this point if everything's normal. What I'd recommend is to repeat the pregnancy test in a few days. Then, if you and Michael disagree on what to do, maybe a counselor could help you sort things out."

He turned to Michael. "And I have to tell you, Michael... I can see that you feel strongly about this, and I can understand that, but the ultimate decision here is Sarah's, and that's the one I'll have to honor. That may seem unfair to you right now but I want to be straight about where my obligations lie."

Michael said nothing but nodded his reluctant agreement. He had to admit that this guy might look young but he told it straight, and Michael respected that.

Sarah reached for her handbag and rose from her chair.

"Thank you, Dr. Cantor. We'll discuss this and get back to you."

She reached again for Michael's hand but this time he ignored her gesture, shoving both hands in his pockets as they walked out.

After they had left the office, Josh leaned back in his chair. He needed some time to think. Two things troubled him about Sarah's situation. First, something was disquieting about her clinical picture. A variety of possibilities could be at work there, but time would tell and no good purpose would be served by making too much of a fuss right now. And second, the prospect of a woman planning to abort her pregnancy always gave him a pang. There were times when he was seized with an impulse to ask them to carry the pregnancy to term and let him adopt the baby.

While he sat reflecting, Bridget appeared at his door to remind him that he had about fifteen minutes left for lunch. She found him staring absentmindedly out the window and massaging his left temple.

"Everything okay, Doctor?"

He answered without turning his head.

"Fine, thanks, Bridget. Just a little headache."

FOUR

They faced each other across a booth in the medical building's first-floor luncheonette. Michael fended off the waitress by ordering coffees.

"Could I get herbal tea instead?" Sarah amended.

"Don't have it, honey. How 'bout reg'lar?"

"Fine, but could you make it decaf?"

"Don't have that neither. Sump'n else?"

Sarah saw Michael clenching his jaw.

"Regular tea will be fine, thanks," she said.

She turned to Michael. "Now, be calm," she begged.

He couldn't keep his voice from rising.

"How do you expect me to react? You just blew me out of the water in there! Why'd you wait until then to tell me how you feel?"

"I'm sorry, Michael. That wasn't the way I planned it. I was hoping I wasn't actually pregnant and I didn't want you to misinterpret me"

"'Misinterpret' you? What's that supposed to mean?"

She leaned forward. "It means that I love you even though I don't think this is a good time for a pregnancy, and I don't want you to think I've changed my mind about us."

He leaned back and sat quietly for a moment, his features softening a little. "Well, I was happy about us having a baby, and I still am. What's your problem with it, anyway?"

"I think you know the problem, Michael. So far, all my family knows about you is your name. Let them meet you first and get used to the fact that you're black. We have to be realistic. The racial issue's going to be enough for them to handle. If we add a pregnancy to the situation, they'll have a fit."

"Yeah, my family won't exactly be thrilled either. It's not gonna go

11

over real big that I'm hooked up with a white woman ... but I thought you and I were beyond that." "We are, but they're not. And then there's the matter of money. You know I hate accepting it from them. And a master's degree will take me another year. Even if I'm working part time, it'll be tight."

"Hey, I'm doin' okay. Let me support you for a while."

She gave him a grateful smile.

"I can't let you do that, Michael. Not yet..."

Michael sighed. "So what, then? You're thinking about an abortion?"

Again she leaned forward and reached across the table to take his hands in hers. "Yes, Michael, but it has nothing to do with how I feel about you. Please try to separate those issues."

"I hear you, but I'd still like to go ahead with this pregnancy. Why can't we take our chances with our families? If they're hung up about it we'll give them some time. They'll come around sooner or later."

A dusky sadness came over Sarah's eyes.

"I don't know, Michael. I really think it'll be a lot to deal with. Maybe we should take the doctor's advice and get some counseling."

They sat without speaking for a long moment, both of them staring out the window at the budding trees.

Finally Michael looked at her again.

"All right, I guess we aren't gonna resolve this thing right now. Maybe you're right. About a counselor, I mean."

Sarah was relieved at his conciliatory tone. She answered gently. "I really think that's what we need right now. Whatever we do, I want to be able to feel what you're feeling, and I want you to understand me too. That way, whatever we decide, neither of us will be left out."

He had begun to resign himself to the idea.

"The thing is, I don't know if I have all that much faith in counseling" -- his voice broke while he tried to control the lump in his throat -- "but I know I love you enough to give it a try." This time he reached for her hand, his emotions beginning to overwhelm him.

"All right, let's go for it ... and whatever happens, I'll be with you .... And Sarah ... I guess I haven't really proposed in a very chivalrous way ... but I'm yours if you'll have me ... and that offer is forever."

In the middle of their tender moment, both of them damp-eyed, their waitress came by to nudge them out of the booth. He hadn't touched his coffee, her teabag sat dry in the cup. "Is everything okay here? Do you folks need anything else?"

They looked at each other and smiled bravely. Sarah answered the waitress while sliding out of her seat.

"No, we're doing just fine, thanks."

12

FIVE

Ever since reconciling himself to their counseled decision to abort the pregnancy, Michael wanted Sarah to return to Dr. Cantor for her medical care. But Sarah refused, insisting on being treated at the Lying-In's family planning clinic. Having chosen social work for her career, she decided that it would be hypocritical to indulge in a higher echelon of treatment than her clients could afford. Plus, she had long since rejected the materialistic values held by her old-guard parents, preferring instead to adopt the mantle of a struggling graduate student. Even her relationship with Michael Wilson was partly a social statement, at least at the start. And although her feelings for him had become genuine, she still took delight in anticipating her family's reaction. They'd flip when they discovered his father was a Boston University professor of African-American studies.

The scene at the evening clinic confirmed Michael's fears. As he took in the chaotic surroundings he couldn't help wondering why Sarah would willingly choose this option. The disadvantaged minority element gathered there was foreign to him, his family having long since boot-strapped their way into the upper middle class. As much as he admired her idealism, from his point of view this was going too far.

Every seat was taken so they were forced to stand against the waiting room wall, jumping aside as an unruly child tumbled past and spilled his french fries. One of the ketchup-laden slices landed in the cuff of Michael's pants. He fished it out and held it gingerly between his thumb and forefinger, shooting Sarah an 'I-told-you-so' look as he dropped it in a trash can. After this he couldn't contain his sarcasm.

"Now tell me again why we're here?"

Color rose in Sarah's face as she hissed her reply.

13

"We've been over this before, Michael. I'm not discussing it again."

Michael shook his head disgustedly. Sarah turned her back.

Finally Sarah's name was called. A Jamaican nurse led them to an examining room, agreeing to Sarah's request for Michael to accompany her. Sarah changed into a skimpy paper gown that began to shred while she squirmed impatiently.

Eventually, a tired looking doctor entered, followed by the nurse and reading Sarah's chart as he shuffled along. He needed a shave. Chest hair flowered out of his scrub suit. Without looking up he spoke to Sarah, ignoring Michael.

"Hello, uh, Sarah. I'm Dr. Conley." He continued talking while perusing the chart, his face only inches from the print. "Looks like your pregnancy test was borderline positive. When was your last period?"

"Around two or three months ago, but I'm irregular."

He looked up at her, squinting through heavy glasses. "Any bleeding lately?"

"Not really. Maybe a little staining ... for the past week, actually."

"Cramping?" "Just some twinges on my left side."

"Okay, let's see what's happening. Are you all set?"

Without waiting for a reply he pulled on a vinyl glove while the nurse positioned her for a pelvic examination. Sarah tensed as an ice-cold speculum entered her body. Within a few seconds the uncomfortable instrument was removed and the doctor proceeded to do examine her by hand internally.

"Hmm. You're not bleeding right now but your uterus doesn't seem to be very enlarged. A little softened, maybe, but I can't really tell that you're pregnant."

Doctor Conley concluded the exam and casually tossed his examining glove in the trash.

"So what would that mean?" Sarah asked. I was examined by another doctor last week and he told me the same thing. In the meantime I've been having a lot of breast soreness and nausea. Am I pregnant or not?"

"I'm not sure," Dr. Conley shrugged. He turned to the sink to wash his hands. "With that 'iffy' test my guess is you're either real early or maybe about to have a miscarriage. Anyway, it's too soon for you to have an abortion. Chances are the pregnancy would be missed and you'd go through the operation for nothing."

"So what happens now?" Sarah asked.

The doctor's hand was on the doorknob. "My suggestion would be to hold off for a couple weeks. If you're not miscarrying now you'll be far enough then, so I guess you can make an appointment at the abortion clinic, okay?"

He was halfway out the door when Michael spoke up.

"Hold it a minute. Can we get another opinion before we go? Because frankly I'm not convinced by this plan."

"You can do whatever you'd like," Dr. Conley offered dryly, "but it'll be a waste of time. This is a straightforward situation. It happens every day."

"Yeah, but it doesn't happen to <u>us</u> every day." Michael jutted his chin at the doctor. "You know, I feel like a goddamn number here. You haven't been in this room for five minutes!"

"Michael, please," Sarah chided him. "It's okay. I can wait."

"Whaddya mean, you can wait? How can you take two more weeks of this?"

After the door closed behind Dr. Conley, the nurse made an effort to soothe them. "Honey, you'll be fine. He's just real busy right now. Go ahead and make an appointment at that other clinic and they'll take care of everything for you."

Over the next fourteen days Michael became increasingly solicitous, calling frequently and spending every night at Sarah's apartment. They'd been dating for eight months and Michael decided this would be an appropriate time to move in, but the days, and especially the nights, were interminable. Sarah complained increasingly of a vague discomfort in her side and Michael sensed that something was wrong.

Even so, she steadfastly refused to get another opinion, believing that to do so would be yet another indulgence too frequently abused by the rich.

For Michael's part, he had been undergoing some serious introspection during Sarah's pregnancy. Even after her insistence on abortion, he asked her again to marry him and have the baby, assuring her that he loved her and that his job would provide maternity benefits. Still, she tenderly rejected his proposal, explaining again that the timing was wrong for a pregnancy now and reassuring him that they could discuss marriage in the future.

All of this left Michael unsettled. For the first time in their relationship, he allowed himself to think that Sarah might not have the courage of her convictions. He wondered if her feelings for him were strong enough to endure the real-world hardships they would inevitably face, if she could stand up to her country club parents. But despite cautioning himself to maintain objectivity, he couldn't dwell on the negatives. She was the love of his life and he would stand by her, no matter what.

SIX

Sarah was prepared for pickets, so she took it in stride as she approached the flurry of activity near the abortion clinic's entrance, eyes forward, chin up. Michael, however, hadn't thought about this eventuality. He was especially struck by the proportion of middle-aged and older men among them. Their cardboard posters flapped in the wind and drew fiery anger from Michael as he read the shocking messages, his heart pounding as they advanced on the picket line. Just as they reached the protesters, Sarah was addressed by a burly fellow wearing a full gray beard and a plaid lumberjack shirt.

"Please don't go in there and kill your baby, Miss. We'll be happy to help you." He tried to place a pamphlet in her hand. "Here's some literature you should read before you make your decision."

Michael slapped the pamphlet to the ground. "Mind your own business, Gomer. And get a job, for Chrissake."

"I wasn't talking to you, sir. I was talking to that lady who's about to kill her baby."

"Well I was talkin' to you! Now step back before you really piss me off."

Sarah was alarmed. "Please, Michael. Let's just get inside."

A young woman holding an infant joined in, her face showing deep concern. "He doesn't mean any harm, you know. He's just trying to save your baby's life."

Michael lashed out again. "Just get the hell out of the way, lady. You can take...."

Sarah grabbed Michael's arm. He turned on her, ready to strike, pulling his punch just in time when her eyes met his. Barely maintaining self control, he allowed her to lead him like a child, past a uniformed policeman and into the clinic.

"Son-of-a-bitch." Michael muttered, railing at windmills. "Fucking people think they have the right to tell you what to do," he grumbled. " Mind your own business!"

Sarah was moved by his distraught state. She squeezed his hand twice, their private sign of strength. "It'll be okay, Michael, it'll be okay."

Michael held his thumb and forefinger to the bridge of his nose, covering both eyes. They stood quietly together while he calmed himself. He moved his hand down so it covered his mouth, then took an audible breath through his nose. Without speaking, Sarah led him to the reception desk.

"Name, please."

"Sarah Moore. I have an appointment."

"Yes, I have you right here. Did you bring your specimen?"

Sarah produced the small container of straw colored urine. The receptionist carefully printed Sarah's name on a sticky label and then pressed it onto the specimen jar.

"Please take a seat, Sarah. We'll call you soon."

They found two chairs together. She patted his knee reassuringly.

Almost immediately the reception door was opened and Sarah's name was called. She and Michael looked up to see a young woman wearing a wraparound skirt and sandals. A cotton tank-top revealed unshaven underarms. She used no makeup. Michael disliked her.

"Hello, Sarah. I'm Dawn, your counselor. You can both come in."

She irritated Michael further by her manner of speech, a contrived slow meter obviously designed to convey professionalism. But she took pains to include him in the conversation and, despite his initial misgivings, he was eventually won over. Explaining Sarah's options, Dawn detailed the abortion process, noting their reactions and allowing enough time to digest each bit of information before continuing. Both of them took all of this in stride, but when she showed them graphic pictures of first trimester embryos, Michael was shocked. He turned to Sarah with a look of disbelief.

"I had no idea it looked so human this early. Maybe we should ...."

Sarah stopped him in mid sentence.

"I don't want to hear it, Michael. I'm barely pregnant." She set her jaw and spoke to the counselor. "Can we continue, please?"

"Are you sure, Sarah?" she answered. "I just need to be certain you're properly informed before you make this decision."

"I'm already certain," Sarah said impatiently. "And I don't need to hear any more. I'll sign whatever you need and then I'd like to get this over with."

The counselor looked at Michael who responded with an expression of resignation.

"All right, Sarah," she continued, "but I need to get some more information before we go any further."

After taking a medical and social history and obtaining a signed consent form, she escorted Sarah to a changing area. Michael asked where he should wait.

"Actually, you have the option of staying in the operating room while the procedure's being performed," the counselor told him.

Michael stood speechless. He heard Sarah's voice coming from behind the dressing room curtain.

"I'd like you to be with me, Michael."

The counselor looked at him for his decision. "Michael?"

He answered numbly. "Okay."

Sarah sat on the end of the examination table, hugging herself for warmth while Michael solicitously draped his jacket over her shoulders. Soon a young woman entered wearing a short white lab coat with a stethoscope draped in chic nonchalance around her neck. Attached to her lab coat was an ID tag containing her photograph and name, and identifying her as a member of the department of obstetrics and gynecology at the Boston Lying-In Hospital. She offered a cool hand to Sarah.

"Doctor Nancy Sanderson," she introduced herself with no-nonsense confidence. Then, with an air of southern gentility,

"I believe you are Sarah Moore, and this is ..."

"My fiancé, Michael Wilson."

Dr. Sanderson favored Michael with a perfunctory smile, then shifted to a brisk bedside tone.

"Okay, Sarah. Are you ready for this procedure?"

Sarah nodded. Michael opened his mouth to speak but Sarah stopped him by reaching over to touch his arm as she lay back on the operating table.

Before Dr. Sanderson began the operation, she did an internal exam to evaluate the size of Sarah's uterus, finding it to be smaller than anticipated. Her eyes darkened. "Was this pregnancy test positive?" she accused the nurse.

The nurse frowned and answered curtly.

"Yes, but this was the weak positive I told you about."

"A weak positive again?" Sarah asked.

Doctor Sanderson looked at her. "Again?"

"I had the same result two weeks ago. Why would that be?"

"I'm not sure," she answered, "but your uterus isn't quite as large as I'd expect and you're doing some bleeding. Most likely you're having a miscarriage," she explained. "I'd say we should go ahead with the D&C and that should confirm what's going on."

"What do you mean? I mean, how will you tell?"

"By the tissue we get from your uterus. Usually I can tell just by looking at it, but if there's any doubt we can send it to pathology for analysis. The point is, you want to be aborted anyway, right? And if you're already miscarrying you'll still need a D&C, so either way you'll need to go through this."

Sarah looked to Michael, who nodded his approval. She bit her lip.

"Okay," she hesitated. "I guess so."

"Good. Now just lie back and relax and we'll take care of this in a jiffy." She changed her gloves and began to arrange the table of sterile instruments. "I'll try to let you know what's happening as we go along. Right now there'll be a little pinch from the novocaine."

A stab of pain shot into Sarah's pelvis like a blunt screwdriver, turning her knuckles white as she gripped the sides of the table. Beads of perspiration broke out on her forehead.

"Unnhh!" she groaned. "I thought that was supposed to be a pinch."

"Sorry," Dr. Sanderson continued, chattering on while she worked. "Just hang on now while we measure your uterus."

While the nurse mopped Sarah's brow, Doctor Sanderson proceeded with the operation. Next she grasped the anterior lip of Sarah's cervix with a tenaculum and then passed a uterine sound to measure the organ's depth. She quickly slipped the instrument through the cervical opening, expecting to feel the top of the uterus at around three inches, but the measurement read five inches, then five and a half ... six ... and still there was no resistance. Immediately withdrawing the sound, she repeated the bimanual examination to estimate the size of the pregnancy once more. The uterus felt barely enlarged, just as it had previously.

A wave of panic hit her as she realized she had perforated the organ. She briefly considered going on with the D&C, taking the chance that she could successfully remove the pregnancy tissue while avoiding the perforation site. Be calm, she thought. Maybe you don't even need to mention it ....

As always she disciplined herself to discount all considerations except statistical probabilities. Quickly calculating the risks and benefits of continuing the procedure, she concluded that the probability of creating further damage outweighed the chance of completing the procedure successfully. Already composed, she removed the instruments and pulled off her gloves. "Sarah, we've run into a problem. I'm afraid I've perforated your uterus."

"Are you certain? I didn't feel any pain just then."

"Yes, I'm sure. Your uterus is small and my measuring instrument went in several inches."

Michael spoke up. "So now what? Is this dangerous?"

Dr. Sanderson folded her arms and directed her answer to Sarah.

"Not usually. Normally we can just observe it and it heals over by itself. We do need to watch you closely, though. I'm going to admit you to the hospital for observation and also to get an ultrasound so we can figure out what's going on."

Sarah and Michael's eyes met. This was getting complicated, she thought. And expensive.

"How long will I have to stay in?" she asked.

"Usually just overnight. I could almost just watch you here but we don't have enough nursing care and there's no ultrasound machine."

Sarah looked at Michael again. "I don't think so. I really feel fine and I think I'd rather just go home."

"That's not a good idea," Doctor Sanderson countered. "You could be doing some internal bleeding without knowing it. I have to inform you that it could be a serious mistake for you to leave right now."

"She's right, Sookie," Michael intervened. "This isn't a time to take chances."

Sarah's eyes misted over. "No, Michael. It'll be too expensive and I'll have to tell my parents. I don't want that."

"I have some money saved up. We can do it ourselves."

"I believe we can help you with that," Dr. Sanderson said. "The hospital has a program to deal with financial hardship cases. The most important thing right now is to give you the proper medical care."

Sarah looked at the doctor for several seconds, the room heavily quiet while everyone waited for her to speak. Suddenly she jumped down from the operating table and headed for the changing room. "Where are my clothes?" she choked through her tears. "I'm going home."

Michael and the nurse were dumbstruck, but Dr. Sanderson remained clinically detached. Shrugging her shoulders, she turned to the nurse.

"Get her to sign a release form," she said.

SEVEN

Michael Wilson didn't sleep that night, having convinced himself that Sarah would be okay if he managed to stay awake and keep watch over her. He placed a chair next to her bed and stood guard, closely observing every breath. By dawn he had memorized every freckle in her alabaster skin.

Amazingly, she got through the night without so much as a toss or turn and awoke to good health. When she opened her eyes she saw Michael's haggard face staring intently at hers. She sat bolt upright.

"Michael! What are you doing?"

"I was afraid to fall asleep. I've been watching you breathe."

She drew up her knees and studied the fatigue in his eyes. "You look exhausted!"

"Never mind me. Are you sure you're all right?"

"Yes, yes. I'm fine. Nothing hurts. But you look awful, Michael. Why don't you put your head down and I'll call your office to tell them you won't be in today."

"Can't do it. Too far behind already. I can crash when I get home tonight. But I don't want you to leave here. I'm going to call every hour to check on you."

"Absolutely not. You have enough to worry about at work. Besides, if there were going to be any trouble it would have happened by now. It's been almost eighteen hours. Go ahead and take your shower. I'll get some coffee going."

Sarah was glad to have some time to herself. After nudging Michael out the door she decided to walk to her morning class and use the time to sort things out. It was an invigorating, cool morning, with ethereal mist rising from the sidewalks and highlighting oblique sunbeams. Drinking in Boston's energy, she began to experience a sense of exhilaration she hadn't felt for a long time. Her circuitous route took her along Beacon Street, past the Common and the Public Garden. She looked instinctively for the swan boats until remembering they wouldn't be launched for a few more weeks. As she glided along the cityscape, passersby did double takes at her bouncing auburn hair and long-legged strides. Her gait increased to workout pace as she fairly leaped her way across Arlington St. Yesterday's dreadful experience was behind her now. She would let some time pass before deciding what to do next. Her karma had turned positive, she sensed, and a solution would be forthcoming if she could just be patient.

That was the trouble with Western thinking. They decided what they wanted to achieve and then went about trying to make it happen. Eastern philosophy was a better idea. They imagined an ideal course of action and then just let it happen. They had faith in cosmic nature. They took the long view. That was the right way. She would share her ideas with Michael and persuade him to just mellow out and wait a while. Everything would fall into place in due time. In the meantime they should cool it until the appropriate inspiration came along. All in all, she had a delightful day, anticipating how she would explain all of this to him, and the feeling of peace that would follow.

"I'm not buying it, Sarah."

Michael wasn't convinced. His deductive reasoning told him there was something wrong and it needed to be dealt with head on. "This isn't a social decision. It's medical. We have a problem. It needs to be fixed by someone who knows what the hell they're doing. All that karma crap isn't going to cure anything. This time we're doin' it my way. I'm gonna make another appointment for you with Dr. Cantor and you're gonna come with me and do this by the book."

Sarah was stunned. After initially attempting to counter Michael's argument, she soon backed off when it struck her that he was going to help her carry this weight. Unexpectedly relieved, she took a deep breath and agreed to his plan.

Two days later Josh Cantor noted with interest that Sarah Moore's name appeared on his appointment list. As soon as Sarah and Michael walked into his office they began to detail her story, taking pains to explain why she had chosen to go elsewhere for her medical care.

"I hope you won't take this personally, Doctor. Sarah has a thing about paying her own way. She really liked you, but..."

Josh waved away Michael's apology with a sympathetic smile.

"Thank you, Michael, but this isn't necessary. My ego's not that fragile. But I do have to tell you both that this story's starting to sound a little suspicious."

"What do you mean?" Sarah interrupted. "Don't you believe us? Honestly, Dr. Cantor, that's just the way it happened..."

"No, no...I'm sorry. I didn't mean that...I'm talking about your medical history. It doesn't quite add up. If you don't mind, I'd like to re-examine you today and see if we can make some sense out of this."

This time the nature of Sarah's examination was quite different. Josh inserted a speculum that had been pre-warmed to body temperature, patiently explaining to her what he was doing.

"Sarah, there's a little bit of bleeding coming through your cervix. Is that something new or have you seen it before now?"

"No, I've been spotting for several days, and I'm also having some pain on my left side. It's hurting right now, actually, just from the pressure of the speculum."

"Okay, let me remove it and then I need to examine your internal organs. We should be done in just a minute and then you can get off this table."

As Josh palpated her uterus, Sarah winced. "That hurts on my side again."

"Okay, can you tolerate a little more? I just want to feel what's over there. Ten more seconds, tops."

Sarah put on a brave smile, trying to lighten the moment. "Yes, I can take ten more seconds, but I'll be counting."

Josh probed towards the left pelvic sidewall. When he felt a hint of a mass he began to consider a differential diagnosis. The standard possibilities of tumors, infections, and aberrant pregnancies automatically clicked through his mind, but when he tried to outline the dimensions of the mass, Sarah couldn't suppress a gasp of pain.

"Oh! Ohmigod! Please stop! Please!"

Josh ceased the examination immediately.

"Okay, okay, that's all. I'm sorry. We're done."

Sarah began to cry. Michael tried to console her, stroking her hand and reassuring her softly.

"I'm sorry, Sarah. I know that really hurt you." Josh said. " Let me give you some time to recover and then I'd like to talk to you both in my office."

Several minutes later she and Michael walked back into the consultation room. Josh placed a box of tissues on the desk and Sarah pulled several of them. He waited until she composed herself.

"I don't know, Sarah. I'm worried that you might have something unusual going on. If you'll hold on a moment, I'd like to talk to one of the doctors over at the hospital. Then I'll explain my thinking to you."

He picked up his phone and dialed a four digit extension.

"Hi, Ronni, this is Dr. Cantor. Could I speak to Dr. Gallagher, please?" He clicked his ball point pen impatiently while he waited.

"Hiya, Cameron. Josh Cantor. Cam, I need to talk to you about a confusing case I have over here."

Sarah and Michael listened as Dr. Cantor detailed her story. After hanging up he turned to them. "That was a fellow named Cameron Gallagher. He runs the ultrasound unit at the hospital and he's willing to see you right away. I'd like to get going on this if you don't mind. An ultrasound should help to clear up the confusion. And I have to tell you, Sarah...I'm afraid you might have a tubal pregnancy."

Sarah felt her heart drop. She had been counseled about this possibility several years ago while she was hospitalized for a pelvic infection. This doctor was undoubtedly right. And it was going to mean hospitalization and surgery. She looked anxiously at Michael.

"Don't even think about it," Michael said firmly. "We're going over there right now, just like the doctor said. There's no way I'm gonna let this go any further without finding out what's going on."

Sarah said nothing. She walked out in a daze, her eyes transformed to shimmering pools of fear.

Thirty minutes later Sarah was positioned on Dr. Gallagher's examination table with a paper drape across her knees and a vaginal ultrasound transducer probing her pelvis. Her head was turned right, facing the monitor. Michael stood to the left of the table, holding her hand and viewing the same image.

Dr. Gallagher kept up a running line of chatter during the examination. "Well, here's your uterus and there's clearly nothing in there except a thickened lining," he said. "And look here, in the cul de sac. There's a pool of fluid back there, probably some old blood from the perforation. There's not much but I'm surprised you're not in a lot of pain. Maybe in the middle of your abdomen or lower back?"

"Not really," Sarah answered. "But I have had some twinges on my left side, and it killed me when Dr. Cantor examined me there."

"Okay, then let's look over there...here's your ovary and that looks fine.....can't see anything in the tube but there still could be an early pregnancy in there.....here's a loop of bowel next to it....that's your sigmoid colon ... say, have you had any ...."

The doctor stopped short as he noted a rhythmic motion behind the bowel. He moved the real time scanner a little higher. Sarah and Michael looked closely but saw only blurry shadows.

Suddenly something flashed across the screen. The image began to clarify into what looked like a hand puppet. Then the puppet turned and showed its profile, waving its limbs.

"Holy shit!" Michael blurted. "What the hell is that?"

"Oh, my God," Sarah murmured.

"There it is." Gallagher was awestruck. "No wonder nobody found it. It's located way out in the abdomen ...."

There was a brief silence as the doctor did some measurements. Michael could barely fathom what he was seeing, but Sarah was transfixed by the embryo's beating heart.

"Sweet Jesus," Gallagher whispered. "You're at least fourteen weeks pregnant." He called to his assistant.

"Ronni, you'd better get Dr. Cantor on the phone."

EIGHT

Nancy Lou Sanderson reached into a cardboard box that contained a dozen lightly anesthetized white rats, all female. Most of the animals lay still, temporarily immobilized by an ether soaked rag that had been thrown in their midst. Some of them, however, were not completely helpless so she wore a leather glove to protect herself from being bitten. She pulled the first one out and matter-of-factly killed it by banging its head on the edge of a stainless steel sink. In the midst of this workaday task she addressed her research assistant about another matter.

"Why me?" she complained. "I have a ton of stuff to do today. Can't somebody else show this guy around?"

Nancy did not appreciate her assignment of hosting a visiting student from Tufts Veterinary School. Continuing to grouse about it, she mechanically sacrificed the remaining animals, then pulled on a pair of latex gloves prior to cutting open their abdomens and removing their ovaries. Half of her subjects had been injected with a potent new fertility drug, as yet unapproved by the FDA, and the relative size of their ovaries was information she planned to present at the annual meeting of the American Fertility Society. Using a delicate laboratory scale calibrated in grams, she carefully noted the weights of the organs before dumping the still warm carcasses into a red plastic bag marked with an environmental hazard warning.

Upon completing this chore her thoughts shifted to the issue of her professional image. The reproductive endocrinology service at the Boston Lying-In had a stellar reputation and her recent faculty appointment had not been easily won. Having been raised and educated in the South, she knew she was not considered a member of Boston's academic elite. In an effort to assimilate she had dropped her middle name but her occasional lapses into Carolina dialect continued to inspire gleeful mimicking by her peers, feeding her outsider paranoia. Nonetheless, she was expected to live up to the department's standard of excellence, so how was she supposed to get her work done if she had to entertain some dopey veterinary student from the university's Grafton branch? What the hell could he want from her, anyway?

She heard a knock on her office door.

"Yeah, what is it?" she grumped.

"Excuse me, I'm looking for Dr. Sanderson?"

The voice rose at the end of the sentence. She hated rising intonation. It reminded her of her own manner of speech, which she was constantly trying to live down. Without looking up from her desk she answered.

"That's me. Whaddya want?"

"Hi, Dr. Sanderson. I'm Philip LeDuc. From Tufts Veterinary School. They told me you would give me a tour of the infertility program?" He tried to sound friendly despite her cold greeting.

Her eyes remained down. "You're early."

"Yeah, I'm sorry. I was afraid I wouldn't be able to find you this easily so I gave myself some extra time. I can wait if you want."

Nancy pushed herself back from the desk. "No, it won't make any difference. Either way it's gonna screw up my schedule." She shot him a disdainful glance. "All right, let's go," she continued. "But I don't have a lot of time today. What's the big emergency behind this visit, anyway?"

Now he was starting to become annoyed. "Look, if this is too much trouble for you, I'll find somebody else."

"I wish," she scoffed. "No, c'mon, I'll show you around."

His voice hardened. "I don't think so. Not with that attitude."

When she turned to take a better look at him she was startled by his appearance. Tall, strapping build, dark hair over smoldering green eyes. He stood firm, legs defiantly apart. Damn! He was gorgeous. And here she was, acting like a bitch.

"All right, I'm sorry," she softened. "They just told me about you this morning and I already had a tight schedule. But we'll work it out. C'mon, lemme show you what's going on here. Are you interested in something in particular?"

He shot her a long stare before answering. "Yeah, I do have something in mind, if you can manage to squeeze me into your busy day."

She parried his defensiveness with perky interest. "Sure. Like what?"

He shot her a long stare before answering. "Well, it has to do with fertility in pigs."

"You're serious?"

"Yeah, I'm serious. It's a big problem for a group of pig farmers in New Hampshire. Their litter sizes are down and it means a lot to their bottom line."

"Really? Like what does that mean? I mean how many babies do they have?"

"Piglets."

"What?"

"They're called piglets."

"Oh, of course. How many 'piglets' do they have?"

"Normally about eight to twelve per litter but lately it's dropped to five or six on several farms up there. They're all located near each other so we figured it was something in their diet or environment but so far nobody's come up with a good explanation."

"So you think we can help you with this somehow?"

His defensiveness was gone now. "Yeah, that's what I was hoping. I've heard about the frequency of multiple pregnancies in these programs and I'm thinking maybe we could use your ovulation agents in pigs."

"I imagine you could, but I've gotta tell you, this stuff is outrageously expensive. Would it be worth it for use in animals?"

"Absolutely. A pig farmer's survival can depend on the size of a sow's litter. Yeah, they'll pay for fertility drugs. If they work. And that's what I'm trying to find out."

Their conversation was interrupted by a burst of noise in the hall. Nancy opened the door to find two ob-gyn residents in the middle of an animated discussion. "Good morning, y'all. What's goin' on out here?"

"Hi, Dr. Sanderson. We just came from the ultrasound unit. Cam Gallagher found an abdominal pregnancy in one of Doctor Cantor's patients. He's got it on tape."

"Really! I've never seen one of those. Is he still there?" "Yeah, we just left. He's reviewing it now."

Nancy turned to Philip. "Would you mind if we ran over there for a minute? I'd like to have a look at that."

"Sure, but what's an abdominal pregnancy?"

"C'mon. I'll tell you about it on the way."

Cameron Gallagher had inherited all the endearing attributes of his forebears; laughing eyes and rosy jowls, a clean-shaven Santa Claus with a personality to match. When Nancy and Philip arrived he was on the phone but took the time to smile and wave, pointing to the image on the monitor. Nancy approached it with intense curiosity, suddenly so absorbed that she forgot Philip was with her. Dr. Gallagher hung up and walked over to them. He extended a friendly hand to Philip.

"Hello, I'm Cameron Gallagher."

"Oh, I'm sorry. Dr. Gallagher, this is Philip ... uh ..."

"LeDuc," Philip finished for her.

"Philip is from the veterinary school," Nancy added.

"How are you, young fella," Dr. Gallagher said. "What do you do over there?"

"I'm in my third year of school," Philip explained. "Right now I'm doing a research elective on swine fertility."

Entranced by Philip's profile, Nancy tuned out while they chatted. A junior in vet school, she thought. That would put him in his mid twenties. A little young for me, unless he did something else for a while.

"So I assume you're here to look at this tape," Dr. Gallagher smiled at Nancy.

His voice snapped her out of her reverie. "Hmm?... Oh, yeah ... I heard about it from the residents. Would you mind running it for me?"

Gallagher beamed with pride. "Certainly. Let me rewind it and I'll tell you the whole story." Nancy had nearly reached for the controls herself but stopped just in time, remembering that Gallagher had a rule about this particular machine. Its cost was well over a hundred thousand dollars and he had fought with the budget committee to get it. Normally he was an easygoing guy, but this piece of equipment made him nervous, prompting him to circulate a memo directing that no one could touch it except him. "Are you familiar with the subject of abdominal pregnancy, Philip?" he asked. "Not really. Dr. Sanderson started to explain it to me but she didn't have time to finish." Nancy cringed at Philip's formal reference to her. Perhaps he thought of her as much older than himself. "Well, basically it means that a pregnancy is growing in the abdominal cavity, completely outside of the normal location in the reproductive organs," Dr. Gallagher continued.

"Right, but how does that occur?" Philip asked.

"Good question. There are a couple of theories. The main one is that a pregnancy starts in the fallopian tube. Your basic ectopic pregnancy. You understand that concept?"

"Yes, we've studied that, but..."

Gallagher interrupted by holding up his palm. "And then, the theory goes, the pregnancy is sometimes aborted out of the tube and into the abdominal cavity. Usually that causes pain and bleeding, the patient gets operated on, and the pregnancy tissue is removed. But in the rare case the pregnancy somehow retains viability and attaches to one of the abdominal organs---like the bowel or the omentum---and establishes a blood supply. Then it continues growing until the patient or her doctor notices that the baby seems awfully close to the surface of the patient's abdomen.

That finding typically leads to an ultrasound, which demonstrates the presence of the pregnancy outside of the uterus."

Nancy found her mind wandering again during Dr. Gallagher's explanation. The video continued to rewind while he spoke. When it reached the beginning she noted the patient's name. It looked familiar. Sarah Moore. Her heart began to pound as she remembered that she had seen this patient recently in the abortion clinic. Damn.

She was the one with the perforated uterus. Nancy nearly blurted out this observation but managed to restrain herself, cringing at the thought that she might have missed something. She made a mental note to review the chart and began to pay closer attention to what Dr. Gallagher was saying.

"But here comes the kicker," Gallagher continued. "Obviously, there's no way out so the baby has to be delivered surgically. And if that were the end of it there'd be no real problem, but the placenta bleeds like hell when you try to remove it so it has to be left in place and that has its own set of problems. Not a happy situation, to say the least."

Gallagher's attention was diverted when his door opened. He turned to see Joshua Cantor entering the room. Gallagher gave him a big greeting. "Good morning, Josh! You've come to view my masterpiece, I see."

Nancy looked up from the screen. Gallagher's welcome went unacknowledged as Josh and Nancy's eyes met. When Josh spoke, his voice was friendly but carried a definite note of reserve.

"Hello, Nancy. Welcome back."

"Hey, Josh. It's good to see you. Sorry I haven't had the chance to look you up." Nancy affected composure, but the subtle emergence of her native drawl betrayed her. She was uncomfortable and Josh knew it.

"Well, you look terrific," he offered generously. "How long have you been back?"

"I guess it's been a couple of weeks." She forced an embarrassed smile, then remembered Philip and moved closer to him, slipping her hand inside his elbow and stifling his surprise by squeezing his forearm.

"Josh, this is my friend Philip LeDuc. Philip, this is Dr. Joshua Cantor."

The two men exchanged a cursory handshake, after which Nancy tugged at Philip's arm. Exiting with her handsome partner, she flashed a plastic smile.

"Well ,I guess we'd better be going. Nice to see you, Josh. B'bye, Dr.Gallagher. Thanks for the demonstration.''

After Nancy and Philip left the room, Gallagher arched his eyebrows roguishly.

"Damn, Josh! You coulda cut that tension with a knife! How long has it been since you two were an item?"

Josh tried to keep a straight face but his fondness for Cameron Gallagher forced a sheepish grin.

"Get outta here, Gallagher. That was a million years ago. I'm an old married man now. C'mon. Show me your fancy movie."

Rolling his eyes a little, Gallagher relented. "Sure Josh, no problem."

The mood turned clinical as they viewed the video.

"What's that next to the pregnancy, Cam?" Josh asked.

"Can you point out the anatomy for me?"

"Sure. That's the sigmoid colon in front of it. It's really hidden back there.

And way up here is the lower pole of the left kidney. Not involved with the pregnancy, though, so I don't think it'll become a factor. And down here is the empty uterus, with some fluid in the cul de sac. Probably old blood. I can't believe she's not in pain right now. Wouldn't you expect that?"

"She's had some twinges, but I'm always amazed at how people come in with these horrendous conditions and don't have a lot of symptoms. I really can't explain it."

"So what happens now?"

"I'd assume we'll be operating on her soon. She was planning to abort anyway. It worries me, though. We're sure to lose a ton of blood from taking this thing out."

"I wouldn't be so sure," Gallagher observed. "About removing it, I mean. You should've seen her face when she saw that beating heart on ultrasound."

Josh let Gallagher's words sink in for a minute, then looked around for a chair and sat down heavily.

"You okay, Josh?" Gallager asked.

"Yeah, Cam, but I just got this dark feeling. This thing isn't likely to have a good outcome. " His left hand moved up to rub his temple.

"God help her, no matter what she decides."

NINE

Aviva Cantor could always sense when something was on her husband's mind, and this was one of those times. Not that it was that difficult -- he had picked at his dinner and was pretty much oblivious during their conversation -- but his level of distraction seemed deeper than usual. It was obvious that he needed to talk about something but she would have to be careful how she brought it up. Josh was vulnerable to criticism about being inattentive, especially since Aviva's recent miscarriage. And perhaps the most sensitive area was how much time he spent at his work. If she ever so much as hinted that he wasn't giving her enough attention it could send Josh into a guilt-stricken tailspin. Clearly he was conflicted about being in a time-demanding career.

In view of all that she tried to make her opening as offhand as possible. She moved her chair near to his and reached over to rub his neck.

"How'd it go today, Joshua? You look tired."

He closed his eyes and leaned back. "What? Oh, yeah, it went fine, I guess. There was this one patient, though...."

She looked at him expectantly.

He turned his head. "You really want to hear about this? I hate to bring my work home with me."

"Go ahead. Just this once," she smiled.

Josh laughed. He knew he was an open book to her.

"Okay, but you asked for it." He turned his chair to face hers. She leaned back and put one bare foot across his knees, her signal for a foot massage which Josh performed while telling his story.

"She's in her middle twenties with this condition that I've only seen once before ... and I have to admit it's got me worried."

Josh went on to explain the concept of abdominal pregnancy and the dilemma it presented for everyone involved, including him.

"So what're you going to do?" Aviva asked. "This sounds like something you'll have to refer to someone else, doesn't it? I mean how are you going to handle something you've only seen once?"

"No one has treated many of these, Viv. They're too rare, so it's not like there's an 'abdominal pregnancy' clinic anywhere. Plus there's the social element. She and her fiancé are disagreeing about the pregnancy. It wasn't planned, but he took it for granted that they'd have the baby. She never told him otherwise, and then while they were sitting in my office she sprung the idea of abortion on him for the first time."

"But you've dealt with that before ..."

"Yeah, but now I get the idea that she's changing her mind, and the longer this goes on, the more dangerous it gets for her."

"And there's nobody who can help you with this?"

"Well, I could work with the perinatal people, but you know Howard Greenwald. He's a real friend and a great doctor, but he can be blunt, and that might backfire with these two. They both seem like pretty strong-willed people." He hesitated briefly. "Plus, I like them, so I want to stay involved even if it's just to be a referee."

They sat quietly for a while, after which Josh stood and started to clear the table. Aviva rose behind him and gave him a playful pat on the rear. "Don't worry about the dishes," she said gently. "You just go hit the couch for a while. And forget about that patient for tonight."

TEN

At 4:45 Bridget Walsh left her desk, walked down the hall, and waited for Dr. Cantor to exit an examination room.

"Doctor, Michael Wilson's in the waiting room. You know, Doctor," she explained, " Sarah Moore's fiancé. He's asking if you have a few minutes for him at the end of office hours."

Josh frowned and checked his watch.

"No appointment? He just showed up?"

"Yes, Doctor."

"Well, I guess we'll have to see. I'm supposed to be at a hospital meeting at 5:30. Why don't you tell him I'll try, but I can't promise."

As his last patient left, Josh called the front desk. "Okay, Bridget, I have a few minutes. Ask him in."

Looking distraught and talking a mile a minute, Michael lurched into the consultation room. "I'm sorry for just showing up like this, Doctor Cantor. I've been worried all day and I just had to talk to you in person about it."

Josh was immediately mollified. "Sure, Michael. I can see you're upset. Please, sit down. How's Sarah doing?"

Now Michael began to weigh his words. "She's okay I guess. But a couple of things are bothering me."

"Go ahead. Shoot."

"Well, first of all, I don't know if I'm madder at Sarah for insisting on going to that clinic, or at the doctor over there who perforated her uterus. I feel like that could have been avoided if we'd have come to you in the first place."

"You know what, Michael? I'd like to tell you that I've never perforated a uterus, but the truth is it's happened to me more than once."

"But how can that happen in professional hands?" he persisted. "It just seems like such a horrendous complication."

"Believe it or not, even some of the blunt instruments we use can go through tissue like butter. I'm sure the reason it happened was that Sarah's uterus was much smaller than expected for the length of her pregnancy. At least the guy who operated on her recognized it immediately and I have to give him credit for that. Sometimes it isn't discovered until a more serious complication occurs."

"It was a woman."

"Pardon?"

"The one who operated on Sarah. It was a woman doctor."

Josh shrugged. "Meaning ...?"

Michael stumbled over his next sentence. "To be honest, I can't help thinking that a male surgeon ... well, you know ...."

Josh couldn't suppress a wry smile. "I guess those stereotypes die hard, Michael, but believe me, gender makes no difference in surgery. And the main thing to keep in mind here is that uterine perforations can happen to anyone. I wasn't patronizing you when I told you I've had some of my own. They happen. It's failing to recognize them that can lead to trouble."

Michael seemed to accept Josh's reassurances, but he continued to stammer.

"Okay, but here's the second thing that's been bothering me. I hope you won't take this the wrong way, but I've been doing some reading about abdominal pregnancies and, frankly, it scares me." He hesitated briefly. "I guess I just have to come right out with it. What I'm trying to say is I'm not sure you've had enough experience in this area and I'd like to know if there's anyone else around who has."

Josh shook his head in agreement. "You're on target this time, Michael. My clinical experience is limited to one case that I scrubbed on in my residency, but believe it or not, that puts me on par or ahead of most doctors. This condition is so rare that no one can build up much of a case load. The best I can offer is consultation with a perinatologist who deals exclusively with high risk pregnancies, but even those guys don't have much experience with these things. They're just too rare."

"Then what do you suggest we do? It sounds like you'd have to be crazy to go ahead with a pregnancy like this."

Josh didn't respond. He sensed that Michael had more to say.

"I mean, what are you gonna tell her? I really don't think it's a good idea to continue. Do you?"

Josh decided to answer at this point. "Given the prognosis for her and the baby, there's no way I could encourage her to continue. But keep in mind we're having a hypothetical discussion here. I have to tell you again that this will be Sarah's decision."

Michael sat up straight and began to tap his foot rapidly. "Yeah, yeah. I know all that, but I don't understand why I can't have a voice in this."

"Because like it or not, that's the law."

"But it's my pregnancy just as much as hers, isn't it? Why shouldn't I have to be consulted?"

Josh thought about his upcoming meeting that was scheduled in a few minutes. This wasn't going to be an easy conversation. . He would have to be blunt. "This process is based on a very practical consideration, Michael. When you have to identify the parents in a pregnancy, the mother is obvious but you have to do an invasive procedure to prove paternity before birth."

"What are you trying to tell me? I'm not the father?"

"No, just explaining the rationale behind who gets to make these decisions."

Michael fell back in his chair. "Well, this really stinks. What am I gonna do if she goes ahead with it?"

"I'm not sure, Michael. I have to admit I've been asking myself the same question."

It was the best answer Josh could come up with at the moment, but to Michael it was a body blow. His shoulders slouched and he dropped his head, eventually forcing a barely audible whimper.

"I'm scared, Dr. Cantor. I love this woman and I'm afraid I'm going to lose her."

Josh tried to reach out in a meaningful way. He began quietly.

"I'm concerned about her too, Michael, so I certainly can't tell you not to worry. I know this isn't easy. But I also know that we can't sit back and allow it to just wash over us. We need to be proactive, to anticipate what she'll need." He waited until Michael lifted his eyes before continuing. "For example, one thing I could use is a world literature search on the subject of abdominal pregnancy. If I remember correctly, you're in the computer field, aren't you?"

"Yeah..."

"Well, the hospital library can normally help but their computer system has been down for the past two days. Would you be able to run it for me?"

Michael brightened up a little. "Sure. That'd be a snap."

Josh offered a handshake. "Well then, how about it? Partners?"

Michael extended his hand cautiously. "Right. Partners."

****

Sarah refused to look at the pessimistic data from Michael's computer search.

"I don't care, Michael. You don't understand. I can't give up this baby now. I've seen it. That changes everything."

"But don't you understand what I'm saying? It's a huge risk to continue this pregnancy, Sarah, and I don't want you to take it."

"But what about how you felt originally? You wanted me to keep the pregnancy, we were going to get married, love conquers all, the whole thing... and now you want me to terminate it?" She shook her head. "I don't think so, Michael. Either way I have to go through an operation, so I'd rather do it later than sooner. At least that way I'll have the baby."

Michael's voice rose. "That's not the way I heard it. Dr. Cantor said it would get more dangerous the longer you waited. And there are no guarantees on the baby, either. I vote we just do this now and try again after you've recovered."

"I know what Dr. Cantor said, but I might not get another chance. My tubes are damaged. What if I can't conceive again?" "How about that high-tech stuff ... IVF, or whatever the hell they call it. If your tubes are blocked they can get around it. I'd rather take that chance than risk your life."

"I don't want to hear it, Michael. You don't seem to understand. I can't abort now. And I won't. This is my decision. My body, my decision. You're not going through this! I am!"

Her adamant stand inflamed him.

"Sonofabitch! I can't believe this shit! In the beginning you were worried I'd make you go through this by yourself and now you're dealing me out? Well, it's my pregnancy too, dammit, and my vote counts just as much as yours!"

Sarah's eyes continued to blaze as her voice turned icy calm.

"Yes, Michael. Your vote counts as much as mine. But I'm the one who has to go through the surgery, so guess who gets to break the tie."

Michael grabbed his head with both hands.

"You know, you're driving me crazy, Sarah! You could die from this thing! It's scaring me!"

Sarah rolled her eyes.

"Relax, Michael. I'm not going to die."

****

Dawn broke as Michael replayed this conversation in his head for the hundredth time. Maybe he should consult with Dr. Cantor again, but to what end? In their initial meeting it was clearly established that Sarah's decision would prevail. Despite spending a restless night, he decided to go to work early. Trying to sleep now was hopeless.

Sarah consulted no one. Now she knew what she was going to do, what she had to do. She was going to have this baby, no matter what. She dialed Dr. Cantor's number.

"Hello, Sarah, how's it going?"

"I'm feeling fine, thanks, and I've made my decision. I want to go ahead with this pregnancy, Dr. Cantor. I understand what's involved, and I just feel right about it."

"You're certain, then?"

"Very certain."

Josh hesitated. "Can I ask you how Michael feels about it at this point?"

"Michael?" Her tone was guarded.

"Yes. Just wondering if you two have worked this out yet."

"As a matter of fact, we haven't," she said, her voice harder now. "Besides, I thought you said this was my decision."

"Yes I did, and I haven't changed my position on that, but he really seems to care for you, Sarah, and I'm thinking you'll need a fair amount of moral support. That's the only reason I asked."

"Well, to be blunt, we've come to an impasse and I guess Michael's out of the picture for now. So let me ask you, then. Is this going to be a problem? Because if it is I'd rather know that up front."

"No, it's not a problem for me, as long as you can deal with it." He hesitated again. "The thing is, this may be riskier than you realize. I took the liberty of discussing your case with a perinatologist, and he's just as concerned as I am, so I can help you to make an appointment there if you'd like."

"But what about you? Won't you be my doctor any more?"

Josh had, in fact, assumed that Sarah's care would be transferred completely to the perinatal service, but her anxiety moved him and he tried to think of a way to placate her.

"Well, I guess I could stay involved as a co-manager, but I have to repeat this, Sarah: This could be dangerous for you, and the prognosis for the baby in these pregnancies isn't very good either. Please be sure you're thinking with your head as well as your heart."

"I understand completely. Please hear me, Dr. Cantor. I want this baby. And I'm ready to do whatever I have to do to get it."

ELEVEN

Nancy Sanderson found herself thinking a lot about Philip LeDuc. Philip had arranged a two-week observation period in the infertility clinic and she began to look forward to seeing him each morning. The problem was she couldn't tell for sure if the feeling was mutual. He was friendly enough, but she wasn't getting the kind of signals she was looking for. This was his second week at the clinic and the majority of his remaining time would be spent working with the laboratory technicians. Soon he would be returning to the veterinary school. She decided he needed a little push.

"Philip, I've been thinking about your research project and I've got an idea we might be able to work on together. Are you free for lunch today?"

"Gosh, no I'm not. I've gotta drive down to Grafton later this morning and I won't be back 'til around four."

"Hmm, I'm tied up then....but let me ask you something....What would you think about having dinner at my place? I'm not a bad cook."

Philip looked pleased, she thought.

"Well, sure. What time do you have in mind?"

"How about 7:30 or so? That'll give me time to get everything together."

"Yeah, that'd be great."

They shared a smile.

"Good. Let me give you directions and my phone number."

Philip was prompt. He drove west on Memorial Drive, a few minutes past M.I.T., and was surprised by the elegance of the neighborhood. He was also in for another surprise. She lived alone. In a plush Charles River

43

Drive high-rise. Compared to the modest accommodations he shared with three other students, this was real luxury. As he rode up the quiet elevator he wondered what this evening was about. Was it going to be strictly business or did she have something more in mind? He was not unaware of the special attention she had been showing him, but he had naively assumed that she was beyond his reach because of her academic standing. He also assumed, correctly, that she must be at least thirty-ish since she had already finished medical school, residency, and a two year infertility fellowship.

Any doubts Philip had about Nancy's intentions were immediately dispelled as her door opened. Nancy's 'researcher' image at the hospital was deliberately conservative: oversized lab coat, wire-rim glasses, hair done up in a neglected twist, ever-present clipboard in hand. But now before him stood someone else, a stunning creature wearing a sleeveless white linen blouse, mid-thigh skirt, and knockout legs in dark stockings. Her hair was down. Silky black. To her shoulders. And the glasses were gone. A little makeup and lip gloss, along with three slave girl bracelets on her left forearm completed a sensational package that had him mesmerized.

Behind her beckoned crystal wineglasses alive with candleflame, and beyond that a panoramic view of the shimmering Charles River, reflecting Boston's sparkling skyline and crowned by the imposing Prudential tower. The scene was breathtaking, but none of it compared to the dazzling smile she offered as she took his jacket.

"I'm glad you could come, Philip. As I told you this morning, I have an idea we might be able to work on together."

Distracted by the elegant surroundings, he was only half-attentive.

"Sure, okay .... Gosh, this is a beautiful place."

Nancy allowed a hint of drawl to creep into her conversation. "Why, thank yew. Don't you love the view? That's why I decided to take this apartment. It's a little inconvenient for work, but I think the commute's worth it."

"I'd have to agree. It's amazing. I had no idea you lived in a place like this."

"I just took it this year. It wasn't practical during my residency and fellowship, with all the night call and stuff. But now I have a little more free time. At night, anyway.... Listen, why don't you sit down and relax. Would you like some wine before dinner?"

Philip eased into the plush sofa. "Great, I could use that. Today was crazy for me. But I have to admit I've been looking forward to this evening. I really wasn't sure what you had in mind."

"Oh, really?" she teased.

44

Again she flashed the brilliant smile. Philip was caught off guard. He felt a blush and knew she saw it.

"Oh, no, I didn't mean to imply, uh," he stammered. "I meant..."

"That's okay," she laughed. "Don't be embarrassed ... Here..." She handed him a glass of wine and sat close to him, exuding a comfortable warmth that began to put him at ease. Small talk led to sharing their personal histories over dinner. Philip described his boyhood on the family farm in Maine.

"Just a typical Canuck dirt farm. Nuthin' fancy. My folks and my brothers and me. We must have grown a million potatoes, but I liked taking care of the livestock. Mostly sheep. I remember my first experience with lambing," he mused. "Middle of a cold spring night, stone floor in the barn with a pile of straw. Steam coming off this little newborn lamb. I think I decided right then to become a vet."

Nancy smiled at the image. "You have a specialty in mind?' she asked. "Like a particular animal species?"

"Not unless I go into academics. In private practice it kind of breaks down into concentrating on large or small animals."

"Like housepets, you mean?"

"Right, but that's not my thing. I'd want to deal with farm animals, but this fertility assignment has me interested. Maybe I could go that route ...."

He considered the prospect as his voice trailed off. Then he perked up again. "You know," he began, "I've been meaning to ask you something. It strikes me that you'd be conflicted over working both ends of the spectrum in your specialty."

"I don't know what you mean," Nancy answered.

"Well, your main effort is in infertility, right? You do everything you can to help women get pregnant, and you seem to be really dedicated to your work. But then you moonlight at a family planning clinic where most of your patients are trying not to get pregnant, and some of them are looking for abortions. Doesn't that pose any problems for you?"

"To a degree, I suppose, but it comes with the territory. During my training I spent a lot of time in the hospital clinic and I'd have to change hats from room to room. You know, one patient wanting desperately to get pregnant and the next one frightened to death about the prospect. I guess I got used to it after a while. And as for my moonlighting, I'm still carrying some loans from medical school and this apartment doesn't exactly pay for itself. So that's the answer. Plain talk, I do it for the money."

Philip raised his eyebrows. "Well, you're honest, that's for sure, but don't you see the irony? Doing abortions to finance your career in infertility?"

She shrugged her shoulders. "It doesn't really bother me. Early on I thought it out. By the time these women come to me they've already been counseled and they're determined to abort their pregnancies. So why shouldn't I do the procedure, especially if it'll finance my fertility research. Means to an end, that's all."

"Umm," he grunted. "And what's the rainbow lead to?"

"In simplest terms, a department chairmanship at a major institution. My name attached to a landmark breakthrough in infertility research."

"Oh, so you're shootin' for the small stuff, huh?" he laughed. Then he leaned forward. "What makes you so driven, anyway?"

Nancy turned quiet at Philip's question. He sensed he had made some sort of faux-pas. "Uh-oh. I said the wrong thing right there, didn't I?"

She looked at him as if trying to make a decision. "Oh, what the hell. This isn't something I normally talk about ...."

"Sorry. Maybe I was out of line."

"No, it's a reasonable question." She brought her elbows up to the table and rested her chin on her interlaced fingers. "First of all, I was adopted."

He gave her a 'no-big-deal' look. "Yeah...?"

"Don't get me wrong. My folks are okay, I guess. The thing is, I have a brother. He was conceived naturally, just after I came on the scene. I'm sure you've heard this kind of story a hundred times. A couple can't get pregnant, so they adopt. Then, bingo. They have a kid of their own. In this case it happened right away. We're less than a year apart in age."

"And you think they treat you differently?"

"They try not to but I've always seen through it. The thing is, he's a superstar. In every sense of the word. Brilliant, athletic, handsome -- and he's his daddy's boy. There's no question in my mind that my father favors him."

"How about your mom?"

"Nice, but real docile, you know what I mean?"

"Not your role model?"

She shook her head resolutely. "No way. I've always been an achiever. Neither of my parents tend to see women in roles outside the home, but that's their problem."

"What about your biological parents. Do you know anything about them?"

Nancy's eyes grew dark. "No, my birthmother wants her privacy. I'd like nothing better than to meet her and show her what she gave up."

Philip tried to placate her with a warm smile.

"Well, for what it's worth, I think you're doing pretty well." He continued smiling while holding eye contact. "Take my word for it ... you're okay."

The intensity of their conversation as well as their inhibitions began to fade after their second and third glass of wine. She waved off his offer to help clear the table and went to the kitchen to make coffee. While it was brewing she returned to the dining room, approaching his back. As she reached him she obeyed an impulse to stop and place her hand lightly on his shoulder. After a moment she allowed her fingers to move up his neck and into his hair. He turned to look up at her and was rewarded with yet another of those fabulous smiles, followed by a tug at his hair which led them back to the sofa. Caught up in a rush of desire, they kissed and fell back onto the comfortable pillows, where Nancy kicked off her heels and pressed closer to him. But when Philip began to unbutton her blouse she brought her hand up to stop him.

He backed off. "I'm sorry. All that wine...I forgot myself."

"No, don't be sorry. It's just a little soon, that's all .... Maybe we'd better get up for a minute."

Philip was feeling awkward now. She was, after all, his academic superior. Perhaps he had overstepped his bounds.

"Sure...okay....actually, maybe I should go. We both have work tomorrow. And I have some driving to do. I'll see you in the morning, okay?"

"Yeah, okay....Philip, I'm sorry. I shouldn't have started that. You're really sweet to understand."

She walked him to the door and kissed him good-bye. "I hope this won't ruin anything between us," she continued. "Please don't let that happen. We'll talk about everything tomorrow."

He kissed her on the cheek. "Don't worry. We'll get past it. I'll see you in the morning. How about coffee? I'll be there at eight."

"You got it. See you tomorrow." She held his hand as he pulled slowly away, then closed the door.

Nancy fought to catch her breath. Forcing herself to start clearing the table, she tried to calm down but she could still feel his kisses and her heart refused to stop pounding. A few minutes passed. She couldn't let go of the moment and finally gave up trying.

Doubts began to plague her. She wondered if she was chasing all the men out of her life. God knows enough of them had been intimidated by dating a 'lady doctor'. Now here was a guy who seemed comfortable with her and she had sent him packing. This was getting to be a pattern.

She was finishing off a glass of wine when a soft knock came from her door. Instantly she ran to open it and found Philip standing there, still breathing hard. She flew at him, wrapping her legs around his waist. As he returned her kiss, neither of them paid attention to the wineglass shattering at their feet, and she raised no objection as he kicked the door shut and carried her to the bedroom.

****

They decided to change the location of their morning coffee date, sharing it instead at her apartment. Philip woke shortly after dawn and made his way into the kitchen, wearing only a pair of dark blue bikini briefs. He was stretching to reach a high shelf.

"Looking for something?"

He turned to see Nancy, who had been admiring the view. She was dressed in only his shirt and her smile. Her legs looked even better without stockings.

"Good morning. Yeah, I was going to surprise you with coffee in bed, but I'm not having any luck here."

"Well, why don't you let me serve you, then. After all, you worked pretty hard last night."

"I'm glad you noticed. I guess that means I'm entitled to a he-man breakfast."

"Anything you want. Just name it."

"I don't usually eat breakfast, actually, but today I have to confess I'm starving. Can you do bacon and eggs?"

"Bacon? You've got to be kidding, Phillip. You can eat that stuff after working with those cute little piggies? I would've thought you'd get attached to those guys."

"Nope, I'm pretty good at disassociation. It's never been a problem for me."

"Yikes! Remind me to never make you mad. This is scary. I just spent the night with a guy who eats his friends for breakfast!" She slithered towards him and nuzzled his neck.

"The problem is that I'm sort of a vegetarian, but I think I can manage an omelet. Will that do for now?"

He smiled contentedly. "How can I refuse?"

Over coffee Nancy shifted the topic of conversation. "You know, we never did get into my research idea last night," she said.

"Oh, you mean you really did plan to talk about work?" he teased her.

"Of course I did, you egotistical S.O.B. You just got me distracted, that's all."

"Oh, I see," he said with mock sobriety. "Well, please go ahead. I'm all ears."

Nancy feigned indignance.

"As a matter of fact, I have a terrific idea, but I don't think I'll tell you about it now, since you're such a smartass."

Philip put on a contrite expression. "Okay, go ahead. I'm sorry. I'm listening. Go ahead. Really."

She studied his face and concluded he was at least attempting to be serious. "Well, I have this idea. You remember that abdominal pregnancy we saw with Cameron Gallagher? Those things are really rare so I was thinking of setting up an animal model. What would you think about using pigs as a research species?"

"It could work, I suppose. In fact, it might work pretty well. Pig abdomens are similar to humans and their pregnancies are much shorter."

"How short?"

"It's easy to remember this one. You just have to use the rule of 'threes'. Three months, three weeks, and three days. About 112 to 114 days."

"Good. Less than half of a human pregnancy. What about ovulating? How often can they get pregnant? Do they ovulate every time they have intercourse, like rabbits?"

"No, they're not copulation ovulaters. They actually have a three week estrus cycle, and they'll only accept a boar over a one or two day span when they're ovulating. But they do get pregnant easily. Their rate of conception is quite efficient, whether it's by copulation or through artificial insemination."

"You do 'A.I.' with them? But how do you get the pig semen? Or should I ask?"

"It's pretty interesting, really. They train the boar to mount a wooden dummy. At first they position a female under it, until the boar starts to make the association. Then he'll mount the dummy without the sow being around. And, by the way, they produce as much as a quart of semen per ejaculation. From a two foot long erect penis. Quite studly, don't you think?"

"Aw, you've got those poor guys not knowin' the difference between the real thing and a bunch of sticks. They must be dumb as hell."

Philip sprang to the defense of his favorite animals. "Not at all, 'Daisy Mae'.

I would've thought you'd know more about farm animals, coming from 'down south' and all."

He stopped to be certain that Nancy could take his kidding. When he saw her roll her eyes good-naturedly, he continued.

"You should know that pig are right near the top of the list in mammalian intelligence. Just after humans, primates, and dolphins. And I happen to think they might be even brighter than dolphins. You can teach a pig to do anything. And they're much cleaner than you think. Did you know some people keep them as pets? And some of them...."

"Okay, okay! I didn't mean to insult all of pigdom! I'm just trying to figure out if they'd be a good subject for the experiment I have in mind."

Philip smiled sheepishly. "Right. And what is it again that you're proposing?"

"Well, I'm thinking of using in-vitro fertilization techniques and then dropping embryos into their abdomens to see if they'll grow. Maybe we could study them to figure out a way to make abdominal pregnancies safer for humans."

"So how will this work? How are you gonna get the embryos into their abdomens?"

"That's the easy part, actually. The problem is retrieving the eggs. From what you're telling me it sounds like the sperm's not a problem, but we need pig eggs to mix with the sperm in a petri dish. Once they're fertilized we could draw them up in a syringe with saline and just inject them into their abdomens and see if they'll grow there. We could follow the pregnancies with ultrasound to watch for problems, and then do surgery to remove the babies" - she held up her hands - "I know, 'piglets'... and then learn how to deal with the placentas. That's the big problem in human abdominal pregnancies, because of the bleeding when they're removed."

"You know, I think someone at school is doing in vitro stuff in the swine fertility unit. Of course they're putting them directly into the uterus. I'm not sure what they're trying to accomplish...maybe some kind of alternative to artificial insemination." "Well, that's convenient. Do you think you can hook us up with these people?"

Philip frowned and drummed the table with his fingers. "I guess I could talk to them, but I see a couple of problems. Like adult pigs are expensive. The typical research animal costs a few hundred dollars. And the bigger problem is getting it past the research committee. They're heavy into ethical considerations these days, especially with animal rights groups breathing down their necks. I'm not at all sure we could get the idea off the ground."

"Hmm, we'll have to think about this," Nancy mused. Meanwhile her thoughts turned to Joshua Cantor. Maybe she could involve him in this project. After all, it was his patient that kicked off her interest, and he was in a position of influence. But she decided to keep the idea to herself. Nancy didn't want Philip to know about her past relationship with him.

Josh had been the chief resident at Boston Lying-In during her first year of training. She was just out of medical school and he represented everything she aspired to. On top of that he was cute, and unattached at the time, and it didn't take her long to make the decision to go after him. Their romance endured for over half of her first year of residency and burned white-hot while it lasted.

All of that was long ago, of course. They had calmed down enough to take stock of their differences and admit that a permanent relationship just wasn't in the cards, and Nancy decided it would be more comfortable to finish her residency across town at the Boston General. Shortly afterwards Josh had entered into a new relationship that led to marriage, but Nancy was certain she still occupied a wrinkle in his temporal lobe. She had sensed it the last time they saw each other.

Philip waved his hand in front of her face, smiling curiously. "Nancy? Are you still with me?"

She blinked back to the present. "Oh! Sorry. Yeah, I'm with you. I guess I was daydreaming." She glanced at her watch. "Meanwhile, we'd better get moving if we're planning on going to work today."

"Right…only what am I going to do about shaving and a change of clothes? Somebody's gonna wonder why I'm in yesterday's wrinkled shirt. And I don't have time to get to my place and back."

"No problem. I've got a razor for you. These legs don't get silky smooth by themselves, you know. And you can change into a scrub suit when you get to the hospital. I've done it lots of times." She began to giggle.

"One night I had to rush in so fast I just threw on a raincoat over my nightgown. Then later that day I got into trouble when I tried to leave. I was wearing a scrub suit under my raincoat and a security guard stopped me because there's a rule against taking scrubs out of the building. I couldn't think fast enough to make up a story so I decided to tell him the truth. When I pulled the nightie out of my pocket to prove it the guy laughed and said fine, just bring the scrubs back in the morning."

Philip grinned. "I wish I'd seen that."

"I'll give you a private showing someday," she winked. Then she pulled back. "So how about my idea? Are you in?"

"Yeah, I think I can see myself working on it with you." She moved closer to him. "You can?" she purred, "Okay, it's a deal." Standing on her tiptoes, she kissed him on the lips. "We'll have to talk more about it later."

TWELVE

Josh and Nancy ran into each other again a few days after their chance meeting in Cameron Gallagher's office. It was 7 AM, the typical arrival time for both of them, but because they entered and worked in different wings of the hospital it was unlikely that they would cross paths. This time, however, they both happened to be on the post partum floor. Josh was making rounds when he saw her in profile at the nurses' station. He called out to her. "Nancy?"

She turned and gave him a friendly smile. "Hi, Josh. Well, isn't this nice. Twice in the same week."

"Right. And after a lot of years," he smiled back. "What brings you over here to the trenches, by the way?" Don't tell me you're delivering babies again."

"Heaven forbid! No, I just came by to check on a former infertility patient. How about you. Someone in labor?"

"No, just making rounds. Actually, I'm nearly finished and I was planning to grab a cup of coffee. Could I interest you in that?"

She looked at her watch. "Sure. Sounds good."

Both of them became aware that they were getting more than a few glances as they sat in the hospital cafeteria. Josh broke the tension by talking about it.

"Looks like we're causing a bit of a stir here, doesn't it?"

"I won't worry about it if you won't," Nancy shrugged. "There's no place like a hospital for creating gossip, is there? I think any two warm bodies of opposite gender can get tongues wagging."

"These days the genders don't even have to be opposite."They shared a laugh.

"So tell me, how've you been, Josh?"

"Doing fine, thanks. Happy with my practice. Pretty much just what I wanted. And you? You look great, that's for sure."

Nancy parried the compliment. "Well, I'm doing exactly what I want. Still love my research."

"So I've noticed. Your name's been all over the journals. I don't think I've ever seen anybody get published that much so early in their career."

She took an exaggerated breath. "Well! I certainly feel good about myself this morning! But you stole my thunder, Josh. I was just about to tell you what great things I've heard about your practice." She tilted her head. "And I hear you're happily married."

"Uh-huh." Then, after noting her quizzical expression, he added, "Very happily."

Nancy took this well. "That's great, Josh. Kids?"

"Not yet." He quickly changed the subject. "That was a handsome guy you were with the other day."

"Mmm. Somebody new, but seems real nice."

Their conversation continued along the same vein, mostly light subject matter with some livelier moments about hospital politics. During the one brief reference to Nancy's research on a new fertility drug, she smiled enigmatically and subtly steered to another topic, quipping that this was a social meeting and that they would have plenty of time to talk medicine some other time. When it was time to go he carried their cafeteria trays and walked with her until they parted directions.

"I'm glad we did this, Nancy," Josh said. "The Lying In's big enough for both of us, but I was hoping we could be comfortable around each other."

"Me too. You take care now. I'll see you soon." She waved goodbye as she walked away. "Education committee next Tuesday, right?"

Josh was surprised, unaware that she'd already gotten that appointment. Why the education committee, he wondered. And what else did she have in mind?

THIRTEEN

Sarah and Michael were barely communicating about the pregnancy now. There were seeds of doubt in Michael's mind. Maybe Sarah really was being selfish. The way she changed her mind without consulting him, and the adamant attitude she displayed, made him think she might not be his perfect woman after all. At the very least she had fallen from his pedestal. At worst he wondered if he really knew her at all. She was beautiful, that was certain. And her values were admirable. There was no doubt about that either. And he knew he was still in love because his doubts melted each time he saw her. But when he forced himself to be objective he could see flaws that he had been blind to in the past. For one thing, she seemed to be giving no consideration to his paternity rights, and he felt her decision to continue the pregnancy was an unreasonable risk to herself. Why couldn't she see his point of view?

Sarah had been wondering about Michael, too. He was being much less attentive than usual. There was a distance between them now. She could feel it. He wouldn't consider her feelings about this baby, always taking the logical perspective without trying to understand her position. She prepared herself for the possibility of a split, deciding she would have to manage without him if necessary. If he was going to back out, so be it. The baby was the most important thing now, more important than Michael and more important than her parents. She knew she had the strength to tell them about this situation if she chose to do so. And even to demand their financial support. They would help. They always did.

So that was it. Her course was charted, no matter who approved or disapproved. This was her baby and her life. Everyone would simply have to understand...and help on her terms. She couldn't allow herself to tolerate any compromises.

Sarah's pregnancy had reached eighteen weeks and she could feel movement now. In fact, she thought she could feel the baby a few weeks ago. Normally, she was told, with a first pregnancy the mother didn't feel the baby until twenty weeks but she was aware of it earlier because of the abnormal location. Doctor Cantor and the perinatologist were following her more closely than usual, recommending frequent ultrasounds in order to follow the baby's progress. One benefit of all this was that they were able to tell her the baby's sex. She was having a boy. But they were concerned about a possible growth retardation because of the placental blood source. As far as they could tell it was attached to the colon, although she had experienced no change in bowel function except the usual mild constipation associated with pregnancy. Still, they questioned her about this. They were worried that the placenta might invade the intestinal wall and cause internal hemorrhage.

"Have you had any bowel problems? Any bleeding? Are your stools dark, or black?"

Sarah was ambivalent about the extra attention. She was reassured with each satisfactory ultrasound study but worried about whether the frequent exposure to high frequency sound waves might damage the baby. Dr. Cantor reassured her that there was no evidence of damage from the level of ultrasound energy they were using, but she couldn't help thinking of it as an x-ray because of the images the machine produced. And there was also the feeling of being a guinea pig. Every visit with the perinatologist prompted a teaching session involving several residents and students. Although they tried to be polite, she always sensed they were gawking at her. All of them wanted to examine her abdomen to see what a pregnancy felt like when it was situated outside of the uterus. Never mind that most of them would never see another abdominal pregnancy in their medical careers. Occasionally, she grew impatient, but always managed to restrain herself for fear of alienating someone. She wanted to befriend every doctor and nurse in that clinic so that she, and ultimately her baby, would get preferential treatment. But outside of the clinic she didn't want to be treated any differently than anyone else. She decided not to tell her parents about the pregnancy at this point. It would just create more problems than she already had to deal with. She didn't want them hovering over her and insisting that she move back to see specialists of their own choosing. She was happy with herself and proud of her image, a single pregnant woman making it on her own.

FOURTEEN

The education committee meeting took place on the first Tuesday of every month. Although the spring and summer agendas were typically less intense than those at the heart of the academic year, the recent addition of Nancy Sanderson to the membership had raised expectations for some lively debate, and June's meeting fulfilled those expectations. The third item for consideration, submitted by Nancy, had to do with changing the future image of the hospital. She was called on to present her point of view.

"This may seem a bit radical to some of you," she began, "but I think it's time for this institution to change its direction. For years, the Lying-In has had the reputation of a first rate service facility. Everyone knows the level of clinical care here is the best in the city, and there's certainly nothing wrong with that, but as you know I've been at the General for the past several years and I can tell you that the Lying-In's image has become a little stodgy. The consensus is that we're starting to slip academically, and the specific reason is the lack of published material that originates from here."

Dr. Leon Landry, the department chairman, responded.

"Your point is well taken, Nancy. In fact that's one of the reasons we were interested in having you join our faculty. We expect that you'll be a 'rainmaker,' if you will, both by your presence here and your contributions to the professional literature."

"Yes, I understand that role, Leon. In fact, when my new fertility drug has gotten past the FDA, I'm planning a gala presentation conference for the medical community, complete with media coverage."

Oblivious to the raised-eyebrow reaction of the conservative committee members, she continued. "But until then I have another idea.

I know you haven't filled the director of education position since Scott Hunter moved to the west coast, and I think that gives this committee an opportunity to accelerate our change of image by replacing him with someone who's more research oriented. For example, one or two of our quarterly conferences could be devoted to research methodology. I think it would make an instant impact on our reputation if we offered a mini course on statistics, or maybe data analysis."

Landry laughed. "I have no doubt that would change our reputation, Nancy, but those conferences have to pull their weight financially, and at four or five hundred dollars a session I'm afraid we'd be presenting our program to a very small audience."

Josh Cantor agreed. "I'd have to second that. I don't think those topics would fill the seats."

Nancy folded her arms. "Well, maybe all the bread-and-butter people out there need to be educated on what's important. And what means more to us? Advancing the status of our institution or worrying about the bottom line?"

Landry gestured toward Josh, indicating he should answer.

Josh weighed his words. "We need them both, Nancy, but to me the bigger question is whether we want to change our mission. The Lying-In does have an excellent clinical reputation and I don't think we should gamble with that. I grant you that we need to contribute our share of research, but I think it would be a mistake to shift the balance too drastically."

Landry nodded his head affirmatively. "That's pretty much my position in a nutshell, Nancy. I'm not ready to turn us into a giant research lab. But there's certainly plenty of clinical material around here. Maybe you could use it for some retrospective analysis studies."

"That's not what I had in mind," Nancy shot back. She slouched in her chair, her arms still folded.

Her pouty expression concerned Josh. He had seen it before and it brought back memories of the headstrong personality he had once known so well. The remainder of the meeting left him uneasy. Nancy's presence was strong enough to alter the committee's course, and this wasn't the way he hoped it would go.

FIFTEEN

After another night on call, Josh came home to find Aviva elbow-deep in books on their dining room table. The number and variety of volumes was astounding - a mixture of their collections dating back to undergraduate school - stacked two feet high, their bulk so ponderous that he wondered how the table-board could bear the weight. Aviva was outfitted in her no-nonsense, house-reorganizing garb: swimming in one of his old shirts, sweatpants, hair persuaded into a pony tail with a thick rubber band. As he entered the room she was lunging to prevent one of the stacks from toppling. He hurried to help her, the two of them barely preventing an avalanche.

"Uh-Oh. She's been in the basement again."

She pushed the pile upright and laughed with him.

"It's still a shambles down there. I don't know what got into me, but once I got started I couldn't stop."

Josh noticed a separate pile on a nearby chair. He could tell immediately that they were all children's titles.

"Stuff from work?"

"Yeah, all out of print now." Her eyes turned misty. "I thought I'd put them aside and save them ... you know ...."

He winced at how rapidly her mood turned. It was taking less and less these days. Even the slightest reference ....

He put his arm around her and pulled her close.

"Pretty soon, Viv. It'll happen for us."

"I know it will, but after the last miscarriage I'm afraid to hope for it any more."

He guided her to the living room where they sat down together. She leaned into his shoulder. "I'm sorry, Joshua. I know you deal with this stuff all day. I didn't mean to hit you with it right away."

"Don't be silly, Viv. This is personal. Work is a million miles away right now." He sat thoughtfully for a moment. "But I will tell you we could have it worse. Like that patient with the abdominal pregnancy. I wouldn't want to trade places with her."

Aviva perked up. It struck him that she always did when he talked about clinical things.

"Oh, that poor girl. I almost forgot about her. How is she?"

"How is she? Well, to look at her, you'd think she was fine. Tough as nails, going ahead with the pregnancy come hell or high water. I don't know if she's heroic or crazy."

"Well, I think she's great. I'd do the same thing in her place."

"No you wouldn't, Viv. I wouldn't let you."

"You wouldn't 'let' me? There's no way you could stop me, Joshua. Even with all the risk."

"You're serious?"

"Absolutely. But I know you can't understand. It's a woman's thing."

He had heard this before from his patients, sometimes as an offhand remark, at other times out of frustration, and it never failed to annoy him. He found it offensive, even sexist. But now it was coming from Aviva, whom he thought he knew so well. He looked at her, trying his best to grasp some sense of what she was feeling, what could possibly motivate her to take such a stand. But try as he might, nothing registered. Not even a clue.

She's right, he thought. I can't begin to understand.

SIXTEEN

Two months passed uneventfully for Sarah despite increasing concern expressed by Dr. Cantor and the specialists at the high risk pregnancy clinic. At twenty-eight weeks her placenta had started to show evidence of premature aging. The doctors showed her the "echoes," small white dots and flecks on the ultrasound image of her pregnancy. They advised her to take it easy and get a lot of bed rest during the day, ideally on her left side. The frequency of ultrasound activity started to rise. They were asking her to return twice a week for more and more pictures and tests. There were discussions about delivering her prematurely, even earlier than the thirty-two to thirty-four week range they had originally hoped for. To complicate matters further, Michael had found out about these recent developments and had been back in touch with her. Over the past week he had been calling or visiting her every day to express his concern and insist that she follow medical advice.

Dr. Cantor had asked Sarah to meet with him and one of the perinatologists to discuss her pregnancy's status and prognosis. When she walked into the office, Bridget Walsh hovered over her as usual, showering her with attention and concern as she showed her into the consultation room.

"Now you listen to Dr. Cantor, dear. We're all worried about you around here"...she softened her voice and placed a tender hand on Sarah's shoulder..."and I want you to know I'm prayin' for ya every day."

Sarah was touched by Bridget's concern. She patted the motherly hand.

"Thank you, Bridget. I really appreciate that."

Josh was waiting with his colleague and friend, Howard Greenwald, Chief of Perinatology at the Boston Lying-In. Greenwald was strictly business. He wasted no time in laying out Sarah's options.

"Sarah, your baby has reached the stage of viability - the point where it could survive - and the placenta is failing. We have to decide whether to let the pregnancy continue or deliver you now."

Sarah was alarmed. "Now? But the baby's so small. People can't even tell I'm pregnant yet."

"That's partly because you're tall, and partly because of the abdominal location."

"How much does it weigh at this point?"

"Only about two pounds. It would have to spend a long time in the intensive care nursery, and there'll be a rocky road in the beginning, but we have to compare that to the risk of leaving it inside. In terms of risk-benefit the baby might be better off in the hospital than the hostile environment in your abdomen."

"What's so hostile inside? I don't want my baby to have to struggle outside with all kinds of machines and tubes stuck in him. I feel like he's safe and warm inside of me. Why can't we let him grow just a little while longer?"

Josh intervened. "Maybe we can, Sarah. The consensus of the perinatal department was to try to get you past thirty weeks. But let me tell you that the idea of waiting wasn't a unanimous decision. Personally I feel it might be too risky, and Dr. Greenwald feels the same way. The placenta seems to be aging rapidly now so we're afraid it might not hold out for two or three more weeks."

While absorbing this information Sarah shifted in her chair before speaking. "I'd still like to try waiting a little longer," she persisted. "My intuition tells me that's the right thing to do, and I believe in listening to my body."

"You'd be wiser to listen to a professional's opinion," Greenwald grunted. "How you feel right now has nothing to do with it."

Now Sarah dug in her heels. "Well, I happen to think it has a lot to do with it. Doctors have been wrong before, and unless I'm mistaken I still have the final say in this matter."

Josh shot Greenwald a "cool it" look and tried for some damage control. "Of course it's your decision, Sarah, but it's our job to put aside emotion and be objective for you. The problem here is the way your placenta looks on ultrasound. It seems to be deteriorating rapidly, probably because its blood supply is failing. And if the placenta isn't working it has a direct effect on the baby."

"I guess I understand that, but it's still hard to believe my system would treat the baby so badly when I feel so healthy. Just let me think about this for a while. I'm going away for the weekend but I'll call you on Monday to talk about it some more."

"You're leaving the area? I don't know, Sarah. I don't like this." Josh stopped to allow himself to think for a moment. "No, let me re-state that. I don't approve. You shouldn't be too far away from the hospital right now."

Sarah tensed again. "Look, I'm just going down to the Cape. Michael's been giving me a hard time about this lately and I feel like I need to get completely away from him for a while, just to sort things out for myself. But I'll be back by Sunday afternoon. Twenty-four hours, give or take. And I won't do anything strenuous, I promise. We can talk again on Monday."

Josh knew this had the potential to turn into a battle of wills, and if it did he was going to lose not only the argument but possibly Sarah's trust as well. "All right," he sighed, reaching for a piece of scrap paper, "but at least take this phone number. It'll reach my pager. When you hear a beep just punch in the number you want me to call back. I'm off duty this weekend but I'll carry it just in case. Who's going with you, by the way?"

"No one. I want some time to think. I'll be okay, but thank you for this number anyway. It makes me feel better that I can get in touch with you if I have to."

On Saturday morning Sarah drove to Cape Cod. It wasn't too far away and it would be just the change of environment she needed to help her think straight. Being near the ocean always put things in perspective for her. Shortly after crossing the Bourne Bridge she reached Falmouth, then continued at random until coming upon an inviting little ma-and-pa seafood shack with a water view, just the kind of spot she liked while spending an unstructured day.

Her mood became increasingly self-indulgent. She allowed herself a sinfully rich bowl of lobster stew, lingering near the window and gazing at the shore. Suddenly she couldn't wait to get her feet in the water. She got back into the car, headed for the town beach, and, after finding a parking space, walked barefoot to the water's edge. Smiling to herself, she squeezed wet sand between her toes while the hem of her loose-fitting sundress dipped into the August surf.

As she sauntered along, her arms swinging in childlike abandon, she turned her face into the sun, squinting her eyes against its irresistible brilliance. Then she turned her attention to the sand, scanning for collectibles. Before long she happened on a peculiar shell that caught her eye, but in the instant that she bent over to examine it, something went dreadfully wrong. Her hand began to tremble, then over-shot its mark. She had difficulty focusing. Her head began to spin. As she stood up to inhale a breath of sea air, blue lights danced in front of her eyes, followed by a rushing sensation, then dim dizziness. She emitted a short cry. A child playing nearby turned her head at the sound and watched as Sarah fell in a heap onto the wet sand.

"Mummy!" the little girl yelled. "That lady fell down!"

Several people rushed to Sarah's aid. One of them was a nurse who kneeled to take her pulse, noting that it was rapid, along with her breathing.

"Are you all right, miss? Miss! Are you all right? Can you hear me?"

A life guard arrived to assess the situation. "Is she okay? What happened?"

"I don't know," the nurse answered. "She collapsed out of nowhere."

"Are you a medical person? Do you know CPR?"

"I'm a nurse. But she doesn't need CPR right now. I'm definitely getting a pulse and she's breathing. She's not answering me, though."

"All right. If you'll stay with her, I'll go call an ambulance."

Sarah regained consciousness as she was being lifted onto a stretcher. She managed to slur out a few words. "Um preg'ant," she muttered softly.....Um preg'ant."

"What? What'd you say, miss?" asked the EMT.

"Preg-'ant."

"Pregnant? You say you're pregnant?"

"Unnh."

"Well, that's good to know. Maybe it's not so serious, then. Fainting spells happen all the time to pregnant women. Has it happened before?"

Sarah shook her head no.

"Is anybody with you. What's your name?"

"Sarah.... No, nobody."

"Okay, Sarah. You're starting to look better. But we're gonna take you over to the hospital to make sure everything's all right."

"Boston ... My doctor ...."

"Yeah, I understand, hon, but there's too much traffic up there. We have doctors down here in the 'boonies' too."

Before she could respond she was hurried into the back of the ambulance. A technician started an IV while receiving instructions from a doctor over the radio. Soon she was on her way to the local emergency room.

Doctor Soo-Yen Park had been having a slow day. She was spending her Saturday working a twelve hour shift in the emergency room at Sisters of Charity, a thirty bed hospital just off route 28. Soo-Yen was a tiny person, small-boned and barely five feet tall, but her image was quickly transformed when she spoke. In addition to being brilliant and quietly confident, she sported a disarming Boston accent that complemented her dry wit. She had graduated near the top of her medical school class, and had earned the unconditional confidence of her colleagues and instructors in her emergency medicine residency at the Boston General. Even her friends tended to be re-surprised by her stature each time they saw her because they never thought of her as small. Now in her third year of residency, she was permitted to moonlight for extra income and she eagerly took advantage of the opportunity to repay her family for college and medical school expenses.

The radio call from the beach came just after notification of a traffic accident on route 6. Soo-Yen calmly directed Sarah's EMT to start an IV line and monitor vital signs. Meanwhile, she and the charge nurse discussed the logistics of preparing for an onslaught of activity.

By the time her ambulance reached the hospital, Sarah had regained nearly full consciousness, although she was still a little dizzy and had some trouble speaking clearly. She looked up to see an attractive Asian face.

"Hi, Sarah. I'm Doctor Park. I hear you fainted. Can you tell me how it happened?"

"I'm preg'ant. In the ab'men."

"What's that, Sarah? Pregnant in the abdomen?"

"Yeah, thass right."

Soo-Yen looked at her oddly. "Okay. Hang on a minute and we'll get you checked out." Then she spoke quietly to the nurse. "Don't we have a fetal monitor here somewhere? We ought to see if the baby's okay. I just hope the kid's brighter than its mother.... 'Pregnant in the abdomen?' .... Where else is she gonna be pregnant? And the way she's slurring her words, I think she's probably stoned."

At that moment the wailing of several ambulances could be heard from just outside the emergency room.

"That's gotta be the traffic accident." Soo-Yen moved to the door. "And it sounds like it's gonna be a lot bigger than we thought. How about getting her on that monitor. And move her out of the way for now. We'll need all the space we can get in here." The accident was worse than originally reported. Five cars and a bus were involved, with eleven people injured, six of them in serious condition. Organized chaos ensued as Soo-Yen tried to single-handedly triage the bleeding, moaning patients, determining which of them needed the most immediate attention. The receptionist called frantically to find help but was having difficulty locating the first backup doctor.

"He's not answering! Where am I going to find someone else on Saturday afternoon?"

The nurse snapped at her. "I don't know, for God's sake! Just keep trying! I'm too busy to do your job for you right now. ... Try some of the surgical staff. Their answering services should be able to find them."

Several hours passed as the understaffed crew worked frantically to coordinate their efforts, readying patients for the operating room, hanging IV's and blood transfusions, interpreting x-rays. By the time they were done it was late at night and the place looked like a battle zone. All of them were exhausted.

"Is there any coffee around here?" someone asked. "I could use some right about now."

"Yeah, me too," Soo Yen said. "If you find some, let me know.... Geez, what a zoo this place was today."

Everyone sat quietly for a moment, letting their heads clear. Then Soo-Yen spoke to one of the nurses. "Say, what happened to that genius pregnant girl we had in here earlier? Did she leave, or what?"

The nurse frowned. "Gosh, I don't know..." Then she drew a sharp breath. "I completely forgot about her! She's in the back room with the fetal monitor." She put down her coffee cup and hurried towards the far side of the treatment area. After a few moments a scream came from that direction.

Soo-Yen jumped up. "What's the matter?"

The nurse came out with her face in her hands, sobbing uncontrollably. Soo Yen rushed into the back room while the others waited anxiously. When she emerged, she stood with her arms hanging limply at her sides, finally managing to force out the words.

"She's cold as ice. She's been dead for hours."

SEVENTEEN

The Falmouth police were faced with a dilemma. A shaken nursing supervisor from Sisters of Charity Hospital had called to report the death of a Jane Doe whose only personal article was a set of car keys found in the pocket of her sundress. Upon inquiry, the investigating officer's leads consisted solely of the facts that the deceased's first name was Sarah, that she was pregnant, and that she had collapsed that afternoon at the town beach. Given the paucity of information, officer Matthew Macri had taken his time about driving to the site where Sarah had been found, reasoning that a moonless night would require deferring his efforts until morning. As it turned out, however, his task was simple. There was only one car left in the parking area and Sarah's keys fit the door. Inside was her handbag, wallet, and driver's license which revealed her full name, address, and social security number.

When Macri returned to headquarters and failed to get an answer at Sarah's home phone listing, he contacted the Boston police who gained entry to her apartment a few minutes after midnight. Initially confounded by the absence of family phone numbers, the detective assigned to the search decided to utilize the next best thing, a black man's picture signed 'Love, Michael' and an address book entry for a Michael Wilson with a star sketched next to it.

Josh Cantor's Sunday brunch was interrupted by a beeper message to return a call in area code 508. The alpha-numeric display also indicated that he should ask for Michael Wilson. Josh's first reaction was that Sarah had changed her mind and invited Michael to accompany her to the Cape, but when his call was answered he nearly dropped the phone.

"Morgue. Shaughnessy here."

"Pardon me? Morgue? Who is this?"

67

"This's Tim Shaughnessy. C'n I help ya?"

Josh held his breath. "My name's Dr. Joshua Cantor. Are you looking for me?"

"Oh, yeah. Jus' a minute, Doc."

Aviva put down the Boston Globe magazine and looked up at Josh, who had turned pale.

"Hello ... Yes, hello, Michael. What happened?"

As Josh listened he began to shake his head sadly. "I'm so sorry, Michael. Would it help if I came down there? ... Are you sure? ... All right, but would you ask the fellow who answered the phone to transfer me to the emergency room? I want to get the medical details if I can. Are you going to be in the hospital for a while? ... Okay, after I talk with them I'll call back and have you paged."

Josh began to rub his temple while he waited. Aviva hadn't taken her eyes off him during the conversation. She mouthed a question. "Not good?"

Again he shook his head gravely, then turned his attention back to the phone. "Hello, this is Dr. Cantor. I'm Sarah Moore's obstetrician. Could I speak to one of your doctors, please?"

EIGHTEEN

It is said that the dead roll over in their grave as an act of disapproval. If so, Sarah Moore would have been spinning in hers to protest her funeral. Had Sarah been given the opportunity to program the ceremonies, her service would have been simple and understated. There would have been no clergy. Her friends would have delivered loving eulogies, speaking of Sarah's inner beauty and waxing romantic about her being laid to rest with the baby still inside her. No one would have worn black. They would have dressed informally and sung of peace and brotherhood, afterwards symbolically spreading wildflowers over her grave. But it didn't go the way Sarah would have wished. Instead there was stifled weeping and the trappings of wealth that she disdained: mahogany coffin, limousines, and dark elegance.

In the midst of this throng of privileged mourners were two young men, both of whom stood out by virtue of their physical appearance. One of them possessed dark, curly hair and Semitic features which prompted several heads to discreetly turn and wonder how he figured into the funeral equation. After he had introduced himself to Sarah's parents, word quickly spread that he was Sarah's doctor, Joshua Cantor. So focused on sympathy and concern that he was unaware of the mild stir his presence was causing, Dr. Cantor moved about the proceedings in an impervious cloud.

The second outsider was a disconsolate young man who, although handsome and appropriately dressed, stood out even more severely. Where everyone else's skin was ivory or florid, his was cocoa. All eyes were on him, wondering what was he doing there. And what was his association with the Moores? A few of the younger people present seemed to be offering him consolation. Josh Cantor also caught sight of him and was chagrined at the raised-eyebrow reaction of the lily white crowd. He made a note to talk with him after the service.

The mourners' curiosity was to be satisfied at the conclusion of the graveside ceremony when the dark stranger turned to the people standing next to him. "Pardon me, could you point out Mr. and Mrs. Moore?"

The queried parties were taken aback. At first they didn't respond. Then an older gentleman in a gray double-breasted suit answered with cool civility.

"They're the couple standing next to Reverend Kehm." He took care not to point but nodded in their direction.

The young man expressed his thanks and then walked toward the Moores, standing aside patiently while the minister consoled them with platitudes. Sarah's parents soon became aware of his presence. Her father turned to him with an expression of mild disdain. "Can I help you?"

An immediate hush fell over those within earshot. While affecting casual nonchalance, they strained to glean gossipy tidbits.

The stranger responded respectfully.

"Yes, Mr. Moore. Sarah never had the opportunity to introduce me to you. I'm Michael Wilson."

At the sound of Michael's name, the Moores stiffened and looked at each other, but Michael continued, initially oblivious to their reaction. "I only want to tell you how deeply sorry ..."

Mr. Moore stopped Michael in mid sentence. "We know who you are, Mr. Wilson."

Michael froze. When he turned to Sarah's mother and saw the same face of abhorrence, the moment was dreadful. Her silence was even worse than her husband's dismissive tone. Without another word Michael turned and walked away, blinking back tears of rage.

Joshua Cantor had witnessed this painful scene and moved quickly to intercept Michael before he reached his car.

"Michael. Can I talk to you for a minute?"

Michael continued his purposeful walking while Josh hurried to keep pace.

"I saw what happened back there, Michael, and I'm sorry. I know how you must be feeling right now."

Michael stopped and faced him, his eyes glistening. "Do you? Have you had the experience of seeing horror in someone's face when they learned you loved their daughter?" He turned away to resume his bitter retreat. Josh followed him.

"No, I haven't, but I'm not a stone. I think I can imagine how you feel."

Michael stopped again.

"No you can't!"

He was at his car now and entered without closing the door, sitting motionless and staring straight ahead while Josh stood helplessly by. After a few seconds he pulled the door shut and rolled down the window, his demeanor now more dispirited than enraged.

"Thanks anyway, Dr Cantor. I know you mean well, but I don't think you could say anything that would make a difference right now." Michael keyed the engine and drove towards the cemetery gate while Dr. Cantor's slumping image shrunk ever smaller in his rearview mirror.

Continuing to stare as the car nearly disappeared, Josh was surprised to see it reverse into a three point turn and head back in his direction. As it rolled to a stop, Michael lowered the window again. "What would you say to having coffee somewhere?"

Josh nodded and got into the car. Still sullen, Michael turned out of the cemetery and drove aimlessly for a few minutes until they reached a roadside bar & grill.

"How about this place" Michael asked. "It looks a little seedy but I'm game if you are."

"Fine with me."

They walked into what turned out to be a dimly lit dive, with Johnny Cash on the juke box revving up a rowdy New England biker crowd. Michael couldn't believe his eyes.

"Would you look at this? I thought I felt out of place at the funeral, but this scene makes me want to go back there."

Josh smiled sympathetically. He sized up the patrons who turned to glance at the two of them but soon turned back to their own boisterous conversations. Deciding that their gawking was more curious than menacing, he reassured Michael.

"I think they'll probably leave us alone, but we can sit next to the door if you like."

Their waitress approached wearing a cut-off tee shirt, exposing a purple Harley Davidson tattoo that covered her entire midriff. Both men managed to order coffees but had difficulty looking away from her abdomen. When she left, Josh was speechless, Michael couldn't help giggling, and the ice was broken. Finally Josh offered an opening.

"Go ahead, Michael. What kind of answers are you looking for?"

"All right, maybe you can tell me why Sarah's parents rejected me out of hand as soon as they saw I was black."

"Do you really think that was it, Michael? I watched the whole thing, and they seemed courteous enough to you at first."

"Yeah, until they realized it was a black man who had gotten their daughter pregnant."

"Well, I can't be sure how they feel about that but, after all, they're in the middle of their grief and maybe they simply view you as the person responsible for their daughter's death ... not that it's logical, but I think it's understandable."

"No, my take on it was definitely racial, but maybe they're right about my being responsible for what happened to her."

"Now how in the world can you possibly feel that way?"

"I don't know, I just can't help feeling that this was my fault. If I had seen things from her point of view, maybe she would've stayed in Boston and she'd be alive now."

Josh sighed deeply. "Not likely, Michael. In the first place, it would have taken a huge stroke of luck for her to be brought to our particular hospital. From what I reviewed about her history, she was mentally compromised when they found her and she was having trouble communicating exactly where she needed to go. Even if she had gotten to a maternity hospital, it's probable the diagnosis would have been missed. The condition's just too rare. But for the sake of argument let's suppose she happened to be examined by someone sharp enough to diagnose the abdominal pregnancy -- a once-in-a-lifetime condition, remember -- and they rushed her to the operating room. In all likelihood, the baby would have been delivered in critical condition and wouldn't have survived because of the bleeding combined with the extreme prematurity. And the worst part is even Sarah probably wouldn't have made it off the operating table."

Michael's eyes came into focus. "She wouldn't? Why not?"

"Because the placenta had begun to separate. To control the bleeding, it would have to be removed, and that's a classic 'no-no' in abdominal pregnancies. The basic principle is to leave the placenta in place because it bleeds uncontrollably when you try to take it out. In her case she was doomed either way, because it would have continued to bleed even if it was left in." Josh's arms were leaning on the table. He gestured by spreading out his fingers. "It would have taken a miracle to save her, and I hate to see you heaping guilt on top of your sorrow."

"But I want the guilt. I'm not ready to let go of it yet ...." A bitter smile twisted Michael's face. "Except for the baby .... Can you believe that? I don't feel anything for the baby." His eyes filled up. "What's wrong with me, Dr. Cantor?"

Josh carefully considered his response. Michael was so vulnerable right now that the wrong word could be crushing.

"There's nothing wrong with you, Michael. I think it's normal for you to feel this way. Maybe you're even resentful about the baby, like maybe it caused Sarah's death."

When Josh got no response he pressed on cautiously. "Look, Michael.

To be honest, I'm not sure exactly what to say to you right now. You're obviously in a lot of pain, and I haven't had any real training in grief counseling." He paused again, sensing that he had come to an impasse. "Can I offer a suggestion?"

Michael was staring down at his folded hands but lifted his thumb ever so slightly, a go-ahead signal.

"You might want to consider a support group to help you deal with this. I can get you in touch with a legitimate therapist if you want."

Michael looked away, staring into middle distance.

"Just think about it," Josh continued. "Men don't tend to do well at this, but I really think it'll do you a lot of good …. and there's something else I want you to know, Michael," he continued haltingly. "Sarah was the first patient to die while under my care." He stopped and swallowed hard. "I know it's different than your loss, but don't be fooled by my apparent objectivity. I've been beating myself up over it just like you have."

Josh had returned to his office that afternoon to deal with a few pressing problems, but as he drove home his thoughts were again with Michael Wilson and the events earlier in the day. He had made a connection, he felt, but he remained ill at ease, wondering if he had really managed to lighten Michael's burden. This type of situation invariably left him with a sense of failure. It was a lot easier dealing with the nuts and bolts of medical conditions than with a person's psyche.

He pulled into his garage and turned off the car's ignition but didn't get out, preferring to sit there and allow his tension to defuse before entering the house. After a minute or two the kitchen door opened to reveal a concerned-looking Aviva.

"Are you all right, Joshua? I heard the garage door go up a while ago."

He breathed deeply. "Yeah, I guess I'm okay now."

She walked to the car and patted his shoulder through the open window.

"Tough day?"

"Yeah," he looked at her with a sad smile. "Real tough day."

NINETEEN

Philip LeDuc had returned to veterinary school in order to finish his research project on swine fertility. He was dividing his time between the school's laboratory and a pig farm in New Hampshire where the owner was at wit's end about the puny litters from his pregnant sows. The pig farmer had come to look at Philip as his saving grace, his only chance to avoid financial ruin.

The farmer's clay-caked boots attested to the perpetually muddy road that led to the property, a rustic hovel nestled at the eastern foothold of the White Mountains. On the porch steps Philip scraped the damp earth from the soles of his sneakers and chided himself for forgetting his roots. He made a note to wear workboots on future visits.

The farmer led him to the kitchen of the tiny farmhouse where Philip explained his idea of using fertility drugs to produce larger numbers of piglets. The problem was that these preparations were expensive, and the farmer was not in a position to afford them.

"This fertility drug thing sounds interestin', but I just can't see how I'm gonna afford to make that kind of investment. Nope, it just don't figger. You're tellin' me that these injections cost fifty bucks apiece and we might need a few of 'em ever' day fer a week or more?" His stuck out a petulant lower lip as he shook his head. "How'm I gonna put out that kinda money on some highfalutin' plan that might not even work? And are ya sure we're gonna get bigger litters?"

"No, I can't honestly promise you that," Philip admitted. "But I don't think I see any workable alternative. I had one of the people at the veterinary school look at the diet factor. The guy has a Ph.D. in swine nutrition and he can't find anything wrong in your feed formula. And the state lab has been up here to evaluate the environment but they haven't come up with any answers either. So what's left? I feel like these drugs are worth a shot."

The farmer pounded the table with his fist. "Sure they're worth a shot! But I don't have the money, I'm telling ya! Damn these cussed hogs. Mis'rable beasts 've got me in a mess!"

Philip winced at this hateful reference. It troubled him that a farmer could feel that way about his animals. Shortly after he met this man he had observed the rough way he handled his livestock, and he was offended by it. While growing up on his family's farm in Maine he had learned to respect all living creatures, even if they were destined for a slaughterhouse.

Their conversation was interrupted by the kitchen telephone. Its ring was nostalgic to Philip, the same sound as the old fashioned phone of his childhood. The farmer looked at it curiously, then picked up the receiver.

"Yeah?"

After listening for a moment he pointed the receiver in Philip's direction.

"For me?"

"Aayep. Some female lookin' fer ya."

Philip took the phone, wondering who could possibly be calling him there.

"Hello, this is Philip LeDuc."

"Hiya doin', boyfriend. Your farmer buddy isn't any too friendly, is he?"

"Nancy! How'd you find me here?"

"The guys in the lab in Grafton gave me this number. I heard some news today and I couldn't wait to tell you about it."

"Yeah? Like what?"

"You remember that ultrasound we saw the first day you arrived here? The patient with the abdominal pregnancy?"

"Yeah, what about it?"

"I just heard she died over the weekend from a massive intra-abdominal bleed.

The perinatal guys are absolutely wild over it."

"You're kidding! I didn't know she was having problems. Was she that far along?" "Not quite seven months, but something obviously went wrong. And there's a big thing about the way it was handled. She died in some E.R. down on the Cape, and the resident who was moonlighting there is in deep shit. But listen, the reason I'm telling you this is that it might open up an opportunity for us. You know, our idea about abdominal pregnancies in pigs. Maybe your research committee will go for it now."

"Gee, aren't you the ambitious little opportunist."

"Hey, what's done is done. And the more I think about it ..."

Philip noticed that the farmer looked annoyed. "Nancy, I'm going to have to get off the phone, but let me give you a call tonight and we'll talk some more about this."

"Good. I'll be at home. You can stop by if you want. I could make us some 'dinner'...."

He could hear her smiling. 'Dinner' had become their code word for lovemaking, ever since that first night at her apartment.

"Sounds good. I'll be there."

"So, what's on the menu?" he teased her from his side of the bed.

"Depends on what side of the river you prefer. What'll it be? Cambridge or Boston cuisine?"

"You mean we're going out? I thought you offered me a home cooked meal."

"You've had all the home cookin' you're gonna get for tonight, Pal. Now get your pants on. We're going out for the evening."

Nancy decided to bring up her idea again over an anchovy special at Harvard Square Pizza. Before broaching the subject, she guzzled a mug of beer, banged it down on the table, and pushed it aside while wiping her mouth with the back of her other hand.

"Damn!" Philip grinned. "Where'd you learn to drink like that, Miss Scarlett?"

"C'mon, now," she replied. "Don't tell me you have this Yankee image of me growing up in pinafores and bows."

"No, but the way you knocked off that beer kind of surprised me. I guess I imagined you sipping mint juleps or something."

"Never mind, farm boy, there's a lot you don't know about me."

The remark caught Philip off guard. Nancy took advantage to redirect the conversation.

"Now what about our research project on abdominal pregnancies?" she went on. "I know you think it's ghoulish to push for this just after that woman's death, but maybe they'll be more receptive to us now."

"Maybe, but I really don't think it's gonna make a difference that she just died.

There's still the matter of the animal rights people. And even if we get over that hurdle, don't forget there's a problem with money. I assume we'll need several adult pigs, and they're expensive, like a few hundred dollars each. And I know the research budget is shot for the fiscal year. But let's just say that we figure out a way to fund it. Then we're back to square one because the animal rights groups are threatening to boycott the products of any sponsor that gets involved."

Nancy wasn't ready to take no for an answer.

"But with IVF it would be so easy to get embryos into pig abdomens. If we could get them to grow we'd have the perfect research model."

Philip was listening carefully but he sat quietly, looking pensive.

"You've got something on your mind," Nancy said. "What are you thinking?"

He pushed his plate aside, clearing the space in front of him. Then he picked up a paper napkin and began to twist it absentmindedly.

"I'm not sure. You know that pig farmer I was with today when you called me?"

"Yeah? What about him?"

"Well, I don't like the guy. I don't like the way he treats his animals... but I'm just thinking maybe he'd be willing to play ball with us. We were talking about using fertility drugs today. You know, to increase the size of his litters. I've told you about that."

"Yeah...?"

"The thing is, he can't afford it. His operation's on the brink right now. He doesn't think the banks would lend him anything because his collateral's already exhausted. He also feels like it's a crap shoot because the drugs might not even work.

So now I'm thinking maybe we could work a deal with him."

"I'm listening. What kind of deal?"

"Like if you could get your hands on some samples of those fertility drugs you've been researching ...we could trade that for a few of his adult pigs and then do our experiments on his farm instead of at the school's research lab."

"Now you're talkin'! Yeah, I could definitely get some samples from the pharmaceutical rep. He's always after me to use his stuff. Hey! This is a good idea!

Good for you, 'Phillipo'. I didn't know you had any devious bones in your body."

"No, not devious. Just practical. After all, it's for a good cause, isn't it?"

"Definitely! Definitely a good cause. Okay! We're gonna do it! Why don't you bounce the idea off 'Farmer Fred' and we'll get this thing off the ground."

Within a few days, Philip had bad news for Nancy. "He didn't go for it." "You're kidding. Why not?"

"He thinks it's still too risky for him financially. If it doesn't work, he's out several pigs at a market value of two or three hundred dollars each."

Nancy was exasperated. "What's he talking about? The drugs are worth a small fortune. He's getting a hell of a deal."

"That would be true if he had some financial reserve, but like I told you, he's nearly bankrupt and he can't afford to lose anything right now."

"So now what? Can't we figure out anything else here?"

"As a matter of fact, he has a counter proposal," Philip said. "But it's complicated. And shrewd. He's not as dumb as he looks."

"So let's hear it."

"He wants proof that the drugs will work. He says if we can show him results with one sow, he'll go for it."

"And he won't donate one pig to find out?"

"In his words, 'Nope.' He's a hard bargainer too."

Nancy slouched in her chair. "Hmm. All right. Why don't we think about it and talk again tomorrow?"

Philip grinned. "Over 'dinner', maybe?"

"Get your brains out of your pants. No, I'll be at the hospital 'til late. I'll try to reach you during the day."

Nancy tracked down Philip just after noon. "I have another idea."

"Well, I'm glad to hear it, because I haven't come up with anything," he admitted.

"Okay, here's the deal. Your farmer guy wants proof that the fertility drugs will work, right? It seems to me that we have to make the first move, but we don't have the female pig to prove it with. One thing we can do is to buy our own animal, but I have a way to do it using one of his own pigs, and it won't cost him anything. Are you following me so far?"

"Yeah, go ahead."

Her voice began to rise. "What we need to do is to provide the drugs and inject one of his sows with it. We can do it up there if you're willing to make the trip. That way he has nothing to lose. He doesn't even have to have the sow removed from his farm. If we get lucky she'll have a big litter and he'll be convinced."

"Sure, that sounds okay, but the problem is that we're gonna have to wait a few months to find out if it works."

"I've thought about that," Nancy continued. "We can predict how many piglets she's carrying by using ultrasound. Within a few weeks we should be able to tell if it's worked or not."

"And where do we get the ultrasound machine?"

"I've thought of that too. There's an old portable machine sitting in storage at the hospital. Nobody's used it for months. It's small enough to sneak it out of the building without being noticed. We could take it up to his farm and just plug it in right in the barn. I'm betting it'll be easy to count the embryos within a few weeks after conception."

Philip was impressed. "You know, that really sounds workable. Let me talk to him again. I'll bet he goes for this one."

Philip made arrangements for several consecutive daily trips to the pig farm that month. The farmer had readily agreed to the proposal, but Nancy was anxious that the precious drugs not be wasted. She asked several questions about swine fertility, especially the female's estrus cycle.

"They ovulate every three weeks," Philip explained.

"Can you predict when?" she asked. "Do you need to do any special blood or urine testing?"

"No, it's pretty simple. Sows will react in a certain way when they're willing to accept a male. All you have to do is to put pressure on their back, by leaning on them with your hands. It's an imitation of a boar trying to mount them. If they're not ovulating, they'll run away. But if they're fertile right then, they'll stop and stay there and their ears will point straight back, waiting for the boar to do his thing. So don't worry. We won't miss the chance to inseminate them at the right time."

"Good. That sounds easy. But I could only get a total of ten vials of drug samples. I got a few of them from the company, but I had to rip off the rest from the fertility lab's refrigerator."

"Well that's great, Nancy. Now you're a crook, too. But will that be enough? I thought you said it required a lot more than that in humans."

"Yeah, it does. But I can't get any more right now. We're gonna have to hope that there'll be a species difference and that pigs will respond to lower doses."

"Okay, we'll just have to go for it. I'll get started as soon as I can."

During the following month Philip injected the farmer's sow several times, taking care to communicate daily with Nancy about dosages and the proper timing for insemination. A few weeks later he called Nancy with unbridled excitement in his voice. "It worked. We counted at least thirteen embryos. Farmer Fred's ready to go! "That's great!" Nancy answered. "Let me see what I can do about getting some more samples."

"I'm afraid not, Dr. Sanderson." The pharmaceutical representative was apologizing about his inability to provide any more medication. "The company only allows me a certain number of samples per quarter. I had to stretch to get you as many as I did last month so I can't appropriate any more for several weeks."

"Can't you get me some under someone else's name? I really need the stuff right now."

"I really wish I could. You can name any other product we make and I can get all you want, but not this one. As much as I'd like to do it for you, I'm up against a wall."

Nancy heard his words but she sensed he wasn't sincere. He was too smug, too slick. She knew he could distribute more of the samples to her if he really wanted to. It was a simple matter of fudging his papers a little. He just wanted to ingratiate himself to as many accounts as possible. She remembered something she learned from her businessman father. At the time, he was instructing her brother in the ways of the world, but Nancy had listened, and the lesson wasn't lost on her.

"In the course of a negotiation there's generally a point where an awkward silence occurs. That's the critical moment. It's like a blinking contest. The first one to speak loses."

She decided to try it. The representative waited for her to ask again, perhaps to protest or threaten. But instead she said nothing. She simply sat where she was and looked at him with an inscrutable expression. In a few seconds his body language started to change subtly, from a posture of self assurance to one of obvious discomfort. She continued her tactic of silence. He squirmed in his seat. She began to enjoy the game. Beads of sweat broke out on his forehead. Now it was his turn to beg.

"Look, I could lose my job over this. The company has a strict policy. They've made it clear that they'll terminate anyone who ignores it."

Nancy's expression didn't change.

"C'mon, Dr. Sanderson, have a heart. This hospital is a huge account and I can't afford to lose it. I have a family to support. Me and my wife have three kids. This could create a serious problem for me."

His family reference made Nancy relent. "All right. I just thought I could persuade you somehow, but if it's that big a deal don't worry about it. I'll figure out something else."

Immense relief crossed his face as he stood to thank her. "I appreciate this, Doctor. If there's anything else I can do for you, just let me know. Anything."

"That's okay. Maybe I'll still be able to use the samples next month if you can get them for me then."

He backed out like a bum with his hat in his hand, bowing and scraping, his eyes filling up with gratitude. "Doctor, you just say the word and I'll have them for you just as soon as I can get my hands on them."

The image of a man in tears gave Nancy a pang of guilt. She stood up and started to babble. "Really, it's okay. It's not that important. I don't know why I made such a big deal over it. I'm grateful for the stuff you've already given me. Don't worry about it. Have a good day. And don't worry. Really."

He gave her a wounded puppy dog smile and thanked her again. As the door closed she sat down heavily.

"Damn! What the hell was I doing?"

After composing herself, Nancy gathered her papers and headed to the clinic. She continued to feel remorse about what had happened, but when she passed by the business office she was shocked by what she saw. Just a few minutes after he had groveled in front of her and been drawing on his family-man image for sympathy, the pharmaceutical rep was leaning across a desk and chatting up one of the young billing clerks, flirting shamelessly, a decadent leer on his face.

Nancy snapped. She rushed at him, spewing verbal abuse. "You lowlife!" she yelled. "You piece of shit! I want you out of here right now!"

The rep began to stammer. "I, uh, ... I ..."

"Shut up!" she said. "Just get out! And if you show up here again I'll report you to your supervisor, you jerk!"

The stunned billing staff watched as he grabbed his briefcase and turned to leave.

"All right, all right. Take it easy," he said, holding out his palm. "I'm leaving."

Without explaining herself, Nancy abruptly stormed off in another direction. When she reached a swinging door she indulged her wrath by kicking it open, and to her satisfaction the door smashed against the adjoining wall and sent echoes of thunder rolling down the hall. Meanwhile, she didn't miss a step as she bolted through the doorway, ignoring the curious stare of a stunned passerby while fervently vowing two resolutions to herself. First, she would get even with this guy. Second, and more important, in the future she would never allow emotional weakness to derail this project's success.

There was a message that evening on her answering machine. She pushed the play button and heard Philip's voice.

"Hi, Nance. Any luck with the samples? Gimme a call."

Still stinging from wounded pride, Nancy did some thinking before returning the call. She couldn't tolerate the image of a sucker, especially in Philip's eyes.

"No, the company has tightened up on their sample policy. I can't get any more for at least a month, and even then I don't think it'll be enough."

"That's too bad," Philip said, clearly disappointed.

Her next thought was delivered tentatively. "Philip, I have another idea, but I don't want to talk about it over the phone. Can you come over here tonight?"

"Uh-oh. This has to be at your place? So what's it about? CIA stuff or what?"

Nancy remained somber. "No, I just want some privacy and I'd like to talk to you face to face."

"Okay. Sure. I'll be there as soon as I can."

Nancy was all business when Philip arrived. She waited for him to sit down, impatiently pacing while he organized himself.

"I've never seen you like this, Nancy," he paused to smile, "except that first day I arrived at your office and you were such a bitch to me."

His attempt at lightheartedness was futile. Nancy continued her pacing without a reply. Her exasperation with their research project had her fuming and she couldn't wait for him to settle into a serious mode.

"I'm just fed up, Philip!"

Noting his expression of surprise, she realized he thought she was angry at him.

"Not with you. Don't be so sensitive. I'm disgusted that nobody's cooperating with our project."

He took a moment before responding. "Well, part of that's because we haven't told anyone what we're doing. Maybe they'll go for it if we're straight with them."

"Right, Philip," she rolled her eyes. "Maybe the animal rights people will magically back off. And maybe the budget will suddenly grow by a million dollars. And maybe monkeys will fly outta my butt! Any other bright ideas, Einstein?"

"Hey! Take it easy! I'm on your side, dammit! Listen Nancy, I've been with you all the way on this and I just dropped everything to drive over here, so don't give me a lot of crap right now."

Nancy was taken aback. "All right.... I'm just really bent outta shape about this." She took a deep breath. "Listen, I've got an idea, but I know I'm not in the right frame of mind to think clearly right now, so I need you to help me with it, all right?"

Letting his guard down a little, Philip leaned back and folded his arms. "Let's hear it. But what's got you so hyped up all of a sudden?"

"It's not all of a sudden. It's been building up for a while. Nothing's falling into place. It's not working with the pig farmer, we can't get the samples, there's a problem at every turn. We need someone to smooth the way for us."

Philip raised his eyebrows. "And you have somebody in mind?"

She hesitated. This was a moment of truth for their relationship. "There's this guy, Joshua Cantor. I introduced you to him at the hospital."

"Yeah?"

"That woman who died of the abdominal pregnancy was his patient."

Her rhythm faltered .... "He's well thought of at the hospital ... I'm pretty sure I could persuade him to back us."

Her discomfort was apparent to Philip.

"So how come you're having a problem with this?"

She met his steady gaze.

"It's obvious, huh?"

His eyes stayed on her until she gave in.

"Okay, here's the story. Josh Cantor and I had a relationship several years ago. It's ancient history now - he's happily married and all that - but I'm afraid you'll hear about it and misinterpret something if we end up working together." She bit her lip and gave Philip a worried look. "So how do you feel about this? Can we do it without messing up what you and I have?"

Philip was impassive. "I think you have to be the one who answers that question."

"Yeah, I know you're right. And I don't think I'll really know if it's going to work until I actually ask him, but if it's all right with you I'd like to give it a try."

They agreed that this was the logical next step and Nancy promised to get back to Philip immediately after discussing the idea with Joshua Cantor.

Nancy checked the operating room schedule and found Josh's name listed for 7:30 on Wednesday morning. The case he had scheduled would take about an hour and she arranged to be in the surgeons' lounge when he would be likely to pass through. She was striking a nonchalant pose with a coffee cup and a newspaper in front of her face when Josh walked in to use the dictation machine.

"Nancy? Is that you?"

She lowered the paper in mock surprise. "Oh, hi, Josh. You have a case this morning?"

"Uh-huh. Just finished. How about you?"

"I was scheduled for a laparoscopy," she fabricated, "but it got canceled so I have a little spare time."

A short lull hovered until Nancy spoke again. "You look good, Josh. Is that a tan?"

"Yeah, a long weekend up in Maine. Great weather. Water was nippy, though."

"Mmmm." Nancy's face brightened as though struck by impulse. "Say, Josh. While we're in here alone, could I ask you something?"

Something about her manner put Josh on guard. His voice lost its chatty tone. "Like what?"

"I have an idea for a research project," she began, "and I was thinking you might be interested in ..."

Nancy's sentence was interrupted by the beeping of Josh's pager, prompting her to start rushing her words.

"Actually, I'm hoping you can help me convince ...."

Josh cut her off. "Hang on a minute. Let me answer this." He picked up the phone for a brief conversation, then turned back to face her. "That's the waiting room. My patient's husband is out there so I'd better go talk to him. But first I have to tell you, Nancy. Between my practice and some personal stuff I'm kind of strung out these days so I don't think I can get involved in a research project right now. Plus, you know me. Research just isn't my thing."

"Sure. I know that. But I have a terrific idea and I can't seem to get the money for it."

"Uh-huh. And you think I can help you with it? Who's standing in your way?"

"Basically, the faculty at the veterinary school. I was hoping you could endorse my project somehow."

"I'm not sure I could do you any good over there, Nancy. I don't think I know a single person on the staff." He looked at his watch. "Tell you what. I'm a little pressed for time right now, but how about drawing up a paper that describes what you're doing and how I might be able to help. Have you tried Leon Landry, by the way?"

Nancy's face fell. "No, I wanted to talk with you first."

"Well, how about trying Leon for now. If he can't help you, let me know and I'll do what I can." He moved towards the door. "Good luck, though. Let me know what happens, okay?"

Nancy delivered the news to Philip later that day at her apartment. He looked at her expectantly.

"Well?"

She avoided his glance. "Basically, he blew me off."

"How come?"

"I'm not sure. He says this will distract him from his private practice, but I'm not sure he's saying everything that's on his mind."

"Like what?"

"Like maybe he's uncomfortable with it because of our previous relationship. I definitely got some vibes to that effect."

"So now what?"

Nancy set her jaw. "So now I'm ready to take some shortcuts."

"Yeah? Like what?"

"I'm thinking we could get right to the injection of an embryo into a sow's abdomen."

"And how're we gonna do that when we don't have either Cantor or the pig farmer?"

"We're gonna do it by forgetting Cantor and the pig farmer."

"And...?"

"And we're gonna use one of the pigs in the research lab."

"And we're gonna get access to that pig by...?"

"By getting in there at night, or on a weekend, and liberating a few pig embryos from that IVF project you were telling me about, and then injecting those embryos directly into a sow's abdomen. And then when she gets pregnant in the abdominal cavity we'll announce what we're doing and your professors will be so impressed that they'll grant us the go ahead to do the research any way we want."

"Are you for real? My professors will be so impressed that they'll give us anything we want? No, Nancy, I think it'll be more like my professors will be so impressed that they'll bounce my ass right out of school! And maybe throw us both in jail in the bargain. I can't believe you could come up with such a screwball plan!"

"Well, do you have a better idea? What're we supposed to do? Just forget it? No, Philip. If this works it'll definitely be publishable. I won't let go of that."

"Now we're getting right down to it. This is about academic advancement, isn't it? 'Publish or perish' and all that happy horseshit."

"Of course it's about that. Partly. But not only that. This could really help women who get this condition in the future. What about that lady who just died on the Cape? Is that about 'academic advancement and all that happy horseshit'? "

"No, I guess not. But Jesus, Nancy. You're talking about breaking and entering, burglary, theft, the whole nine yards."

"What breaking and entering? You have a key, don't you? If I understand the law, that eliminates the factor of breaking and entering. If someone decides to press charges I think it would be categorized as malicious mischief or some other misdemeanor. I mean, really. It's not such a terrible thing. People have done worse and gotten away with a slap on the wrist. C'mon. Think about it."

Philip sat quietly and allowed her argument to sink in. He had to admit he was getting caught up in the idea.

"All right. I'll think about it......think about it. No promises. And give me a couple of days. I don't want to be rushed into this."

Ecstatic at this concession, Nancy ran to the couch and flung her arms around his neck. At first he pulled back, feeling uneasy about her wild ideas and unpredictable moods. But as he yielded to her advances his resistance melted away.

He knew he was going to agree to her crazy plan.

TWENTY

Of the many repercussions of Sarah Moore's death, there was one that caught Josh by surprise. One day, out of the blue, Bridget Walsh timidly handed him an official-looking mailer from the law firm of Pauley and Westergren, known in Boston as specialists in medical malpractice litigation. Contained inside was a document demanding that Dr. Cantor forward a true copy of the medical records of Miss Sarah Moore, and naming Sarah's parents, T. Lyle Moore and Grace Patterson Moore, as the plaintiffs.

Josh stood holding these papers in both hands, staring dumbly, unable to believe this was really happening to him. Even though he knew that he was in a high-risk specialty and that this day would surely come sooner or later, he never imagined that it would arise out of this case. This case which he managed so closely and which he took so personally.

And now they were requesting his records? To what end? Did the Moores need to be satisfied that he had done everything properly? He could answer that. He would have been happy to discuss it with them personally. They didn't have to go through attorneys, unless they had a lawsuit on their mind, which they apparently did.

His mind continued racing. Now what should he do? Just send the records? Should he talk to an attorney first? But which attorney? Perhaps he had better contact his malpractice insurer. Maybe they could guide him. Of course they could. That was their job, why he paid his exorbitant premiums. But why him, and why this case? He hadn't done anything wrong. How could they be accusing him of that?

Now hold on a minute. Calm down. Maybe it was just an inquiry. Right, that was it. Once they reviewed the records they'd see the case was properly managed and that Sarah's death was a tragic example of maloccurrence, not malpractice.

That was it exactly, he reassured himself. He'd send the records and it would be obvious, although perhaps he should send a note of explanation along as well. No, better not do that. Might be misinterpreted.

Finally he asked Bridget to place a call to the office of his malpractice underwriter, where a receptionist took his name and connected him with a client representative.

"My name's Tim Skolnik, Dr. Cantor. Can I help you?"

The voice was young, but confident, and put Josh somewhat at ease.

"Yes, thank you, Tim. I just got an attorney's letter requesting a patient's medical record, and to tell you the truth, it has me pretty upset. I guess I need you to guide me through this."

"Certainly. Why don't you fill me in on the particulars."

Josh took a breath and began to summarize the case of Sarah Moore. "Well, let me warn you that it's going to sound pretty bad at first, but if you hang on I'll try to explain how things happened."

"No problem. I won't be judgmental. Just tell the story and we'll discuss it afterwards."

While Josh detailed Sarah's history, Skolnik allowed him to speak without interruption, except for an occasional thoughtful comment or expression of sympathy. Before long, Josh realized that this young man was doing a masterful job of positive listening, and, despite the state of near panic he had been in only minutes earlier, he broke into a knowing smile at how well he was being handled. After nearly half an hour, much longer than was actually necessary for purposes of information gathering, the conversation ended with Josh feeling somewhat unburdened. Skolnik had made it clear that anything could happen in these cases, but the inquiry was often dropped with the realization that there were no legitimate charges to be made. Of course should the litigants choose to pursue it, a competent defense attorney would be in touch immediately.

When Josh hung up he leaned back in his chair and closed his eyes. This wasn't the end of the world .He just had to keep it in perspective. He glanced at his wristwatch. And right now he had patients to see.

Monday's office schedule was interrupted by an intercom message from Bridget. Josh was in the middle of entering a chart notation when her voice came over the intercom.

"I have Mr. Skolnik on the phone, Doctor."

Josh put his pen down and picked up on the blinking line.

"Hello, Tim. Good news, I hope?"

"More like neutral, I'd have to say."

Josh tightened his grip on the receiver.

"Yeah? What's 'neutral' mean?"

"Well, you know, the Moores' attorney has decided to do a little digging. Pretty routine, actually".

"I'm listening."

"Basically, the legal term is 'discovery'. Their lawyer gets the opportunity to question you about the case, and your lawyer - I've contacted her already, by the way - her name is Julie Dardano - does the same with the plaintiffs. Dardano will be in touch to go over all of this with you, but as I said, it's pretty routine."

"Routine for you guys, maybe, but I'm getting a migraine as we speak."

"I understand, but we need to count on you to hang in there while we do the infighting."

Josh sighed. "I don't like the sounds of that, Tim. 'Infighting?' Doesn't anyone care about the facts in this case? Why can't I just explain what happened directly to Sarah's parents."

"I only wish it worked that way, Doctor, but if you'll try to be patient we'll guide you through the legal process."

Josh gave no response to this reassurance and the phone line hung quiet for several seconds. "Dr. Cantor? Are you there?"

"I'm here. I'm just can't say I'm very happy right now." Josh took another breath. "All right, Tim. Just please try to expedite this stuff as soon as possible. I feel like there's a mountain on my back."

"Got it. I'll call Dardano right away."

Attorney Dardano had asked Josh to come to her office an hour before the interrogatory appointment. After making him comfortable and offering a soft drink, she began to explain what to expect.

"This will be a formal, on the record, question and answer session," Dardano told him, "with a stenographer who records every word. You've heard of this. It's called a deposition. Usually it starts off reasonably non-confrontational. Their attorney will begin by asking you about your background, how you met Sarah Moore, etcetera. And you should be yourself. Answer the questions in a straightforward manner, give only what he asks for, and try not to get angry. Which reminds me. The litigators have assigned a guy named Clyde Stanton." Dardano couldn't resist an expression of disdain. "He's a real moron, and he's obnoxious, so you'll really have to do your best to exercise self control because he'll definitely try to provoke you. I'll be there to object if he gets out of hand, but just keep in mind that it's a normal business day for him, even though you might feel like going for his throat."

Stanton was forty minutes late. He entered with a flourish and without apology, wearing an impeccably tailored dark suit and carrying a soft gloss aluminum briefcase which he clunked carelessly onto the conference room desk. To Josh's surprise, civil greetings and pleasantries were exchanged between the two attorneys. Then, when Dardano introduced Stanton to Josh, there was a flash of gold from a filigree wrist bracelet and matching cufflink. Josh accepted the handshake reflexively, then cut it short, wishing he hadn't responded.

Stanton wasted no time getting started. He sat down, adjusted his chair noisily, and turned to the stenographer.

"Ready?"

When she nodded, hands poised over her little silent typewriter, he put on a pair of lightly tinted glasses, glanced briefly at Josh, and then looked down at his papers as he spoke, all business now, oozing with self importance.

"For the record, this is Thursday, September 6th, and we are meeting in the offices of attorney Julia Dardano. I am attorney Clyde Stanton, and Doctor Joshua Cantor is about to give testimony in the case of Miss Sarah Moore, whose parents, T. Lyle Moore and Grace Patterson Moore, are the plaintiffs." He looked up again at Josh, this time with a pompous glance over his glasses.

"Dr. Cantor, please state your full name."

By now Josh's apprehension had been largely replaced by hostility. He took more time than necessary to answer.

"Joshua Aaron Cantor."

"And your date of birth."

"July 17th, 1972."

"And where did you attend undergraduate school?"

Josh went on to answer a set of perfunctory questions establishing his training, his date of board certification, and the year he opened his office. Eventually he was asked to describe his initial meeting with Sarah Moore as well as a long chronicle of events leading up to the week before she went to Cape Cod. Josh noticed that each question was designed to neutralize the quality of care he gave, and on two occasions, when he began to elaborate beyond what was called for, Julie Dardano stopped him with a gentle nudge under the table.

The questioning droned on for nearly an hour, during which Josh was working noticeably harder to retain his composure. Ultimately, Stanton shifted to a change of tone, indicating to Dardano that he was preparing to ask the crucial questions about the Cape Cod conversation. At this point Dardano put her hand on Josh's arm and interrupted the proceedings.

"Clyde, I'd like to give my client a ten minute recess here."

Josh started to open his mouth to say he'd like to get it over with, but he winced when he felt a vice closing on his elbow, and before either he or Stanton could say another word, Dardano was escorting him out of the room.

When the door had closed behind them, Josh turned to Dardano who had just released her death grip.

"Hey!" Josh complained. "That hurt! What'd I do wrong?"

"Nothing yet, but you were about to lose it, and that's just what Clyde's looking for. Now go visit the bathroom, or have a seat in my office, or whatever. He's just about to get into the crucial stuff, so get yourself under control before we go back in there."

Josh decided to take Dardano's advice. Literally. He walked to the bathroom and took the time to wash his face with cold water, then went to Dardano's private office where he sat and closed his eyes, allowing his mind to clear. When it was time to return to the conference room, he felt refreshed. He actually smiled as he entered, and thought he saw Stanton's legal demeanor sag just a bit at the sight of his newfound confidence. But if Stanton was momentarily distracted it took him no time to recover. In an instant he had resumed right where he left off, again peering over the top of his glasses in a way that Josh found highly irritating.

"Can we resume now?"

Josh nodded, a comfortable expression on his face.

"All right, then. Dr. Cantor, I'd like to discuss how it happened that Sarah Moore traveled to Cape Cod while carrying a potentially lethal pregnancy. Can you tell me why you allowed her to travel that weekend?"

"I did not 'allow' her to travel, Mr. Stanton. I advised her against it and she opted not to take that advice."

"I see. You advised her not to go to the Cape, you say?"

"That's right."

"Would you say you strongly advised her?"

"Yes, that's an appropriate term."

"Don't you think you should have forbidden her to go?"

"I don't forbid my patients. I believe in treating them as human beings who have the right to make an informed choice."

"But you would agree it was potentially dangerous for her to leave?"

"Yes."

"Potentially very dangerous, would you say?"

"Yes, potentially very dangerous."

Stanton feigned a puzzled expression and started shuffling papers. "You know, it's strange, Dr. Cantor, but I can't seem to find anything in Ms. Moore's medical records that verifies such a conversation."

Josh's eyes narrowed. "That's because I didn't enter it."

"Oh, I see. But would it not be appropriate to record such a conversation, if it actually occurred?"

Josh started his answer with a slight edge to his voice, but he remembered Dardano's coaching. Stay calm, stay calm.

"I suppose it would have been appropriate if one were protecting himself legally, but that was not my concern at the time."

"Umm-hmm," Stanton raised his eyebrows. "But you're certain this conversation took place?"

"Absolutely certain."

"Do you think you could repeat that conversation word-for-word at this time?"

"Not word-for-word, but I remember the crux of it very clearly."

"The crux, you say?"

"Yes, and I remember a great deal more than that," Josh shot back. He felt Dardano nudging him under the table again but this time he wouldn't be deterred.

"I remember the day of the week, the time of day, her facial expression, and the dress she was wearing at the time. I remember her tone of voice. I remember how resolute she was about going, and why she felt it necessary to go. I remember having signed out to another doctor that weekend but giving her my beeper number in case she needed me."

Josh slowed now and leaned forward. Out of the corner of his eye he saw Dardano holding her breath.

"And I also remember that my colleague, Dr. Howard Greenwald, was present when Sarah and I had the discussion about going to the Cape. I'm sure he'd be happy to verify it."

Dardano exhaled loudly, trying in vain to stifle a snicker by coughing.

Stanton was speechless for a moment, his eyes darting while he shuffled his papers to buy some time. Then he came back with a desperate retort.

"But you didn't write any of this down."

"No, I didn't."

Stanton drew himself up and began to stack his papers again. "That will be all. This concludes our session." He nodded to the stenographer, hurriedly threw his materials into the aluminum briefcase, and left without another word.

Josh looked to Dardano. "Is that it?"

"That's it. You can go home now.... And Dr.Cantor ..."

Josh looked at her again.

"Ya done good," Dardano smiled. "I can't believe the way you just shot down Clyde Stanton! I'm sure he'll feel compelled to depose Dr.

Greenwald, but after that I can assure you he won't be bothering us any more."

Dardano's prediction turned out to be right; after Greenwald's deposition the litigation was dropped. But the matter didn't end there for Josh. He told himself not to take it personally - that it came with the territory, a rite of passage - but he knew better. This was an assault on both his professional competence and his integrity, and it could rise up again with any patient who walked through the door.

It left a scar that would stay with him for the rest of his career.

TWENTY - ONE

Soo-Yen Park had also been named as a defendant by Sarah Moore's parents, prompting attorney Dardano to advise Josh not to contact her in any way, at least until they had both been deposed. Now that this had been accomplished, Josh took it upon himself to pay her a visit. At his suggestion they agreed to meet at the end of her shift at Boston General Hospital. He parked in the emergency room lot and walked past a row of ambulances, one of them still flashing its warning lights. A pair of automatic doors opened as he neared the entrance. Inside, a baby-faced security guard chatted with a flirty teenager, allowing Josh to pass without a glance. Josh approached the receptionist.

"Pardon me, I'm Dr. Cantor. Would you let Dr. Park know I'm here?"

"Yes, doctor. She's waiting for you." She pointed to a door marked 'STAFF'. "Go through that door. She'll be in the consultation room on the left."

Soo-Yen jumped up when he walked in.

"Dr. Cantor?"

Josh tried to put her at ease. He shook her hand. It was tiny, and cold.

"Yes. How are you, Dr. Park?"

"Nervous, to tell the truth."

"I can't blame you. I'm sure you've been going through a tough time lately." He turned to close the door, then sat down, inviting her to do the same.

Soo-Yen perched on the end of her chair and stole a fleeting look at Dr Cantor, her eyes darting away when they made contact.

"I know this must be painful for you, Dr. Park, but I'm not here to judge you. This meeting's for my benefit as well as yours."

Soo-Yen dared to look at him a second time. His expression was gentle as he spoke again.

"I know things were pretty crazy at the Cape that day. Do you think you can tell me the story?"

She took a deep breath, then leaned forward, knees together, hands tightly folded. Her words came in choppy fragments...

"I don't know.... It was really busy....big car accident...not enough help...."

"Take your time," he encouraged her. "Let me hear everything."

She took another breath and exhaled through her nose.

"This is hard...."

"I understand. Just tell it in your own words."

"All right, here goes ... It started off as a quiet day down there. You know the kind of place, a remote ER that usually treats mostly scrapes and bruises. I've worked there three or four times and never came across anything that was beyond the hospital's capacity. Then out of nowhere we got a call about a traffic accident from out on Route 6. Normally the ambulances would go to Hyannis, but this happened so close that they chose Sisters of Charity. When I first heard about it I wasn't concerned because it didn't sound too bad."

Soo-Yen looked at Josh for reassurance. He nodded for her to continue.

"Then, while we were waiting, in comes this pregnant woman who had fainted on the beach. When I met her she was confused and slurring her words a little, but her vital signs were reasonably stable, pulse initially recorded at 92 and regular, respiratory rate 24, skin dry and warm, pressure was 100 over 60. Overall she looked pretty stable. I thought she might have been drinking or something."

Josh wanted to remark that Sarah would never have been drinking, but decided to hold the thought.

"When I examined her abdomen it wasn't tender. She wasn't contracting or bleeding, and the fetal heart sounded fine. Stronger than usual, in fact. And the baby seemed unusually active, too. At the time I took all of that as a good sign, but since then I've read up on abdominal pregnancies and I know now that those were clues that I missed. If I'd been sharper I could've made the diagnosis and handled it differently."

Josh gave her a sympathetic smile.

"Are they still teaching the old adage about when you hear hoofbeats in North America ... ?"

"Right. You think of horses, not zebras."

"Exactly. Well, this case is the ultimate 'zebra'. A well-trained obstetrician would've been hard pressed to come up with it, so I don't think you need to be so hard on yourself."

"Maybe so, but I can't help it right now."

"All right, we'll come back to that if you want, but first can you detail the rest of what happened?"

Soo-Yen nodded. "Right then several ambulances arrived with the accident victims. It was much worse than we expected. Four really sick people and not nearly enough help. Typical Saturday afternoon. I don't think there was one other doctor in the hospital. Eventually some help showed up, one general surgeon and an ENT guy, but even then we were swamped. One of the accident victims had a crushed thorax with a flail chest. I had to throw in a chest tube to stabilize him. And there was blood all over the place, mostly from a woman with a horrendous scalp laceration. The sickest was a kid with an acute abdomen. Ruptured spleen. He needed to be prepped for the OR right away. The nurse couldn't get an IV going because he was shocky and his veins were collapsed, so I had to do a cutdown to get some fluids and blood in him.

"Meanwhile we had wheeled Sarah Moore's stretcher to a side room. By the time the smoke cleared from the accident and we got back to her, it was too late. I couldn't believe it..." Her voice trailed off. "I just couldn't believe it...."

As he listened, Josh found Soo-Yen's story credible. He had no difficulty imagining himself in her place. When she got to the part about finding Sarah dead, she described the specifics in clinical detail, her voice a numb monotone. Then she sat still, her eyes unfocused.

Josh gave her a moment, then spoke softly. "You know this is going to be reviewed by the state's maternal mortality committee?"

She nodded her head..

"Are you going to be there?"

She smiled weakly. "No, they requested my version in writing, but when I asked if I could be present I was told that it wasn't 'customary'."

"I can understand that. I'm sure they feel a lot more objective about analyzing a case when the doctor of record isn't present, but I do know they take pains to keep their conclusions private so that they can't be used later as evidence. All I can tell you, Soo-Yen, is that I find your story believable. As I was listening to it, my reaction was 'There, but for the grace of God, go I', and I think the committee members will have the same reaction."

She looked at him hopefully. "Has anything like this ever happened to you?"

Josh immediately thought of his reaction to the litigation inquiry brought by Sarah's parents. "Not exactly, but I know how disheartening the criticism can be. Maybe it'll help you to know I've been asked to attend the review session, and I can assure you I'll be in your corner."

Soo-Yen stood and extended her hand again. "Thank you, Doctor Cantor. I really appreciate..." She swallowed hard and bolted from the room before breaking down .... "Excuse me...thank you," her voice cracked. "Thank you..."

The Massachusetts Maternal Mortality Committee held its regularly scheduled meeting on the second Wednesday in October. Its members consisted of several high- powered academicians and one or two private obstetricians from the Boston area, plus smaller contingents from Worcester and Springfield. They prided themselves as being among the most prestigious medical organizations in the state. Either outstanding professional accomplishments or political connections were necessary to receive an invitation to serve among its luminaries.

In the first half of the century the committee had a great deal of work to do. Babies died routinely, and even maternal death was considered a standard risk of childbirth. The committee's task was to analyze large scale trends in the hope of learning from mistakes and ultimately to share their wisdom with rank-and-file physicians via the prestigious New England Journal of Medicine.

In more recent decades the situation had changed. The incidence of catastrophes was dramatically reduced, so that poor outcomes were infrequent enough to become the subject of intense medical and legal investigation, especially in the case of maternal mortality. Unfortunately the committee was often thwarted by a lack of clinical material, mainly because medical records were tied up in the legal process. However in the case of one Sarah Moore, who died under unusual circumstances earlier in the month, the records had somehow found their way to the committee for review before the usual legal machinery had the chance to intercept them.

The committee's current chairman was Dr. Caleb McAdam, a patriarch of the Boston Obstetrical Society. Although Dr. McAdam's medical career had not been particularly noteworthy, his family history was indeed rich, both historically and financially. Several hospital wings and medical school scholarships in the Boston area bore his surname and he carried himself with old-guard demeanor, including his manner of speech and dress. His outdated but immaculate dark suits, frayed collars and bow ties, combined with his family's name, afforded him an unusual degree of esteem among his peers, despite his lackluster reputation as a practitioner.

The hubbub in the conference room came to an abrupt halt as Dr. McAdam entered. A protracted moment passed while he made his way deliberately to the head of the table. He looked about the room with regal bearing, noting who was there and who was not. Despite the professional stature of those in attendance, his commanding presence caused all of them to shrink from his gaze. All of them, that is, except an outside physician who was attending this meeting by specific invitation. No one knew much about the new man except that it was his patient whose case was the subject of today's agenda.

Dr. McAdam took his time about seating himself and arranging his papers. Finally he looked up and again surveyed the group.

"Good afternoon. I'm pleased to see all of you again."

He adjusted his half-moon bifocals, allowing another moment to pass. Then he spoke again...slowly, deliberately.

"And I see we have a guest today." He looked down to his papers, then back up again to scan the distinguished assembly.

"Dr. Joshua Cantor?"

All heads turned to the new face. Josh responded by raising his hand and nodding respectfully.

Dr. McAdam continued. "Good afternoon, Dr. Cantor." McAdam then addressed the committee members. "I should explain that Dr. Cantor is here today for a review of the death of his patient, Miss Sarah Moore." He turned back to Josh. "I'd also like to relate that my old friend, Wallace Parsons, advised me that he trained you during your residency, Dr. Cantor, and that you were an outstanding house officer. In fact he told me you have an exceptional head on your shoulders. I pray your service to the medical community will be as long and exalted as your mentor's."

"Thank you, Dr. McAdam," Josh answered. "Dr. Parsons has been a great role model and I've learned a lot from him. I hope I can live up to his standards."

"Good, good." Dr. McAdam nodded approvingly. He was gratified that this young pup would show genuine respect to a member of his generation.

"Now then," he continued. "We have a most interesting case for review this month. It seems a young woman has died of hemorrhage from a rare abdominal pregnancy. Out on the Cape, I understand. Falmouth, was it?" He paused to shuffle his papers. "Unfortunately there is a disturbing element to this story. Apparently this occurred right under a doctor's nose and the patient's body lay undiscovered for several hours following the catastrophic event."

Again he paused, allowing his dramatic statement to work its effect. "I have asked our colleague, Dr. Albert Rowe, to review this case in some detail and report his findings and conclusions to us. Albert, will you be so kind as to illuminate us on this most unfortunate story?"

Albert Rowe was the second in command at one of Boston's Harvard-affiliated hospitals. He had held that position for nearly fifteen years, through three changes of department chairmanship, thus gaining a perennial bridesmaid's status. Each time he was considered for advancement there was some failing or other that caused him to fall just short. Nevertheless he was well regarded among Boston's academic elite. He was one of them, and could be counted on to defend their rituals and traditions. As he rose to dissect the debacle of a maladroit provincial, his cohorts perked up. Blood was in the air, and they looked forward to a well-deserved lynching-in-absentia.

"I would like to tell you that I have discovered some element of saving grace in this situation," Dr. Rowe began, relishing the spotlight. "Unfortunately no such factor could be found despite the most forgiving perspective I could muster. This case clearly represents an example of the darkest side of our profession, a patient who trusted her welfare to a supposedly responsible professional, and whose trust was rewarded with gross incompetence and neglect." He enunciated the key words in his next sentence, using a deliberate, high-volume monotone and gesturing with karate chops for emphasis.

"The woman / arrived / at an emergency room / in stable condition / and was ignored / while she proceeded / to bleed / to death!"

The air hung heavy until he continued, this time with lower volume but containing even more derision. "The doctor in question is a female resident over at the Boston General, but I shudder to think she is perceived as one of our colleagues."

He allowed another moment to pass before delivering his coup-de-grace.

"Without belaboring the point, I must recommend that summary revocation of this doctor's medical license would be an appropriate action on the part of the state licensing board.

"Am I being too harsh? I think not. You have all read this case history and, frankly, I anticipate unanimous agreement. So there you have it. That is my opinion and my recommendation. I have nothing further to add, except to call for an immediate vote on this matter."

Dr. McAdam removed his glasses and rubbed the bridge of his nose, remaining in this contemplative posture for an interminably long moment while the committee members held their breath. Finally he pursed his lips, sighed heavily, and launched into his own terse pronouncement of condemnation.

"I don't believe I can recall such an open-and-shut case in recent history. Dr. Rowe's assessment is harsh indeed, but I'm afraid I concur entirely. I will accept a motion to recommend revocation of this physician's license."

"So moved!" came the hearty chorus from several academicians.

The private practitioners exchanged glances but were cowed into submission by the blitzkrieg of opinion from the professors.

"Is there a second?"

"Second the motion."

"All those in favor?"

"Aye," came the same chorus.

"All those opp....."

From the far end of the table a dissenting voice interrupted Dr. McAdam.

"Before we conclude this matter, I'd like the chance to say something."

Everyone turned in the speaker's direction and to their shock, it was the committee's guest, Dr. Cantor. Eyebrows were raised. Dr. McAdam looked simultaneously annoyed and amused. He placed his eyeglasses on the table in front of him, leaned back in his chair and folded his hands over his vest, waiting smugly for the brash intruder to speak his piece.

"All right, Dr. Cantor. Let's hear what you have to say."

Josh rose to his feet. "First of all, let me apologize for interrupting you, Dr. McAdam. I did not intend to speak today. I recognize that I am a guest here, and it was my intention to quietly observe until I learned how this process works. However I don't believe I can remain silent now in light of what's happening in front of me.

"On the surface I have to admit that this case looks indefensible. But I took the liberty of doing a little digging and I can tell you that there are some extenuating circumstances here. This patient had a rare obstetrical condition, and that information was not available to the physician in charge at the time. In addition, this doctor was moonlighting at a normally low key emergency room. The hospital doesn't even have a maternity unit. The ambulance driver took the patient there because it was the closest medical facility to the beach. Her vital signs were only slightly altered, mainly in the form of a rapid pulse, but her blood pressure was stable and she wasn't shocky.

"Unfortunately there was another pressing problem that occurred at that moment, namely a major traffic accident that completely overwhelmed this doctor and her staff. It's certainly tragic that all of this occurred as it did, but I would view the situation as extraordinarily unusual and I don't believe the physician in question deserves censure, or suspension of her license, or anything of the sort, especially without an opportunity to defend herself."

Dr. Rowe was incensed. He jumped up from his chair. "Well! I must agree with one thing Dr. Cantor said, namely that he is 'a guest here', and it would be prudent to withhold comment until he understands how this committee works. But since he has raised these questions, I feel I must respond ...

"I would hold that a physician who is staffing an emergency room is obligated to familiarize himself...or herself... with a working knowledge of all specialties, since any manner of problem may present itself in that setting."

His voice began to rise again. "It is clearly apparent that this patient presented with intra-abdominal bleeding caused by a separating placenta. I certainly don't feel sympathy for a physician who lacked a sufficient knowledge base to recognize a problem when she saw it. And as for being overwhelmed by the simultaneous traffic accident, that speaks to a lack of preparation on the part of both the physician and the hospital." He poked at the air with an accusatory forefinger. "No, there is no excuse for what happened here. No excuse! I want a vote on this matter now!"

This time Josh was incensed. "Now just a minute! This inexperienced physician-in-training may not have recognized a once-in-a-lifetime situation when she saw it in the midst of chaos, but I can tell you that I recognize what's going on here. This is nothing more than a kangaroo court, intent on frying a young physician who was busting her ass against overwhelming odds. There's no way I'm going to allow this vote to be taken today without a formal protest. In fact, I believe the matter should be tabled until your next meeting and this doctor should be invited to give a first hand account of her side of the story before jumping to conclusions."

Josh's impassioned remarks gave one of the other private practitioners the courage to speak up. "I have to agree with Dr. Cantor. This case was complicated. I don't think we have the information necessary to vote today."

The entry of another party into the argument opened the flood gates, pandemonium breaking out as partisans from both sides quickly jumped into the fray. Dr. McAdam sat calmly and clapped his hands several times to regain control.

"Gentlemen, gentlemen! Let me remind you of where we are. I would appreciate it if you would all calm down."

All of the doctors, save one, complied with Dr. McAdam's call to order. Albert Rowe was out of control.

"I call again for this decision to be completed today! We were in the middle of voting when Dr. Cantor interrupted!"

"The vote is moot," Josh retorted. "It was introduced before we were permitted to have any discussion."

"But this is the way things are done here, Dr. Cantor. By the book. And by Robert's Rules of Order." Dr. Rowe's features twisted into a sarcastic smirk. "Perhaps you and your colleagues from the hinterlands haven't heard of them in your plebeian world of private practice."

A self-conscious hush fell over the group. They all held their breath as Josh gathered his papers with exaggerated care and pushed back his chair. When he spoke, his words carried an ominous undertone.

"What we have heard of, Dr. Rowe, is common courtesy and common sense. And we've also had the experience of working in the real world. You should try it sometime."

He marched to the exit. "Thank you for inviting me, Dr. McAdam, but this meeting is over for me." Then, addressing the secretary, "And I want to go on record as protesting these proceedings."

The committee sat stunned as he stomped out and slammed the door. Dr. McAdam's bifocals slipped off the end of his nose.

TWENTY - TWO

T hursday morning from 7:30 to 8:30 was the time slot for weekly grand rounds at the Boston Lying-In hospital. The topics were arranged well in advance but there were occasions when an unusual situation prompted the department chairman to make a program change. Such was the case during the weeks following Sarah Moore's death. Her story had created such interest that, in anticipation of expanded attendance, the location was changed from the usual conference room to a larger auditorium.

Joshua Cantor informed Michael Wilson of the date.

"It's coming up next week, Michael. I thought you might be interested in attending."

"Yeah, I'm definitely interested, but what exactly do you mean by the term 'grand rounds'? I thought 'making rounds' referred to a doctor going around the hospital and visiting his patients."

"You know, you're right. It is confusing. 'Making rounds' is just what you described, but 'grand rounds' refers to a formal meeting in a classroom or lecture hall setting, usually with a case presentation followed by a group discussion and critique of how the case was handled. That's the format for next week. One of the senior residents will detail Sarah's medical course, then I'm going to be presenting a world literature review on abdominal pregnancies. Since you helped me to compile it, I wanted to acknowledge your input."

"Well, I appreciate that, but maybe I'd better ask how graphic this is going to be."

"Pretty graphic, Michael. Descriptions of the autopsy and all the rest, including color slides. If you want, you can skip that part and just come for my review."

Michael hesitated. "I don't know. I think I'd better pass on the whole thing. Thanks anyway, but I'm just not ready for that kind of objectivity yet. Probably never will be."

"Okay, but if it's all right with you, I'll acknowledge your assistance anyway."

"Sure. I hope it'll do some good for someone else."

The atmosphere was anticipation-charged as Josh's conference was enthusiastically received by an appreciative audience consisting of hospital staff, private practitioners, and medical students. At its conclusion, he graciously accepted the congratulations of a host of well-wishers, including Nancy Sanderson, who had made a special effort to attend. She waited until the others had finished, then approached him with a gushy hug. "That was great, Josh. Whatever happened to that guy who wanted to avoid the 'publish or perish' rat race?"

He blushed slightly, both at Nancy's uncharacteristic public display of warmth and her friendly dig. His thoughts were brought back into focus when Nancy asked if she could prevail on Josh for a favor.

"Sure, Nancy. What'd you have in mind?"

"I wonder if you'd mind lending me your notes from today's presentation. I'd like to photocopy them and then I could get them right back to you."

"I suppose so. Sure. But why the interest? You don't have another patient with this condition, I hope."

"No, just general academic curiosity. You never know. One of these could crop up any time. Never hurts to be prepared."

Josh had no time to dwell on Nancy's motives because as he was handing her his notes he felt an arm around his shoulder. He turned his head to see the department chairman, Dr. Leon Landry.

"Josh, that was an outstanding presentation. I think it's worthy of submission to one of the major journals."

Josh answered cautiously. "Thank you, Leon, but I think you know that's not my thing. If you'd like my material, I'd be happy for you to submit it in the hospital's name, but I'm afraid of getting bogged down in academics. I want to keep my priorities on the clinical side, and reserve some time for teaching."

Landry smiled indulgently. "Yes, I think I know how you feel about that, Josh, but let me remind you of another discussion that we've had more than once in the past, and let me be candid this time. Your opportunity to teach is going to be limited unless you advance academically, and that advancement is going to depend in large part on your publication curriculum."

"But why does the system have to work like that, Leon? Do you really think it'll make me a better communicator if my name appears in print?"

Landry patted his shoulder. "Josh, Josh. We've gone over this so many times. I didn't invent the system. Why can't you just go along with it? Look at Nancy Sanderson. She already holds an assistant professorship because of what she has in print."

"Gimme a break, Leon. Nancy's one type of doctor, I'm another. Why can't we both be allowed to do our thing?"

Exasperation crept into Landry's voice. "Look, Josh. Idealism's fine, but it's already to the point where I have to go to the wall for you when your name comes up for academic promotion. As it is you're behind some others who don't have your talent. You'll just have to decide whether the compromise is worth it to you."

His frankness jolted Josh into a strategic retreat. "All right, Leon. Let me think about it and get back to you."

Landry was pleased. He genuinely liked Joshua Cantor and this was the first time he had conceded so much as an inch on this issue. "Good, Josh. I really hope you can see it my way. Let me know what you decide."

After a session of self examination, Josh recognized that he had come to a crossroads. He concluded that he would ultimately have to agree to Landry's recommendation, but he didn't like it and he refused to take it lying down. Knowing that Landry normally arrived at the hospital sometime after 9AM, Josh tested the waters by asking for a 7:30 appointment. To his satisfaction, Landry agreed to meet the very next day.

Despite arriving ten minutes early, Josh found Landry waiting for him with a steaming carafe of coffee and an array of danish pastries on a silver tray. The usual plastic utensils and throwaway styrofoam cups were replaced by ornate china and tiny silver spoons, along with a cream pitcher and sugar bowl. Upon seeing this display, Josh couldn't contain a gentle laugh.

Landry smiled. "What's so funny, Josh?"

"I have to admit something to you, Leon. I was all charged up when I walked in here. But look at this! Where'd you even get this stuff? You've taken the wind right out of my sails."

"I guess my hunch was right, then. I sensed you were going to challenge me today. And that's okay. I'm always up for a spirited discussion. But I've always liked you, Josh, so if we're going to have a confrontation, I'd like to keep it civilized. Have a seat. Tell me what's on your mind."

Josh took a chair and collected his thoughts. "First of all, Leon, let me thank you for this. It's really a nice gesture and I appreciate it." Josh reached for the coffee pot and began to pour a cup for Landry.

"No thanks, Josh. I'll have some in a little while. Go ahead, though. Help yourself."

Josh put the pot down. "I think I'll wait also. First I want to get this off my chest." He shifted in his chair and coughed nervously before launching into his presentation.

"Leon, before you took this chairmanship I was in residency training under Calvin Birch, and I think you know he could be unpredictable at times. One day during grand rounds I quoted something I had read in a recent journal. He challenged me to name the author and when I did he blurted out:

'Oh, for God's sake, Cantor, don't you know he's a liar?'

Just like that! And right in front of the entire department. Well, I was shocked by it, I guess, and I was standing there with this stricken expression on my face when Calvin scoffs and says 'Aw, grow up!'

"Later that morning I caught him in his office and asked what that was all about. He got all puffed up and blustery and said 'Now look here, Cantor! I'm a man in search of the truth! And you can choose to join me on that search, or you can put your head in the sand. It's up to you. So tell me now. Are you with me or not?'

"That sounds like Calvin," Landry chuckled.

"I didn't know what to do. At first I was sure he was putting me on, but when he kept a straight face I decided not to say anything and just kept looking at him, hoping I wouldn't commit some kind of blunder. He went on to say that he was fed up with all the crap that was being pumped into journals, and didn't believe in getting involved in a research project unless it could make a real difference.

"Now I have to tell you, Leon, what he said that day struck a nerve in me.

It motivated me to formulate a set of criteria that I vowed to apply to my own research ideas. As a result I've published very little, because ninety percent of what I designed didn't stand up to my own standards. And now I'm sure you know what I'm getting at ... I don't think I should be penalized for failing to contribute a lot of pablum to the professional journals, and I don't think those who have submitted that stuff should be rewarded for it."

"All right, Josh, you have a point. So where would you like to go with this?"

"Well, for starters I think we need to break with the tradition of rewarding people solely on the length of their bibliographies. And then I think we need to establish our own department standards for promotion in the area of teaching. And last, if I may be so bold, I propose that we re-work the position of director of education."

"How do you mean, 're-work' it?"

"Unless I haven't heard, the position's still vacant since Scott Hunter left."

"That's correct. We're in the process of reviewing applications right now."

"From outside the institution, I assume?"

"Yes...."

"What would you think of filling it with someone currently on the staff?"

"Who, for instance?"

Josh put his hands together, fingers pointing upwards in mock servile petition, and bowed his head.

"I'm at your service."

The idea took Landry by surprise.

"Are you serious, Josh? You know this would mean a significant time commitment?"

"I know I'd have to cut back on my practice, and I'm willing to do that." Josh read the uncertainty on Landry's face. "You don't have to answer right now, Leon.

I'm just asking you to consider it."

Landry pondered the idea for a moment. Then he gave Josh a response.

"All right, let me offer you this for now: What I'm thinking is that I'd like you to submit your work on abdominal pregnancy. I'm sure it would be published, and then the committee on academic advancement would look a lot more favorably on your proposal."

"Because a journal article would carry my name?"

"An important journal article." Josh knew instinctively that this was the best he could hope for. He reached across the table to shake Landry's hand. "That's a fair deal. I'll have it ready in a couple of weeks."

"Terrific, Josh. Now how about some coffee?"

To Josh's surprise, there was an immediate acceptance of his paper from the prestigious Journal of Obstetrics and Gynecology, the so-called "Green Journal" that was considered the flagship of ob/gyn literature. Its publication was a huge feather in his scholastic hat, and his name began to circulate in academic circles. Before he knew it, reprint requests began to pour in, followed by solicitations to speak around the country, even an invitation to participate in an international conference in Geneva.

Ironically, this made Josh nervous. He still didn't want to be dragged into that world. All he wanted was to concentrate on his primary interests;

clinical practice and teaching. However, he was immensely pleased when Landry made good on his promise by presenting Josh's proposal to the next executive committee meeting.

This was a step in the right direction; the opportunity to teach without getting bogged down in the politics of academia.

TWENTY - THREE

Josh interrupted Aviva just as she finished arranging the kitchen chairs and was about to make her usual after-dinner phone call to her mother.

"Hold on for just a minute, Viv. I want to show you something." After squeezing in the last dish and starting the dishwasher, he walked across the room to retrieve his briefcase and pulled out a single sheet of paper which he handed to her.

She reached for her reading glasses. "What's this?"

"Just look it over and tell me what you think."

Josh had decided to hold off on telling Aviva about his notion of becoming the hospital's Director of Education until he thought there was a real chance that it could happen. Two days earlier, Leon Landry had informed him that the university's committee on academic advancement had approved the idea of choosing the director from the current hospital staff, and that a memo would be circulating shortly. He watched Aviva's face as she read it:

CALL FOR APPLICATIONS
POSITION OF DIRECTOR OF STUDENT AND
RESIDENT EDUCATION AT BOSTON LYING-IN HOSPITAL

The Dean's committee on academic advancement announces their decision to choose the next Director of Education from within the existing staff at the Boston Lying-In. Interested applicants should apply through the office of Dr. Leon Landry, Chief of Obstetrics and Gynecology.

Aviva looked at Josh. "So I'm assuming you're interested?"

"I think you know I am. And I need to know how you feel about it."

"We'd better sit down for this one. C'mon in here for a minute."

She led him into the living room of their old stucco home. The Cantors had specific ideas about decor, but because their taste was running ahead of their budget,the large, half- empty room looked even bigger than its actual dimensions. It contained only three pieces of furniture: a forty-year-old Steinway baby grand gifted by Aviva's parents, a mahogany bookcase filled to overflowing, and the latest addition, a six foot long antique brocade sofa that begged for a coffee table and accessories. The floor-to-ceiling windows were undraped and more than half of the wooden plank floor remained empty. Aviva turned on the room's solitary lamp as they sat down. She drew up her knees and faced him on the sofa but said nothing.

"Well?"

She remained silent.

"Aviva?"

"Joshua, I have my doubts. You're already too busy."

"This would be part-time. Two or three hours a day, so I could continue practicing also."

Aviva was immediately exasperated.

"And what happens when we have a baby, Joshua? We agreed I'd take some time off from work. Am I supposed to handle everything myself while you keep expanding your career?"

Josh felt his temper rising.

"We'll worry about that when ..."

He stopped himself, realizing that he was about to say something he'd regret.

He softened his voice and reached for her hand.

"No, Viv. When that happens, I plan to cut back."

"Then what about the financial part? Your education loans and all that."

This time he had more trouble controlling his temper. Well that's great. Do you think you could put a little more pressure on me?"

"What pressure, Joshua? Are you the one going through all these miscarriages? And now you want to set up a schedule that'll keep us apart even more?"

She had pushed the critical button. He melted immediately.

"No, I'm sorry, honey." He reached for her hand again. "Look, I would be taking a salary cut, but nothing devastating. We'll just take a little more time paying off the loans.... And there'd be some benefits we haven't talked about yet."

"Such as?"

"For starters, we'd have a lot more time together."

"Oh?" she brightened.

"Well ... I'd have to cut back on obstetrics," he leaned back and stretched out his legs, "and, who knows, maybe I'll even split my call schedule with someone."

Aviva reacted in mock surprise. "Wait a minute! Get outta here, mister, and stop impersonating my husband!" She threw her arms around him. "What brought this on?"

"I don't know, Viv. I'm starting to realize my patients know I'm only human, and they seem to be receptive to the idea of someone else sharing night call with me."

His tone became more serious. "And I can't help thinking if I gave you more attention, you'd have better luck with these pregnancies."

Aviva put the memo down and kissed his cheek tenderly. "We both know that's not the way it works. But thank you, Joshua."

He returned her kiss, then looked at her expectantly.

"So what's the verdict?"

"I don't think it could hurt to apply," Aviva patted his hand. "Then we'll wait and see."

****

Josh looked forward to his next teaching assignment. A new crop of medical students had just entered the Lying-In for their obstetrical rotation. Having heard about his recent grand rounds presentation on abdominal pregnancy, they asked that it be the subject of one of their elective lecture topics. He agreed, but advised them to be prepared with a working knowledge of the subject before their session.

Josh did not lecture in the formal manner nor believe in spoon feeding his students. His preferred method of instruction was via a modified Socratic method, whereby teacher and student examined a topic through a series of provocative questions and answers. He also sometimes employed the technique known as Socratic irony, using the pretense of ignorance to expose the fallacies in an opponent's logic or fund of knowledge. Students tended to be lukewarm to this approach because it was often used for browbeating, but this wasn't Josh's style. Although he tended to be a tough grader, he saw no good or useful purpose in humiliating students in front of their peers.

As he anticipated the teaching session, Josh was struck with an idea. Socratic discussions were far less predictable than didactic lectures. Perhaps he could introduce an element of fate into the decision to alter his career direction. If this session went particularly well it could be a sign that he was destined to assign a significant part of his time to education, but if it went badly perhaps he should stick to private practice and continue in his limited capacity as a teaching volunteer.

The meeting began promptly at noon. As per the custom at the Lying-In, there was a cafeteria cart that contained sandwiches and soft drinks. Everyone picked something from the cart as they walked in and then took a place at one of the classroom style chairs that had been arranged in a small circle. At Josh's request, one of the students read the patient's history while the others listened attentively. Josh interrupted the clinical account before it came to the description of the physical examination. He called on the student sitting opposite him.

"Brian, can you tell me what you'd be thinking when this patient presented with the history you just heard?"

"I guess I'd want a pregnancy test."

"Okay, that's already been done and it turned out to be equivocal, sort of a weak positive, so what's next?" He nodded to the student to Brian's left. "Could you turn your nametag around, please?"

When she did so he continued. "Okay, Amy, what's your next move?"

The student hesitated. "Uh, maybe an ultrasound?"

"Uh-huh. And what would that tell you?"

"How far pregnant she was?"

"Yeah, it would do that, but can you tell me what an ultrasound study costs?"

When she hesitated again Josh continued. "Anybody? The cost of a pelvic ultrasound?"

One of the others ventured a guess.

"A hundred dollars?"

Josh smiled. "Actually, ultrasound machines are super expensive and the techs are paid pretty well too, so believe it or not a study of this type can run several times that amount."

He waited a moment for this to sink in, then he turned to Amy again.

"So Amy, any other way that might be less expensive to determine how far pregnant this patient might be?"

She broke into a smile. "Oh yeah, I forgot. A pelvic exam."

He snapped his fingers.

"Right. We always have to come back to the basics. History and physical exam.

It might be a good idea to make that your mantra for a while.

'History and physical. History and physical.' You'd be amazed at how often that's all you need to manage a patient. And keep in mind that lab tests can be quite expensive, so if they're not really necessary, why order them?"

The students began to get comfortable. It was obvious that this guy was there to share his knowledge without making them feel like a bunch of fools.

"Okay, now we've taken our history and done our physical exam, and this patient's uterus is barely enlarged despite the fact that it's been two or three months since her last period. Her cervix is closed and she's bleeding lightly. Now where are we? It's apparent that this isn't your routine healthy pregnancy, isn't it?"

The students' heads bobbed in unison. Josh turned back to Brian. "So now what, Brian? What would you be thinking at this point?"

Brian warmed to the challenge. "Well, I'd be trying to compile a list of what sort of problems could be going on."

"And what do you call such a list?"

"A differential diagnosis."

"Good. How about breaking that down for us?"

"Sure," he replied. "It would have to start with the various natural accidents of pregnancy, like threatened or incomplete abortion."

"Okay. Anything else?"

"How about tubal pregnancy?" Amy called out.

"Bingo! And now what sort of information would be helpful?"

Amy cowered and made the sign of the cross with her index fingers. "Ultrasound?"

"Right, Amy," Josh laughed . Now's the right time for ultrasound. And in this study the sonographer is prompted to look around a little further because the patient is complaining of pain in the region of her left flank. What would he or she be looking for?"

Brian spoke up again. "Kidney stone, maybe?"

"Actually that's a fair possibility, but in this case it's not there. What we find this time is a fourteen week embryo that's located in the abdominal cavity, and that's the way it happened with my recent patient who had an abdominal pregnancy. But what's more likely? What Brian said about a kidney stone or finding an abdominal pregnancy?"

They answered together this time.

"Kidney stone."

"Good. How often do we find abdominal pregnancies, by the way?"

"Rarely."

"Any idea of the frequency?"

"One in multiple thousands."

"Close enough. The average practitioner might see one or two in a career, maybe none. Can anyone quote the principle about how to prioritize statistical possibilities in a differential diagnosis?"

Brian volunteered again.

"When you hear hoofbeats in North America, you think of horses, not zebras."

"Great. Okay, then. Those are the basic messages for today ... the importance of history and physicals, the prudent utilization of ancillary testing, and the consideration of probabilities in a differential diagnosis. Now we have a few minutes left for questions."

The students sat forward on the edge of their chairs, insisting on every detail of Sarah Moore's case and growing completely engrossed as he described Soo-Yen Park's predicament. When the conference came to an end it was well past one o'clock. Josh glanced at the notepad of the student sitting next to him and smiled when he saw the three quickly scribbled entries:

H & P, H&P, H&P

Labs only if necessary ... consider cost !!!

Diff Dx ... Horses / Zebras

Next he surveyed the rest of the room and realized that nobody had touched their lunch. His own sandwich wasn't even unwrapped. He took this as a sign. He was meant to be an educator. A total of nine members of the staff indicated their interest in being appointed director of education. All but two were full time faculty. At his discretion, Dr. Landry lowered the field to five candidates and recommended that the residents make the choice by means of secret ballot. There were six residents per year, twenty four in all, and when the votes were counted no individual candidate had a clear majority. Of the top two, one was Josh Cantor, and Josh was surprised to see that the other finalist was Nancy Sanderson. Until now, Dr. Landry had kept the names confidential. At Landry's request, Josh sat in his office to discuss the situation.

"I've already talked to Nancy about this, Josh," Landry began. "It's her intention to concentrate on research and I have no doubt that she views this teaching position mainly as a means of advancing her career, either here or elsewhere. But I have to tell you, even though she's a new faculty member she's proven herself to be an excellent teacher and the residents respect her, so I consider her a legitimate candidate.

I just wanted you both to be aware of where we are with this because now there has to be a choice between the two of you. I could exercise my prerogative to make the appointment but I think that might lead to an impression of favoritism, so I've decided to run a second closed ballot."

Josh shifted positions in his chair. "This makes me a little uncomfortable, Leon. You know we dated several years ago, so the idea of campaigning against her poses a dilemma for me."

"It might be a problem for you, Josh, but I can tell you it doesn't seem to be bothering Nancy. I happen to know she's already buttonholed a bunch of residents."

Josh's dismay was evident. He remained quiet for a moment before rising from his chair. "Okay, Leon, I hear you. Thanks for your time."

Josh decided to take the high road. He wouldn't campaign but would answer questions if specifically asked. On the day before the balloting, one of the senior residents stopped him in the hall. "Dr. Cantor, can I ask you something?"

"Sure, Jeff. What's on your mind?"

"Some of us were wondering just how interested you are in tomorrow's election. I mean, Dr. Sanderson has been actively putting out the word on herself and we haven't heard much from you."

Josh shrugged. "To answer your question, I'd have to say that I'm very interested. Don't take my lack of campaigning as an indication that I don't want it, Jeff, because I do. It's just a difference in style."

The resident smiled. "I'm glad to hear that, because some of us have gotten the wrong impression. If you don't mind, I'd like to set everyone straight before tomorrow."

"As a matter of fact I'd appreciate it. Just please don't get into any mudslinging. I don't want it to get out of hand."

The election results were announced at the department's business meeting later that week. As the first item, Dr. Landry indicated that Josh Cantor would be appointed to the position of Director of Education. As Landry was speaking, Josh caught a glance of Nancy out of the corner of his eye. Her complexion had turned blood red, causing him to have a flashback of one of their encounters when they were dating. At a department conference during their residency, someone gave Josh credit for a project that had been initiated by Nancy. Nancy's face had taken on a frightening mask of scarlet anger, and even though Josh had set the record straight in front of everyone, she continued to treat him coolly for days afterward.

Josh thought about this incident for the remainder of the business meeting, and as soon as it was adjourned he tried to catch Nancy in the hall. When he called to her she ignored him, however, continuing on her way even though Josh was certain she had heard him. Now he was angry.

"Nancy! Stop, dammit!"

Nancy halted but didn't turn around, remaining still with her back turned to him. Josh walked around and faced her. "Look, I know you're upset about this, but I'm not going to let you carry a grudge over it."

117

She looked back at him but said nothing. The anger in her face had been replaced by defeat and frustration, causing Josh's heart to soften.

"Nancy, why don't you work with me on this? You'd be an enormous asset to resident education in this hospital."

Her faced darkened again. "And how would that look on my C.V.? 'Member of the education committee?' No, I don't think so, Josh. If I haven't held the chair, what good will it do me? Thanks, but no thanks." She began to walk away but stopped and turned back to face him again. "You know, Josh, I don't think you really understand how important my work is. If you did, you wouldn't stand in my way like this."

His expression turned incredulous. " 'I wouldn't stand in your way?' What do you think, Nancy? The rest of the world's going to lie down so you can roll over them? This is about medical education, for God's sake. How can you manage to twist it around so it's part of your career advancement?"

Suddenly he realized they were standing in the middle of the hall and their conversation was becoming a spectacle, but Nancy didn't care.

"Forget it, Josh," she sneered. "You don't have a clue."

Josh restrained himself as she walked away. Apparently he didn't know Nancy as well as he thought Or come to think of it, maybe he did.

TWENTY - FOUR

One of the responsibilities of the Director of Education was to develop a teaching schedule for the staff with the subjects ranging from infertility to cancer, and high risk obstetrics to medical ethics. Since assuming the director's position, Josh had discovered that this nuts-and-bolts task required a lot more time than he anticipated.

The reason was not so much the actual paperwork involved, but the myriad personalities and constant schedule changes that seemed to pop up every week. The private practitioners in particular had unpredictable schedules, so managing the logistics could be both frustrating and time-consuming. Fortunately for Josh all of this was a labor of love, his commitment to education making it worthwhile despite the headaches.

When it came to Nancy Sanderson, however, the challenge was more daunting. Shortly after their altercation on the day of his appointment she had informed him that she would require a temporary reprieve from her teaching duties, and she had remained on inactive status ever since. It was when a small crisis arose that Josh tried to re-approach her. A physician who was scheduled to conduct a resident conference had given him just two days cancellation notice and Nancy was the most appropriate substitute. Uncertain about how she would respond, he called her to explain the circumstances and asked if she would reconsider her position.

"Nancy, I wonder if you could fill in for Bill Driscoll. He was scheduled to run a conference on surgical procedures for infertility and you'd be the logical person to teach this topic."

Nancy's tone was cool. "I don't know. What day are we talking about?"

"Day after tomorrow. I know it's short notice, but do you think you could help me out here?"

She delayed her answer again. Josh imagined her rolling her eyes.

"I suppose so, but I can't do this on a regular basis, Josh. I'm really tapped out right now."

"I understand. There's one more thing, though. If you're agreeing to do this I need to make a suggestion."

"Such as?"

"The dean's office has asked that we use their teaching model of case presentation. That's my technique anyway - you know, a modified Socratic method - so I was happy to accommodate them, but as I recall you use a more formal lecture style."

"So?'

"So you'll need to adopt a different format, at least for this one session."

"Just a minute, Josh. Let me be sure I understand this. You're asking me for a favor, and now that I've consented you want to tell me how to do my job too?"

"I know, it sounds a bit obnoxious, but I'm in a bind. I can review the technique with you if you want."

"That won't be necessary. I'll do my best to live up to your lofty academic standards."

Josh took on a sharp tone. "Look, Nancy. Don't do me any favors. There are plenty of people busier than you, including full professors who are donating their time without making a big thing about it. In fact they consider it a privilege. So if this is too much for you just say so and I'll find someone else."

Nancy responded with a condescending smirk, giving Josh the impression that she had taken a twisted satisfaction from agitating him. "Well, I'll say this," she began. "If it takes nerve to do your job, you're more than qualified. But I'll tell you what, Josh. I'll do it. I'll even do it your way. Just don't forget this the next time I need a favor," she snipped. "You owe me one."

TWENTY - FIVE

The university's animal research facility became the subject of intense discussion between Nancy and Philip. It was a free-standing cinder block building with simple external architecture; rectangular, one story, flat roofed. A parking lot bordered the south end with patches of dense woods abutting the remaining three sides. The interior layout was much more complicated. Nancy was having difficulty getting a feel for it from Philip's descriptions and diagrams.

"I need to see it myself before we try to pull this off," she said. "Is there a way you can get me in there when nobody else is around?"

"I'd rather not do that," Philip protested. "I know the place well enough for both of us. We're gonna do this thing together anyway, so what's the advantage of your seeing it beforehand? Plus, the only time for you to get in without being seen is after hours, and if we're going to do that we might as well carry out our experiments at the same time."

"All right, but at least let's drive down there to look at the neighborhood. We can't just park in the lot and walk in, even at night. We're going to have to approach the building through the woods and I definitely want to get a feel for that in daylight before we try it after dark."

On the following Saturday afternoon they prepared to drive to Grafton. Nancy was dressed in her usual weekend garb, black denim jacket and jeans. This time she added a Red Sox baseball cap worn backwards. Philip grinned when he saw the hat.

"Oh, a Sox fan, eh?"

"Not really. Baseball's a little slow for me. Hockey's my game. I wear it this way at 'The Gahden' when I root for the Bruins."

"I don't know. We're gonna have to get past that when Montreal comes to town."

"The Canadians? Those prima donnas? I guess they can stick handle okay, but they don't ..." -- she delivered a playful blow to Philip's chest with her forearm -- "...body check like the Bruins. That's what gets me where I live. I like hard-nosed hockey."

Philip dropped into a boxer's crouch. "So you're a little tomboy, eh? This winter we'll have to do some skating. Maybe bring a hockey stick along."

"You just say when, 'Pretty Boy'. I'll kick your 'Canadian' butt!"

They made the trip in Nancy's Mustang convertible, a bright yellow street machine with dual exhausts. She slid in behind the steering wheel and pushed a button to lower the top. As it was folding down she took off her cap and shook her hair loose.

Philip raised his eyebrows.

"A little brisk for a top-down day, don't you think?"

She turned the key and revved the engine.

"I always drive this way. Just bundle up and blast the heater. Love it!"

He shrugged his shoulders and buttoned his jacket.

"Whatever you say."

They cruised the Mass Pike well over the limit, Nancy's black hair whipping in the wind, low autumn sun flashing off her tinted glasses. Philip was uncomfortable -- he was freezing and her aggressive driving style made him nervous -- but he sensed she was testing him. He'd have to tough it out.

Finally they reached Grafton and parked near a playground a block away from the school. As they began to walk towards the research facility Nancy insisted on stopping from time to time, looking around to see of they were being watched. Then, after assuring herself they were alone, she took a small camera from her pocket and began to surreptitiously take shots of the path leading to the building.

"Don't you think you're carrying this just a bit too far?" Philip said. "We're not robbing a bank here."

"I don't want anything to go wrong, Philip. There's too much at stake. Maybe I was unrealistic about how much trouble this could cause. It'd be awful if this kept you from graduating."

He was having trouble keeping up with Nancy's mood swings. "Well this sure is a change of heart. What happened to that 'malicious mischief' theory you had? Are you getting cold feet now?"

"I guess maybe I am, now that it's becoming reality."

"Well, it's funny but I'm going the other way. Somehow I'm not as worried about it as I was before."

"You're not?"

"Naah, if we get caught we'll apologize and offer to make restitution. But if our sow turns up pregnant, the school's name will get lit up in all the journals. I'm betting the faculty will eat it up."

Nancy was psyched. "All right! That's our plan!"

"Okay, so I'm in. When do you want to do this?".

She took his hand and led him back to the car, talking ever more excitedly. He listened with a bemused expression at her enthusiasm.

"Now don't forget any of this, Philip. If you have any questions, check with me. In the meantime, you'll monitor the pig IVF study and let me know when the embryos are ready. That's when we'll make our move."

On the following Wednesday afternoon, Nancy answered a page for an outside call.

"I peeked at the IVF project," Philip said over the phone. "They've got embryos in there now at the two cell stage. How soon do we need to do this?"

"Two cells, huh? Well, that's when we start transferring them in humans. They go through one or two cell division every twenty four hours so that would mean at least four cells tomorrow and eight cells Friday."

"So we'll do it tonight?"

"Not necessarily. We often do four cell transfers and sometimes eight, so we could wait a day or two if necessary......No, wait. You told me that pig gestations are a lot shorter than humans, so that might mean that cell division at this stage is faster also. I guess we've gotta do it tonight or tomorrow, at the latest."

Philip grew more enthused. "I'm ready when you are. How about tonight then?"

"I don't know. Somehow it doesn't feel right. No good reason, just intuition I guess. Would you mind if we waited a day? Thursday night just sounds better to me somehow."

"Sure, if you don't think that'll be too late."

"No, it shouldn't be a problem. It might even be a slight advantage to wait for an extra cell division since we're placing the embryos in the abdominal cavity rather than the uterus. Maybe that'll even give them a survival advantage. I just don't want to wait so long that the IVF researcher uses them all before we have a chance."

"All I can tell you is that he has a ton of embryos growing here. I also found out that he's using super-ovulation techniques to retrieve plenty of eggs. He injected one of the sows with so much medication that her ovaries blew up to the size of melons and she started bleeding internally.

They had to operate on her to remove her ovaries. Then they didn't have any more use for her so she got sent to the butcher. Cruel world, huh?"

"Really. Although sometimes I wish we had those kind of options in humans when we screw up."

He laughed. "Whoa! You've got a dark side, don't you? I just hope it doesn't surface some night when I'm asleep."

Her tone became tender. "Don't worry. You're definitely on my good side, Philip. I want you around for a long time."

This was the first time in their relationship that either one of them had verbalized genuine affection. Up until now it was strictly physical and decidedly cautious on both sides. Philip was caught off guard by this change of mood. He wasn't sure what to say and there was a long silence over the phone line. She decided to break the tension.

"Hello? Are you there? I didn't scare you away, did I?"

"No, I was just a little surprised, that's all. I'm not saying I didn't like it, though."

"Well, that's nice to hear."

"Yeah? I guess we haven't talked about this stuff up until now, but I have to confess I've thought about it more than once."

Another short silence ensued. Philip decided to break it this time. He cleared his throat.

"Anyway, what about our plan? Is it gonna be tonight or tomorrow?"

"My instinct tells me tomorrow night, although I'd be hard pressed to tell you exactly why. Is that okay with you?"

"Absolutely. I'd never question a woman's intuition. I'll be there."

Ultimately they decided to time their escapade for early Friday morning. Nancy's alarm went off at 4:00 AM and within minutes they were on their way. To their dismay the early autumn weather was rainy and unseasonably cold. Low clouds streaked by, visible just overhead, and staccato pebbles of wind-driven rain flailed their faces while treetops swayed gracefully, then violently, according to the whims of the storm.

Determined to stick to their plan of a pre-dawn raid, they drove to the playground and arrived just before five o'clock. Their tools were minimal, consisting of a flashlight and an assortment of needles and syringes which Nancy carried in a fannypack. The dark conditions forced them to use the flashlight for short bursts to make their way through the thick trees and underbrush. Philip went ahead, stopping frequently to hold branches aside until she passed. They exchanged gestures and hand signals until reaching the edge of the vegetation. There was a thirty foot border of grass separating them from the building, but they had managed to exit the woods directly opposite the door. Allowing herself a self-satisfied smile, Nancy nudged Philip in the ribs, her way of bragging about the foresight of using her photographs in their tactical planning. Then she faced him, gesturing that he should go ahead and open the door while she waited in the woods. When he didn't understand she motioned for him to lean over towards her, cupping her hands over his ear and whispering. "You go first and unlock the door. Once you're inside, leave it open just a crack and I'll follow."

Momentarily distracted by the sensual warmth of her breath, Philip controlled himself as he turned to inspect the property. Seeing no one, he dashed across the grass. Upon reaching the building he pulled the key from his pocket and dropped it onto the cement step, causing a small clatter. Before picking it up he stood still and waited for a response. When none came he bent over to retrieve the key, quickly unlocked the door, then defused the alarm. Nancy immediately scampered across the grass and closed the door behind her.

They had successfully completed phase one. Now that they were safely inside the building, Philip held her close, their bodies moving together as they caught their breath. From Philip's sleeve, Nancy picked a flaming red maple leaf that was soaked from the storm. She pressed it to her cheek.

"I'm going to save this for a memento," she said.

He looked down at her and felt an irresistible impulse...

"I think I love you, Nancy."

Nancy's face showed astonishment at first, then broke into a warm smile.

"Well, that's great, Philip," she whispered. "But this is a hell of a time to tell me that."

He was even more surprised than she was.

"I know it. It just came out."

"Well I hope you meant it anyway."

"As a matter of fact, I did. How about you?"

"Yeah, me too."

They gazed into each other's eyes until she took his face in her hands and reached up to whisper in his ear again.

"In case you haven't noticed, it stinks in here."

Philip cracked up. "Okay. Let's go do our thing and get the hell out."

They came to a small room with a computer-printed sign on the door.

EGG LAB
CLEAN ROOM

This was the site where the IVF researcher was combining swine sperm and eggs in a small petri dish and incubating them so that fertilization and cell division could take place. Any type of bacterial or viral infestation of these cultures could cause a failure of growth. This fact necessitated extreme efforts in sterile technique, including a "sticky mat," tacky-surfaced floor covering which pulled the debris from the soles of any footwear crossing it. A fresh mat was laid down at the end of every workday. In addition, all who entered were required to wear sterile gowns, caps, masks, and even shoe covers. Anyone handling the specimens directly wore sterile gloves.

Nancy knew about these conditions, of course. The egg lab at the university's human IVF facility had similar rules. She had discussed this with Philip when they were making their plans. They agreed to walk around the sticky mat so as not to leave a footprint trail, and also to skip the sterile precautions because of the cumbersome logistics they would present. It occurred to Nancy that this might be sabotaging another scientist's work, but she immediately put the thought out of her mind.

Guilt was an emotion that could get in the way of her career. She had learned to ignore it.

Once inside they worked quickly, taking stock of the room's contents. Contained within was a long counter, on the center of which sat an exotic looking microscope with a double head designed to allow two investigators to view the same field at once. Next to it was an incubator with a centigrade thermometer piercing its top. Nancy directed her flashlight beam so that she could read it.

"This one's working. Thirty seven degrees, perfect for an in-vitro petri dish."

She opened the incubator door and saw several saucer-like clear plastic devices with raised edges, each one measuring only six centimeters in diameter and containing a small amount of fluid. Picking one at random, she placed it under the microscope. The mounting stage of this instrument was programmed for a constant temperature of thirty - seven degrees centigrade, like the incubator, because of the cold sensitivity of the dividing embryos. At this point she turned the scope to the high power lens and peered through it.

"Philip. Take a look at this."

Through the second eyepiece he easily viewed six embryos, all at the eight cell stage. Nancy opened her fannypack and took out a sterile ten cc syringe and a small-bore, flexible plastic catheter. After connecting them she drew up half of the solution, observing the process through the microscope to insure that at least three of the embryos were included. Then she recapped the syringe and slipped it inside her bra to protect it from chilling. She smiled at Philip and punched the air with her fist.

"To the pigs!"

As they approached the pigpens they could hear the grunting of a new mother as she was calling her piglets to nurse. Nancy found the scene irresistible and asked Philip to stop for a moment. The huge sow was cordoned off in a relatively small space within her own pen. Surrounding her was a three foot high grating that allowed enough space to move back and forth, and a little more room for lateral movement, but she could not turn around or get to the other side of the pen where nine piglets lay on top of each other and slept under a warming light. Her persistent grunting stirred the piglets into motion and they marched around her rear end in military-like formation to get at her engorged teats. For a long while they rooted aimlessly as though they couldn't see, but then each of them latched on and sucked lustily. Through it all the sow grunted contentedly.

"Oh, look how cute!" They're so small, Philip. How old are they?"

"Born Wednesday morning. Not yet forty eight hours, but believe it or not, their sibling dominance is already established."

"What do you mean? How can you tell?"

"It actually occurs within six hours of birth. The piglet nursing at the front is always the boss. And it stays that way. You've heard of getting the 'hind tit'? The ones at the back get the least amount of milk and remain submissive to their brothers and sisters for life. And by the way, there's no pattern of sexual dominance. A female is just as likely to get to the front as a male."

"But don't the males grow bigger and faster?"

"No, not at all. Both sows and boars can weigh damn near half a ton. And Nancy - they're not real cute when they get to be that size, believe me."

"I can imagine. I hope we're not going to have to wrestle one of those monsters tonight."

"No, the typical research animal goes about two-twenty-five or two-fifty. We'll be at their pens in a minute."

"Before we go, tell me why the sow is cordoned off in such a small space."

"Oh, that. It's called a farrowing crate and it's designed to keep the sow away from the piglets so they won't get crushed. This sow weighs about five hundred pounds and the piglets are only two pounds at birth. All she has to do is step on one or lie down the wrong way to wipe out the whole litter. And some sows are cannibalistic. They'll just eat the little critters. So they're kept in the farrowing crate for a few weeks until the piglets can fend for themselves. The piglets grow several pounds a week so it doesn't take long."

"Poor thing, she must be miserable in there."

"They don't seem to complain, and I don't know of any better way to protect the piglets .... Okay, enough of that. Those embryos are getting cold. Let's go do our injection."

They walked down the row of pigpens, inspecting the animals as they passed by. Nancy stopped short.

"Which one? And how do you tell the males from the females in the dark?"

"They're all females in a research facility. The boars can get mean."

Philip continued to analyze the stalls. "Look over here," he called to her. "In the last pen. This one's by herself."

The two of them stood still for a moment, assessing the pig as it stared back at them.

"Whaddya say, Nancy? She's bigger than the others, but she's in there alone."

"Looks as good as any. Let's go for it."

"Okay, I'm gonna go into the pen and close the door so she can't take off. Then I'll nudge her over near the fence and pin her against it. That's when you're gonna have to do the injection. And remember, she's gonna squeal like hell when you stick her, so do it quick 'cause we won't get a second chance." He took a critical look at Nancy. "Can you see okay?" he asked. "Do you have enough light?"

"Yeah, I can see fine. Just wait a minute until I get my equipment organized."

She opened her fannypack once more and unsheathed an imposing six inch, fourteen gauge needle.

"Jesus, lookit that mother!" Philip recoiled. "You didn't need a needle that size for this job. A smaller one would've done fine."

"Too big, do you think? I thought I'd have to get through a pretty thick abdominal wall."

"It really won't be that thick because you'll want to go from the side, rather than underneath. Just stay back far enough that you're behind the ribs and you don't get into the thorax." Philip dissolved into giggles. "You'll probably kill the poor girl if you stick that spike of yours in her chest!"

Nancy looked at Philip, then at the needle, and finally at the pig. As the absurdity of the situation struck her, her shoulders began to shake with helpless laughter. It took a while before either of them could speak.

"All right, stop!" she pulled herself together. "She'll do just fine. I'll get her in the abdomen and hopefully she'll grow us a few babies in there."

Philip had to take a deep breath and exhale hard before he could get serious.

"Okay, here goes."

As soon as he entered the pen, the pig began to grunt and retreat. After closing the gate behind him he moved slowly towards the animal, soothing her by speaking softly, but as he came closer she grew increasingly agitated, rocking side to side while her grunting grew more frantic. Eventually he managed to coax her near the fence where Nancy waited with the needle bared, her thumb on the end of the syringe, set to inject as soon as the abdominal wall was pierced.

"Are you ready, Nancy? I'm gonna push her against the rail and then you'll have about five seconds max to empty that cannon."

Nancy braced herself. "Yeah, I'm ready."

"Okay, on the count of three.......One...two..."

Philip shoved with all his might, slipping on the straw as he did so but managing to press his shoulder to the animal's ribs and pin it against the fence. Nancy seized the opportunity to shove the needle into the opposite flank, just behind the rib cage. She was surprised at how little resistance she encountered, requiring little effort to plunge it all the way to the hub. But as Philip had predicted, the pig let out a frightening squeal and immediately began to violently twist and turn. Nancy lost control of the syringe as the terrified animal pulled away, the needle still sticking in its side. Meanwhile, Philip had jumped away in time to see what happened and had the presence of mind to shove the plunger into the syringe's cylinder before yanking it free.

At this point the pig became enraged and turned, bull-like, ready to charge. Philip looked briefly at the gate but then made a snap decision to jump the fence and did so while wielding the long needle in front of him. Nancy watched as he began a graceful hurdler's leap, front leg extended, then held her breath as his trailing foot barely nicked the top rail. To her horror, this seemingly minor error caused him to trip and fall awkwardly against the opposite pen's gate, simultaneously banging his face against the metal latch and jabbing the needle into his thigh.

He came up reeling, blood streaming from his nose. Nancy froze, not sure what to do first. Philip instinctively pulled out his shirttail and brought it up to his face. She ran to him and pinched his nostrils while helping him to sit down. After a few minutes he regained his senses and his bleeding diminished, but his nose was pointed sharply to the left, clearly broken. She helped him to his feet and they started for the door.

Philip mumbled nasally. "My leg ..."

Nancy looked down to see that the needle had completely pierced his inner thigh just above the knee, exiting his jeans at the back of the leg. The point rested in a patch of grimy straw that reeked from the nauseating stench of pig manure. As she stared at the gruesome sight, the likelihood of infection occurred to her immediately, both because of the bacteria-laden straw and the pig's blood on the needle. She wished she had antiseptic material and antibiotics with her, but there was no time for worrying about ideal conditions. She steeled herself for the act of removing the bent needle, praying that it wouldn't break and lodge in his thigh.

"Philip, I'm going to pull this thing out now. It's gonna hurt, so brace yourself."

He grunted, continuing to hold his bleeding nose. After wiping away the filthy straw with her fingers, Nancy pulled the needle, twisting it to follow its bent angle. Philip stiffened and let out an involuntary groan but Nancy ignored his pain, forcing herself to concentrate on straightening the needle in order to insert it in its sheath and replace the whole apparatus back in her fannypack. She pulled him to a standing position and studied his eyes. They were clear.

"We have to get going. It's gonna get light soon. Can you make it?"

He attempted to compose himself with a deep breath, his eyes now closed, cold sweat dripping from his forehead. "Yeah, let's go."

Walking quickly, she steadied him by grasping his arm while they found their way to the door and set the alarm. Now Nancy was grateful for the storm, reasoning that the rain would wash away any blood Philip might shed while dashing across the grass to the woods. Fighting off breathless panic as the thick underbrush grabbed at their legs, they finally reached the car, and then, witnessed solely by the deserted playground, stole away through rain-soaked streets, their fiasco dissolving into Friday's gloomy dawn.

TWENTY - SIX

"What the hell happened to you?"

Philip was to hear this astonished comment repeatedly that day. His nose had been set by an ENT resident, a friend of Nancy's, but his mid-face was grotesquely swollen and multi-colored. In addition, he was limping noticeably. Nancy had liberated an ample supply of broad spectrum antibiotics and a vial of tetanus vaccine for his leg because Philip refused to visit an emergency room. He argued, logically, that he would be able to explain away the broken nose by concocting a story about falling in the shower, but that wouldn't work for the nasty needle wound in his thigh.

After completing these initial phases of his treatment, Philip decided to visit the swine research facility to see how their prize patient was doing. He was concerned that there would be a tell-tale bruise in the animal's side where they had inserted Nancy's large bore needle. But as he passed down the walkway between the pigpens he was in for a shock.

A large group of students was gathered around the last pen, the one he had been inside last night. His immediate reaction was panic, thinking that the animal was injured or had died as a result of their experiment. Soon, however, he saw that the pig was, in fact, in excellent health and was the subject of a lecture by Dr. Daniel Farnsworth, a member of the faculty who had a special interest in genetics.

"So you see," Dr. Farnsworth was saying, "he is quite an unusual specimen, genetically engineered to produce large litters, and each of his offspring will be a low-fat animal which will grow rapidly to reach market weight in less then five and one half months."

"He?" Philip repeated to himself.

Dr. Farnsworth continued. "Fifty thousand dollars may seem to be an outrageous sum for a pig, but his semen commands high fees because it can be used to impregnate several sows with artificial insemination, and their litters will produce huge economic returns for the modern farmer."

Philip moved closer. Someone had hung a humorous sign around the pig's neck.

"HAMLET," it read.

Philip could scarcely breathe, but by looking closely he was able to detect a subtle bruise on the animal's left flank. Immediately he exited the building, rushed to his car, and flipped open his cell phone. Inside the car, his breath began to fog the cold glass. He dialed Nancy's number and began to shake his leg as he waited impatiently for an answer.

Finally, Nancy's voice.

"Hello?"

"Nancy! We fucked up!"

"What do you mean? What happened?"

"We fucked up, I said! Shit! The pig's a male! It's a goddam prize stud that sells for fifty thousand dollars!"

"You've gotta be kidding! A fifty thousand dollar pig? I never heard of such a thing!"

"It's a genetically altered male that's used for breeding, just like a stud horse or bull. We injected a boar, Nancy! All that trouble for nothing! All our work and planning, my goddam nose and leg, and we injected a boar! And a prize boar at that! Damn! I don't believe it!"

"But you said they only used females in research facilities. What was a boar doing there?"

"Hell, I don't know. This guy Farnsworth is a geneticist, so he must have arranged to bring it here for some kind of study. I should have known when I saw it by itself in the pen. I can't believe how this turned out."

"How could you have known? It was so dark in there. Besides, I'm worried about your leg right now. You've gotta be sure to take all those antibiotics. We'll deal with the rest later."

Nancy kept him on the phone until he calmed down, hoping that by remaining composed she could reassure him. Eventually he came around.

"I guess you're right...don't worry...no, I won't do anything crazy.... All right, I'll see you later."

Through the perspective of time and distance Nancy and Philip were eventually able to see some humor in the situation. They shared a laugh over it one evening and decided their scheme just wasn't meant to be. Still in a lighthearted mood, Nancy posed a question. "How did they ever come up with the name "Hamlet" anyway?"

"Just a little veterinary humor," Philip chuckled. They tend to use 'ham' in all the boars' names. You know, 'Hamlet, Cunningham,

Billingham' ...."

"You really are a bunch of wild and crazy guys."

"I know it. Vets can get pretty corny sometimes. It tends to lighten things up, though. The profession can be stressful when big money is involved."

Nancy's attitude did help Philip to accept what had happened with Hamlet. Still, he found himself looking at the exotic pig every time he was in the research facility, imagining what would have happened if they had seriously injured him during that wacky four A.M. episode.

Two weeks later Philip was still recovering from his own wounds. His face looked nearly normal and his leg had escaped serious infection, but on his thigh there was a curious puffiness that persisted despite a lack of fever. Nancy was concerned as she inspected it. Underneath the skin was a pea-sized nodule of spongy texture.

"Ouch!" Philip winced as Nancy tried to examine the mass's dimensions.

"Sorry. That really hurt, huh?"

Nancy's concern was evident to Philip.

"Yeah. But why are you looking so worried? Wouldn't you still expect a little tenderness? It hasn't been that long."

"Not with a mass. There's something there. I think it needs to come out."

Philip was calm. "All right, so let's get it out. Who do you want to do it?"

"I guess a general surgeon. But I have a funny feeling about this. I'm worried about what we're gonna find."

"Like what?"

"Like some kind of foreign body reaction from pig skin or muscle that got lodged in the needle when we injected Hamlet. We may have a little trouble explaining that to a pathologist if it looks atypical."

"Can't we skip the pathologist?"

"Only if we do it ourselves. Everyone else will order it routinely." She looked at him. "Are you willing to let me carve it out?"

"Sure. Let's do it."

"Just like that? Aren't you even a little bit worried?"

"Naah, I'm sure you're capable. Gimme some novocaine and get this thing outta my leg."

Philip waited while Nancy left to get together a small surgical tray. When she returned she locked the door to her office, prepped Philip's leg with antiseptic solution, and isolated the area with sterile towels. Next she positioned a small scalpel over the area and cut through skin and subcutaneous tissue until she came upon the spongy mass lying just above the muscle. Although bloody, it shelled out easily and she was able to control the bleeding with hemostats and ligatures. She finished quickly and left a neat row of sutures in his skin.

Philip sat up and inspected her work while Nancy applied a dressing. "Nice job," he smiled. "Didn't hurt either."

"Yeah, well you're gonna be sore for a couple days but at least it should heal now. Meanwhile, I'm gonna have to come up with some kind of story to get this analyzed in pathology without telling them where it came from."

Philip stopped in at Nancy's office two days later to have his leg inspected. "It's healing nicely," she assured him, "but I've gotta talk to you about the pathology slide. I got one of the techs to prepare it, then I read it myself."

"And?..."

"And my hunch was right. It was even more bizarre than I thought."

"Like what?"

"Like placental tissue. Some of the cells from the pig embryos must have lodged in your thigh from the needle."

"So what's that mean? Whadda we need to do about it?"

"I've been thinking. Basically you're gonna need to have blood drawn for pregnancy tests every week for a while to make sure none of that stuff's still in you."

"So what's that mean?" he laughed nervously. "My leg was pregnant or something?"

"No, no. Nothing like that. Just to check if there are any placental cells left in the muscle."

"And if there are?"

"You'll need to be treated with some kind of swamp water like methotrexate, but if it comes to that we'll have to come clean with the whole story because that stuff can be tricky to use. I wouldn't want to treat you myself. We just have to hope that won't happen."

Fortunately for Philip, several consecutive blood tests turned out to be negative and his leg healed without incident, allowing him to continue his observations in the research facility. One day, while walking through the building, he noticed another group of people gathered around Hamlet's pen. This time there were no students. It was Farnsworth and three other faculty members, and they looked worried. Busying himself nearby, he eavesdropped on their conversation.

"I don't know," Farnsworth was saying. "We tried yesterday also, and he showed absolutely no interest. Most unusual for a boar of his age.

I wonder if our genetic alterations have affected his libido somehow. He used to mate with any sow who'd hold still. He'd even mount the copulation dummy without the least bit of encouragement. But now he's just not showing any interest. The problem is that we've already taken advance cash payments for his semen and there are a bunch of unhappy pig farmers who're ringing my phone off its hook."

Philip felt a wave of remorse as he listened, feeling certain that Nancy's six inch needle had damaged Hamlet's internal organs in some way. Or maybe the ill-fated animal had developed some type of infection. He decided to take a chance by asking Farnsworth what was happening.

"Excuse me, Dr. Farnsworth, I couldn't help overhearing. Do you have any idea what's wrong with him? I've read that listlessness is sometimes due to hidden infections. Could that be it?"

"No, I don't think so, Philip. We've worked him up for that already. His temperature and white cells are normal. We're just stumped right now. If you have any other suggestions I'd be glad to hear them, though."

Later that day Philip spoke to Nancy about Hamlet's behavior, looking for her input, but she was equally baffled.

"I don't have the slightest idea. It certainly doesn't seem likely that there'd be a connection after this long. If we had damaged some internal organ it would have shown up long before this. I just can't imagine that his behavior is related to what we did."

To the consternation of everyone at the research facility, Hamlet continued to languish over the next several days. In addition to his lack of sexual activity he was off his food and had begun to lose weight. Philip felt comfortable about hanging around the animal since his conversation with Dr. Farnsworth, but he was just as much in the dark as the rest of them. Then one day, while examining Hamlet's abdomen, he noted what looked like two lines of small tumors running parallel along the length of his ventral side, all the way from the front of his chest to his groin. He examined them carefully. Then it struck him. These "tumors" were in fact enlarging nipples, and there were small mounds of breast buds beneath each of them. Philip examined the pig's testicles. Definitely shrunken! He felt an exhilarating sense of revelation. Barely able to contain himself, he hurriedly punched in Nancy's number on his cell phone. When she answered he took a furtive look over his shoulder to be sure no one was within earshot.

"Nancy! You won't believe it! I think Hamlet's pregnant!"

Nancy was astounded as Philip described the changes in Hamlet's appearance and behavior.

"I just can't believe it! How could this happen?"

"You're gonna have to tell me, doctor," he laughed. "What do I know?"

"Well, we have to confirm this somehow. The first thing we need is a pregnancy test, and if that's positive, I'm really gonna wet my pants!"

They forced themselves to calm down and think logically, but Philip couldn't help laughing again. "All right, how do I go about doing the pregnancy test?"

"We can do it in one of two ways, either on blood or urine. The urine test is less sensitive but I assume it will be easier to collect."

"Actually, it's not that easy. A pig won't exactly urinate into a collection cup for you."

"Yeah, I guess not. So how do you get a urine sample?"

"One way is to catheterize them, but you need to anesthetize the animal for that. The easier way is to get them into a metabolic crate. That's a contraption that limits mobility and has a wire grid for a floor that'll allow fluid through but will catch solids. There's a pan underneath it that collects the urine."

"That sounds okay, but what about blood? Is that a problem to collect?"

"No, there's a nice sized vein near the ear, so I can get that if you prefer."

"That's even better. Blood tests are more accurate anyway, and we won't have to worry about contamination. Okay, then. It's settled. I'll run an HCG on his blood."

"HCG? What's that?"

"It stands for 'human chorionic gonadotropin'. It's a hormone that's produced by the placenta."

"Human chorionic gonadotropin, huh, Nancy? Does anything about that term bother you?"

"Oh, shit! I forgot we were dealing with a pig. But don't you think there'd be a crossover? Or better yet, aren't there any blood or urine pregnancy tests for pigs?"

"Nothing practical, believe it or not. We've been using ultrasound to diagnose pregnancy lately, but an embryo won't show up for about a month after conception."

"I just can't wait that long to find out. And with a pregnancy out in the abdomen somewhere, we won't even know where to start looking for it. Undoubtedly it's gonna be hidden somewhere. Philip, it could be another month before we can find it."

"Okay, I'm open to suggestion. How do you want to do this?"

"I guess we should give the blood test a try. If we have any kind of luck at all, pig pregnancy hormones and human ones will be similar enough that the test will work. And it occurs to me that we were using HCG tests on you to monitor that pig placenta in your leg. If that concept turns out to be invalid, we'll have to re-test you in some other way."

The next morning Philip walked into Nancy's office with a red-top vacuum tube containing five cc's of Hamlet's blood. Nancy's face lit up when she saw it. "Good goin'. I'll get a qualitative pregnancy test done in no time."

An hour later she met him back in her office. He stood to greet her but she couldn't contain herself, jumping on him as he staggered backward while trying to hold her without falling.

"Positive! It's positive! We have an abdominal pregnancy in a male pig! We've made history! Do you know what this means?"

Philip caught his breath. "I'm afraid to ask! What do you have up your sleeve now?"

She stepped back and held him by the shoulders. Then she dropped her bombshell.

"Philip, this is the biggest thing since penicillin! I'm betting this concept will work in humans. We're gonna get men pregnant!"

TWENTY - SEVEN

Josh Cantor was on the brink of exhaustion. He had pulled his second consecutive all-nighter and now, at 11 AM, was barely able to function. His office hours that morning had been wiped out by a cesarean section and an emergency surgery for a tubal pregnancy. As he walked into the office he could see that Bridget was sizing him up. She took a look at the bloodshot eyes and drooping lids and wasted no time taking charge.

"You're in no condition to see patients today, Doctor. I'm going to re-schedule this afternoon's patients and arrange for Dr. Greenwald to cover any emergencies.

You're done for the day."

Bridget knew that Josh would worry that his patients would be upset. Many of them had waited several weeks for their appointments and not everyone understood the unpredictability of solo practice.

Again she spoke before he could protest.

Don't worry, Doctor. This has happened before. I'll accommodate everyone and they'll take it just fine."

Josh knew from the tone of Bridget's voice that she was doing a little fabricating in order to placate him. Never mind, he thought. If Bridget couldn't make them happy, no one could. And besides, he had neither the strength nor the enthusiasm to protest.

"No argument here, Bridget.. I'd just like to have a bite to eat and then get a little sleep this afternoon." He thought of his wife, whom he hadn't seen for over forty-eight hours. "Actually, I think maybe I'll try to get Aviva to have lunch with me before I head for home."

He thought himself lucky to have a speed dial option on his office telephone.

Otherwise he wasn't sure he could have remembered Aviva's work number at that moment.

"Hi, stranger," she answered. "You still among the living?"

Josh produced a comic groan. "Just barely. I have enough energy left to meet you for lunch, though."

"Oh yeah? You think you can get a date just like that, huh?"

"Yep. Figured I could take you for granted."

"Well ... all right," she teased, "but this is the last time I'll be able to accept on such short notice."

"Most understanding of you. And would it be convenient for madame to call for me here at the office?"

A surprise silence caused Josh to look at his phone as if it had gone dead.

"Viv?Are you there?"

More silence.

"Viv?"

Then a subdued, "Yes, I'm here, but I'd rather meet somewhere else if you don't mind."

"Really? I was just thinking it'd be more convenient - "

"I know what you were thinking, but I said I'd rather meet somewhere else, all right?"

"Okay, Viv. We'll meet wherever you want. But would you like to tell me why you responded that way to such a simple request?"

Another brief silence, followed by a long breath. Josh thought he heard a catch in the inhale.

"What is it, Viv? Tell me. Please."

One more hesitation, then a torrent of verbal pain.

"I can't, Joshua. I just can't walk into your office anymore. All those pregnant women, all those baby pictures on the wall. It's just too hard. Please don't ask me to do that."

By the time she was finished she was in tears and Josh was kicking himself.

"Viv, you sit tight. I'm coming over there right now."

A rainstorm was brewing while she was waiting for him on the sidewalk outside of her building, wind squalls forcing her to clutch at her trenchcoat. When he pulled his car up to the curb and pushed the passenger door open, she slid in and leaned across to kiss him.

"I'm sorry I acted like that over the phone, Joshua. I know you're exhausted today."

"It's okay. Maybe we'd better talk about it, though. This stuff is making us both a little crazy."

"Tomorrow maybe. We haven't seen each other for two days and I don't want to talk about our pregnancy problems right now."

He reached to take her hand, allowing the car to idle in the parking space, oblivious to the hypnotic sweeping of the windshield wipers.

"Well then, let's talk about my practice schedule again. I was thinking on the way over here that I need to make some more changes. My plans with the education thing aren't working out and we're not seeing nearly enough of each other, Viv."

She brightened a little. "Like what kind of changes? A partner, maybe?"

"Yeah, that's what I'm thinking, but I have to admit it worries me. It could create some problems, even for Bridget."

"Especially for Bridget. I'm not even sure she could adapt. You know, it's just a good thing she's not younger. I could get jealous of the way she treats you."

Josh smiled. "I know it. She's a gem, though. Really, she thinks of both of us as family."

"It's true. Sometimes I think I'm talking to my mother when I call."

They sat quietly for a moment until Josh spoke again.

"You know, Viv, there's more than that. I'm really not sure I could deal all that well with a partner. Do you remember that story I told you about my father? He sent me off to medical school with an old Russian proverb: 'If you want to know about a condition, ask the patient, not the doctor.'"

"And ...."

"And I don't know if I can find someone else who thinks like that."

"Is that it?"

"No, there's more. Like I'm forever hearing doctors in the hospital talking about how they dismissed such-and such a patient from their practice because they wouldn't take their advice."

Aviva gave him another quizzical look and waited.

"I'm thinking of Sarah Moore. She ended up paying a terrible price for wanting to control her destiny, but I still believe patients have the right to make their own decisions. Do you see what I'm getting at, Viv? I'm afraid I'll have my hands full with my own issues, let alone working out compromises with someone else."

The corners of her mouth rose almost imperceptibly into a knowing smile. "Are you sure that's what you're worried about, Joshua? When I think about it, you've never been too happy about change of any kind."

"What do you mean?"

"Well, like the idea of computerizing your office, for example. Most of the world has already gone that route, but you and Bridget are still bumping along with an appointment ledger. Not that it isn't working right now, but if you expand you'll have to consider conversion to a hi-tech system. I'm just wondering if it isn't the prospect of change that worries you more than anything else."

Josh shrugged his shoulders and gazed through the rain-streaked car window at the passing traffic. "Maybe you're right, but the question is whether I can adapt. The world's moving faster than ever."

"Sure it is, but there's nothing new under the sun. You're a solid thinker, Joshua. Just don't let anything throw you before you think it through."

He turned to look at her. Their eyes met and held while both of them broke into smiles. He had married the right woman.

Finally she turned away to look at her watch.

"Well, now that we've solved the world's problems, I guess it's a little late to get lunch."

"Story of our life. Will you be okay?"

"Sure, I can get a sandwich delivered."

"I mean about us. Will you get through the afternoon all right?"

"Do you love me?"

"What a question! More than anything. You know that."

"Then I'll be fine. Go get some sleep. We'll talk some more later."

As he watched her walk away, it occurred to Josh that Aviva hadn't said a word about her own career. Having worked for a number of years as an editor in the field of children's literature, her star had been rising when she met Josh. Then, for the sake of their relationship, she had passed up several advancement opportunities and was currently treading water in a mid-level position. Meanwhile she was struggling with the problem of recurring miscarriages while trying to achieve a successful pregnancy and ultimately raise a family. And although it had undoubtedly occurred to her, she hadn't reminded him just now that a partner could ease her load should any of these possibilities be realized. Nor had she thrown it up to him that the original plan to lighten his schedule wasn't working out.

A wave of guilt washed over him and he nearly called out to her just before she re-entered the building, but instead he made a silent resolution.

I really do have to think a lot harder about a partner.

TWENTY - EIGHT

Nancy's plan hit Philip like a ton of bricks. Even though he was unconflicted about animal research, the concept of experimenting on humans was totally foreign and repugnant to him. He couldn't understand how she could think this way.

"This is nuts, Nancy. What we've done up until now was on the edge, but at least it had the potential to do some good. This idea is a leap in thinking that I just can't accept. What you're considering is dangerous as hell, and I'm afraid I can't see any merit in it besides the gratification of your curiosity."

"Hey! Take it easy! There's plenty of merit in it. What about the woman who can't carry a pregnancy because of medical complications? Why can't her husband carry it for her? Think about it, Philip. Is this really an ethical problem for you, or is it maybe just a gender thing? What's the matter with you men, anyway? Even with infertility cases there's a big thing about whether it's the male partner's 'fault'. Well, frankly I'm sick of that macho bullshit, and I think there are plenty of guys out there who are beyond that problem, even if you're not."

Wounded, Philip retaliated.

"No, the problem, Nancy, is that you're heated up with a lot of blind ambition right now. I don't see where you've thought this thing out nearly far enough. You have one bit of promising information and you're ready to run with it, even though you don't have the appropriate data. You're like a guy with no resources who comes into a little money and immediately blows it on something frivolous. 'Nigger Rich' we used to call it."

"Philip! I can't believe that just came out of your mouth! But I will say my opinion of you has just plummeted. And they say southerners are bigoted!"

143

Immediately contrite, Philip held up his hands in the surrender position.

"I'm sorry. I take it back. That wasn't really me talking. I was just upset. But my point still stands, Nancy; you've gotten way ahead of yourself scientifically, let alone ethically."

"Look. Give me a little credit for common sense here. I'm not ready to do this tomorrow. I don't even want to talk to anyone else about it yet, but I am willing to put my other work on the back burner."

She stopped to compose herself. "Here's my thinking. For a pregnancy to grow there are a few basic requirements. We know it can be sustained temporarily in a test tube with the proper temperature and nutrients. After that it's a matter of maintaining body temperature, establishing a blood supply, bathing it in physiologic body fluids, and providing an expandable space. With some hormone support there's no reason why it has to be gender specific. A male abdomen should be just as efficient as a female abdomen when it comes to nurturing a pregnancy. Look how that stuff was even growing in your leg, for example. The problem is that abdominal placentas can't be easily removed, and that's where patients run into trouble. That's one of the specific problems I want to study in pigs. I know it'll take some time. I don't even know what's going to happen with Hamlet. We'll have to observe him for a while and then do the same thing with several other boars to see if this can be re-created."

"Well, that's another problem, Nancy. It was horrendously bad luck to choose this particular pig. The fact that is was Hamlet has this project 50,000 dollars in the hole before it's even started."

"I know it. We'll have to work that out somehow. But let's not lose sight of the fact that we've created the first ever pregnancy in a male mammal. The fact that it happened by mistake is beside the point. This is a classic case of serendipity, just like the way penicillin was discovered; by chance, while researchers were working on something else. Please, just don't panic on me. I need you to stick with this project and follow Hamlet's progress."

Philip threw up his hands. "That's one more problem. Farnsworth is liable to figure this out. Like I said, they're testing the hell out of this poor animal. They've also noticed the breast development and the shrunken testicles. So far they're thinking he has some sort of hormone imbalance, but I think they're gonna figure it out."

As he spoke, Nancy's mind was racing. She decided she would have to use Philip to suit her own purposes. What he didn't know wouldn't hurt him. "All right, so we'll have to deal with that, too. Just tell me you'll cooperate with me by observing Hamlet."

Philip again felt himself being drawn into an abyss. "Okay...but just for now. I'm sure I'll have a lot of trouble with the idea of getting men pregnant. Don't count on me for that."

Three days later Philip and Nancy ran into another crisis, this one literally deadly. Philip was frantic as he burst into Nancy's office. When he saw that she was alone, he blurted out the news.

"Hamlet's dead!"

"What?!"

"You heard me! He's dead! They found him this morning. And now they're planning an autopsy! I'm in trouble, Nancy! They're gonna find out!"

As she watched Philip's anxiety evolving into terror, she instinctively forced herself to keep control.

"Calm down, Philip Tell me as slowly as possible what happened."

"That's all I know. I was afraid to ask too many questions. What am I gonna do? They're gonna do an autopsy, and when they do they'll find out he was pregnant. And I've been paying way too much attention to him. They'll link me to it for sure. Damn! I'm gonna get kicked out of school... and worse. They'll probably have me up on charges of some kind. This is bad, Nancy!"

Nancy spoke deliberately. "I'm not sure it's all that bad, Philip. The very fact that you've spent so much time with Hamlet is going to be our saving grace." Her gaze locked on his. "Now listen. Are you paying attention?"

As she stared at him, he could feel his energy being consumed by hers. "But I mean close attention, Philip. We can't allow ourselves the luxury of panic right now."

He nodded soberly.

"Good," she said. "Here's exactly what you are going to do." She paced back and forth, lecturing him as his eyes followed her.

"You are going to help Farnsworth with the autopsy on Hamlet. All the time you've spent studying him will make it perfectly reasonable that you'd be interested. In fact, you'll get there well ahead of time and open the abdomen before Farnsworth arrives. You'll explain this later by telling him you wanted to spare him the routine work involved in the autopsy. That'll give you time to find the pregnancy. Chances are that there's been an acute bleeding episode of some sort, so you'll encounter a lot of blood. When you find the pregnancy you'll remove the embryo along with its membranes and cord, and then hide that tissue for me to study later. But you'll leave the placenta in place. Now don't forget that. It's the most important thing. It'll probably be attached to the bowel. You'll just need to rough it up a little to make it unidentifiable to the naked eye. The microscopic pathology report will describe placental tissue, but since this is from a male they'll most likely conclude it was a choriocarcinoma. That's a hormone- secreting tumor that looks something like placental tissue. It'll also explain the hormone theory for the physical changes Hamlet was undergoing, and you'll be off the hook." She turned up her palms. "No problem."

Philip was astonished, both by Nancy's genius and also by this scheming side of her personality. He numbly agreed to her plan, knowing this was probably his best way out for now, but once more he felt a premonition of lurking judgment. And he sensed it would exact a price.

TWENTY - NINE

Hamlet's autopsy was scheduled for Friday at six A.M. Dr. Farnsworth insisted on the early start because he had a full schedule that day, meaning that Philip would have to arrive even earlier in order to carry out Nancy's instructions in time. Thursday night was a sleepless one for him. By three o'clock he hadn't closed his eyes and he couldn't wait any longer. Impatiently kicking off his covers, he dragged himself out of bed, threw on some working clothes, and arrived at the research facility twenty minutes later. Having accomplished a previous illegal entry helped to steady his nerves a little, but on this occasion he was alone, and the pre-dawn silence and odors rendered an eerie atmosphere to the musty building.

Organizing the actual post mortem examination required several logistical details. He would have to move Hamlet's huge body, over 400 pounds of dead weight, from a slab in the cooler to a three foot high autopsy table, but because of the equipment designed for this very purpose, he was able to accomplish it alone.

At his disposal was a large hydraulic hoist with a moveable arm. This machine moved about the main autopsy room on tracks which extended between the cooler and the examination table. Proceeding to move the hoist into position, Philip opened the door and rolled out the sturdy metal shelf supporting Hamlet's body. At the end of the hoist was a heavy chain which he strapped to Hamlet's left rear leg. As he cranked the lever arm upwards, Hamlet's bulk slowly lifted off the cooler slab and groaned its way aloft until it was hanging vertically, head down.

Rolling the hoist to the examination table was surprisingly easy. Once there, Philip maneuvered the carcass and lowered it gently, guiding it into position so that it unfolded into the dorsal recumbent position, back down with the distended abdomen facing the ceiling.

Next came the task of opening the abdomen. This was accomplished with the use of a foot-long knife, a ponderous instrument with a stainless steel blade and a thick plastic handle. Philip pulled on thick rubber gloves, grasped the knife handle like an icepick, and plunged the long blade through the abdominal wall just below the sternum, using his strong triceps to pull it downwards in one swoop, all the way to the pelvis. This action laid open the abdomen and he was immediately gratified to see that Nancy had been right; the abdominal cavity was filled with liquid and clotted blood. Using a small plastic beaker, he dipped into it several times, each time emptying the dark red glop into a plugged-up sink.

Then he was able to inspect the internal organs. The location of the pregnancy was not immediately apparent so he had to run the bowel, passing the long, sausage-like tissue through his fingers. Near the end of the ileum he found a large hemorrhagic mass. After wiping the clotted blood away he could easily identify a pig embryo with an umbilical cord attached to its spongy placenta. The placenta had aggressively invaded the bowel wall and its primary artery which displayed a gaping hole in its side, the obvious source of Hamlet's massive bleeding. Philip shook his head in acknowledgment of the utter accuracy of Nancy's prediction. Following her instructions further, he dissected away everything but the placenta, including the membranes and cord, then proceeded to rough up the tissue so that it wouldn't be immediately identifiable. Then he transferred the embryo and its associated structures into a heavy plastic bag which he tied securely and placed in his green bookbag. Removing his rubber gloves, he looked at the clock, noting that it would be over an hour until Farnsworth arrived. He took a deep, satisfied breath and rewarded himself with a cup of coffee.

"What's all this?" Farnsworth frowned as he entered the room.

Philip had fallen asleep with the styrofoam cup in his hand. He awoke with a start at Farnsworth's entrance and jumped up out of his chair, spilling the cold coffee onto his jeans. Confused and stammering, he pawed at the coffee while trying to rescue some semblance of credibility.

"Uh, good morning, Dr. Farnsworth. I got started to save you some time..er..trouble...I mean I wanted to do the routine stuff for you...uh, before you got here....you know, uh, to save you time..."

Farnsworth's features softened into an amused smile. "That's all right Philip. I appreciate your effort. Just fill me in on what's happened so far."

Philip breathed easier. "Oh, sure, Dr. Farnsworth. Basically I opened the abdomen for you and I was going to stop right there, but when I saw all the blood I thought I'd at least clear it out so you could get right to the organ examination."

"I see. That's quite a lot of blood in the sink over there. All of it from the abdominal cavity, eh?"

"Yes, sir. It took a while to scoop it out with that 100 cc beaker over there. But I stopped at that point so I wouldn't interfere with your evaluation. I hope that's okay."

"Yes, excellent, Philip. Good work. You've saved me a lot of time here. Quite a bizarre case, don't you think?"

"Yes, sir. I can't wait to see what you find." Philip felt a curious mix of guilt and pride at his subterfuge.

"Well, let's get to it. I want to solve this as soon as possible."

Philip felt another surge of pride as Farnsworth conducted his examination in exactly the same manner as Philip had done earlier. As Farnsworth came to the end of the ileum, Philip held his breath.

"Well, well. What do we have here?" Farnsworth raised his eyebrows. "There's some sort of soft tumor that's invaded the small bowel. And look here, Philip. There's a huge perforation in the iliocolic artery."

Philip feigned fascination. "Gosh, that's amazing. What kind of tumor do you think that is?"

"I'm really not sure. We're definitely going to have to send it to pathology for a microscopic reading. And with the weekend coming up, I'm afraid we won't know much for several days, unless I can convince one of the pathologists to give us a rush reading. Before we remove it, though, I'd like to get some photographs in its anatomical setting. I have a feeling that this may be one for a textbook, or at least a journal article." Farnsworth was obviously filled with glee at this prospect.

Philip's guilt returned as he imagined the misleading information that might evolve from his devious caper, but he forced himself to keep up his bubbly visage while assisting Dr. Farnsworth with his work.

Later that day he dutifully reported the news. "I have to hand it to you, Nancy. It went exactly like you said it would. Farnsworth bought it completely."

"Of course he did. It was the only logical conclusion a legitimate scientist could come to. But what about the pregnancy? Did you remove the embryo like I instructed you?"

"Yes, I have it here in my bookbag."

Nancy's eyes lit up as she grabbed the watertight plastic pouch. Without another word she abruptly turned and walked away , in her own world now, eager to get to the laboratory.

As he watched her, it struck Philip that his role in this experiment had become little more than a cog in her research machine. He thought of a candid conversation from early on in their relationship. "I have to warn you," she had cautioned him. "I come with a lot of shit."

Philip wondered at his reaction to Nancy's dismissive behavior. Normally he would have been offended, but instead he found himself reacting with feelings of concern. In his previous relationships he had always had the upper hand by virtue of his good looks and educational advantage. He had casually dropped other women for even minor transgressions, but this situation was different. Nancy was not only beautiful, she was clearly brilliant ... and nobody's fool. He also had to admit that he was attracted by the sheer intimidating force of her personality, though at times it could also infuriate him. He had always scoffed at the image of the dependent, sensitive male - farmboys from Maine didn't go in for that stuff - but now he was working with, or maybe for, a woman to whom he was being inexplicably pulled. On nothing more than a whim she could make him soar, then bring him crashing down. He had never known a woman like her. He was confused. He was hooked. He was in love.

THIRTY

Dr. Farnsworth was on a rampage. "There's just no way it could be placenta! This was a male pig, a boar! What'd you people do, mix up your specimens?"

The veterinary pathologist, Dr. Timothy Collins, stood his ground.

"Listen, there was no other specimen sent to me that day. I did the gross description on the spot, then fixed the slides myself because you requested a rush reading. This was placental tissue. No ifs, ands, or buts. So you can tell me all you want about what it can be and what it can't be, but I'm telling you what it was, and that's placenta. End of story!"

"Now you listen, Collins! There is no way in hell that placental tissue can come from a male animal. So you go back to your microscope and come up with a diagnosis that makes sense, or, I promise you, I'll hire someone who can!"

Tim Collins was not a guy who backed down easily, but this kind of ultimatum from the normally reserved Farnsworth was not to be taken lightly, and he sensed that he had backed himself into a corner.

"All right, I'll look again if it'll make you happy. But I assure you that there was no mix-up with the specimen."

Farnsworth was unrelenting. "Well, something's wrong with this picture, Collins, and I can't accept a completely implausible pathology reading. I'll be in my office, expecting your modified interpretation. And don't keep me waiting. I've got an unhappy insurance agent who has to come up with a fifty thousand dollar payoff, and I'm sure he's not going to be anxious to cut us the check when he hears that the official explanation for this prize boar's death was an acute attack of placenta!"

Collins didn't laugh. He turned and brooded his way back to his lab, thinking all the while about how he could simultaneously save his job and his self respect.

Philip tracked down Nancy in the hospital. "There's some trouble developing over Hamlet's diagnosis. The pathologist is convinced the specimen was placental tissue, but Farnsworth won't accept the report."

Nancy face flushed with impatience. "For God's sake, Philip. Don't you remember our conversation about this? Go back there and suggest the diagnosis of choriocarcinoma to them. Christ! Don't they have any imagination? You're just gonna have to rub their simple noses in it. Tell them you've been reading an endocrinology text and you came across the subject of choriocarcinoma. Then tell those morons that it can look similar to placenta and secrete pregnancy type hormones, blah, blah, blah. That should be enough, even for those simple-minded doofuses."

"They're not stupid, Nancy. This case wouldn't make sense to anyone. And I don't like your condescending attitude toward people I respect."

Nancy responded with a mocking, sing-song taunt.

"'I don't like your condescending attitude toward people I respect.' Aw, whatsa matter, did I hurt the wittle boy's feelings?" Abruptly, her countenance turned dark. "Look, Philip. I don't have the time to tolerate bruised egos, yours or anyone else's. So go do exactly as I instructed you, and see if you can be part of the solution from here on, because right now you're part of the problem."

Philip's eyes narrowed. No matter how much he cared for her, this was intolerable. He pointed a menacing finger. "Hey! Maybe you're forgetting who you're talking to! There's no way I'm gonna take that kind of crap from you or anyone else. If you were a guy I'd be kicking your ass right now!"

He yanked the door open, then paused to deliver a parting shot.

"If this project is so important to you, try sleeping with it for awhile instead of me!"

THIRTY - ONE

Bridget Walsh greeted Dr. Cantor with her usual cheery good morning, but somewhere behind it was a hint of concern. If Josh had been challenged to define what he sensed that gave it away he probably couldn't have done so, but it was there nonetheless.

"Good morning to you, too, Bridget. What's wrong?"

Bridget raised her eyebrows. "How did you know?"

"Never mind. You never could keep a secret. Out with it, madam."

She sighed. "I hate to have to tell you this, Doctor, but Dr. Greenwald just left a message to call him back. He says it's about Aviva, and he sounded concerned, Doctor."

Josh went straight to his phone. "What's going on, Howard? Something about Aviva?"

"She's here now, Josh. It looks like she's about to have another miscarriage."

Josh's heart jumped. Until now he hadn't even known about the pregnancy. Reflexively, he shot off two rapid-fire questions. "Is she okay? Is she bleeding?"

"No bleeding, but I just did an ultrasound and there's no heartbeat. I'm arranging a D&C for tomorrow, hopefully before she starts to hemorrhage." Greenwald delayed momentarily. "She wants to talk to you, Josh. Hang on a second."

Josh listened to the background noise as Greenwald reached across his desk to pass the phone. Then he heard Aviva's broken-hearted voice.

"I'm sorry, Joshua. I didn't want to tell you until I knew everything was normal this time."

"It's all right, Viv. Don't worry about any of that. I'm coming right over there."

"You don't have to. I'm doing fine. Just upset, that's all."

"No way, honey. I'm not gonna let you drive yourself home. I'll be right there."

After hanging up, Josh slouched in his chair and contemplated how much Aviva had been through. This would be the sixth miscarriage, four of which required D&C's. Every one of them had been devastating, and now there was an increasingly likely prospect that they might never be successful in having a biological child of their own.

For the hundredth time he thought about their options. One was to use a surrogate mother, someone who might have better luck with carrying their donated embryo, but there was the ever-present concern that the surrogate might have a change of heart and decide to keep their baby. Josh shuddered at the image of Aviva's face when they discussed that unthinkable possibility.

Of course they had also seriously considered adoption, but the driving force behind Aviva's desire for her own children was her family history: aunts and uncles, grandparents she had never met, who had perished at the hands of the Nazis. She had seen the pictures, heard the stories over and over from her survivor parents, both of whom had been imprisoned in the camps and still lived their private hells every night. Aviva had told Josh these stories as well, to the point where he could identify with them as though they were his own flesh and blood. And now Aviva was going through her own pain, knowing that these people could never be replaced but wanting so desperately to have them live on through her progeny.

Josh felt the weight of history settling over him. Until now he had been reluctant to have Aviva subject herself to aggressive research technologies, but now he was seeing things differently. If something new came up, and if she truly understood the associated problems, he wouldn't stand in her way.

THIRTY - TWO

Philip brooded for the next week over his encounter with Nancy. He definitely had feelings for her, and they weren't going away. The problem was how to handle it from here. It wasn't his style to make the first move. She would have to be the one to give in.

Three more days passed without communication between them. He decided that was it. He'd go to her apartment and move his things back to Grafton. To avoid confrontation he called first, hanging up twice when Nancy answered. On Thursday evening he got the answering machine. Nancy was probably on call at the hospital. It was as good a time as any.

He was in the bathroom organizing his shaving kit when, to his surprise, he heard the front door unlocking. Walking into the living room, he saw Nancy entering with two bags of groceries in her arms. As they stopped to look at each other, Nancy broke the silence.

"What are you doing?"

"Gettin' my stuff together. I'm moving out."

Nancy remained calm but Philip thought he saw her face fall just a little. She spoke again.

"Are you sure you want to do this? Don't you want to talk first?"

He put his hands in his pockets and shifted his weight to one leg. "I'm listening."

"With an attitude, I see."

He shrugged his shoulders. "I haven't heard from you for a week. That's long enough for me."

"You never considered calling me? You were the one who walked out."

"Yeah, after you acted like a bitch. You can't yank me around like some kind of toy, Nancy. I won't take that kind of crap."

After a short staring contest, Nancy correctly assessed that Philip's pride would never let him make the first move. She decided to give him an opening by divulging the slightest hint of a smile.

"So I was a bitch, huh?"

She had chosen the right strategy. He cracked a grin. "Major league."

She put down her packages and slithered towards him, instantly the sultry temptress. "Maybe I'd better say I'm sorry. Otherwise you'll leave me, won't you?"

His eyes narrowed. "The thought had crossed my mind."

She put her arms around him and kissed him passionately. "Do you think I could convince you to stay?"

He returned her kiss. "Umm-hmm. Maybe."

"I really am sorry, Philip. I don't know how it got this far."

"Me too. Let's just try and forget it. We have more important things to worry about."

She pulled him towards the sofa. "Right, but let's worry about them later."

THIRTY - THREE

Dr. Farnsworth presented Hamlet's case the following Tuesday morning at the weekly clinico-pathological conference, or "CPC", as it was commonly referred to. He had invited the entire faculty and student body, and arranged to have the editor of a prominent journal of veterinary medicine in attendance.

"Ladies and gentlemen, I believe today's case is the most unusual one I have ever encountered. I will forego the usual format of presenting the history and havingyou try to figure out what unusual disease process killed this animal. I'll wager that most of you have heard this story in advance anyway, so let me get right to the point and introduce the brilliant student who showed the way to a bunch of stodgy, short-sighted professors and helped us come to the proper diagnosis on a most perplexing problem. Please welcome the soon-to-be Doctor Philip LeDuc, who is about to embark on what I am certain will be a stellar career in veterinary medicine."

The entire assemblage had already heard of Philip's diagnostic coup and they stood to give him a thunderous ovation. Philip's sense of shame over this situation punished him with a wave of nausea. He was afraid he'd actually get ill in front of his unsuspecting audience. As he had done in the past, he forced himself to use Nancy's strength as inspiration. Rising to present his fabricated case of Hamlet's medical condition, he did his best to downplay his own contributions and shift the credit to Dr. Farnsworth, but Farnsworth wouldn't hear of it. Instead, he stood to lead everyone in another round of applause. The session ended with a round of handshakes and backslapping. Several of the area's veterinarians gave Philip their professional cards and offered him a position in their private practices. All of this blurred past him while he mumbled his gratitude and tried in vain to make his way out of the room. After a while he gave up and began to see the humor in the situation. He thought of what Nancy had advised him:

"Philip, if they're dumb enough to buy into it, then what the hell. Take full advantage and just go along for the ride."

By keeping this in mind he was actually able to enjoy himself temporarily, but by the end of the evening doubts began to plague him once more. There was just no getting away from it. He knew he'd hate himself in the morning.

THIRTY - FOUR

Nancy Sanderson sat in the courtroom listening intently as the prosecution presented their case against her. Why can't they understand, she thought. Risk is an integral part of medical research. Without it we'd still be in the dark ages, succumbing to diseases that have long since been eradicated.

She wanted the trial to be over, to be vindicated for what she had done. As Samuel Foster's wife was called to testify, Nancy's thoughts digressed to when she had first met Samuel and Ellen Foster ....

The infertility service at the Boston Lying-In Hospital saw many human interest stories come and go. Many had a happy ending, resulting in successful pregnancies and adding immeasurably to the quality of life of the fortunate people who benefited from the high tech facilities. Others were not so fortunate. One such couple, Ellen and Samuel Foster, had gone through three years of devastating disappointments consisting of failed attempts at ovulation induction, artificial insemination, surgery, and in-vitro fertilization. Ellen's medical condition involved an advanced case of endometriosis which had occluded her fallopian tubes and left her with a "frozen" pelvis, a situation consisting of virtually inoperable adhesions around her reproductive organs. Ellen had managed to conceive once, in her late twenties, but lost the pregnancy to a devastating miscarriage. Now in her mid thirties, she and her husband were both frantic about the increasingly likely scenario of being childless. To make matters worse, she had recently begun to develop her family's inherited tendency toward high blood pressure, and medication was being considered to control it. These factors, in addition to the age related possibility of chromosome problems in a baby, painted a bleak picture of potentially serious complications if she ever managed to get pregnant.

Nancy had inherited the Foster case since returning to the Lying-In.

She had come to know both Ellen and Samuel very well, and now she was faced with the task of informing them that the situation seemed hopeless. As their appointment drew near, she considered their desperation and the shattering effect this news would have on their marriage. Samuel seemed even more caught up in this than Ellen, and that fact strengthened Nancy's resolve to take a bold step. On the day after their appointment Nancy called Samuel Foster at his office.

"Mr. Foster, this is Dr. Sanderson ... we spoke yesterday at the hospital."

"Yes, of course, Dr. Sanderson. How are you? Please call me Samuel."

"I'm fine, thanks. Samuel, I'm calling about a rather touchy subject. I have another option for you and Ellen, but I'd like to talk with you about it personally. And confidentially, if you don't mind."

"Okay, but you know we're not ready to consider adoption yet. Neither of us wants to quit trying, at least for now."

"I understand that. But this isn't about adoption. Actually it's about a new technology that isn't fully perfected but I thought you might be interested."

There was silence on the other end of the line. For a moment Nancy wasn't sure if Samuel was still connected.

"Samuel?" Nancy queried.

"I'm still here, but can you tell me a little more about what you're proposing?"

"I really can't. At least not over the phone. I wonder if I could talk to you somewhere in private, perhaps in your office, but it would have to be completely confidential. Maybe I could pose as a client or something."

"Forgive me, but this sounds just a little bizarre. Are you sure it's on the up-and-up?"

"I guess you'll have to decide that for yourself. All I can tell you for now is that you will be the first person to whom this has ever been offered."

"Well, now you really have my curiosity up. You can come over this afternoon if you'd like. How about four o'clock?"

"Fine. And please, not a word to anyone for now, even Ellen. I'll be there at four."

Nancy had chosen carefully when she decided to approach Samuel Foster. The medical situation with Ellen was certainly a big factor, but Samuel's personality and political background had the largest bearing on her choice. His personal philosophy was ultra liberal. He had a long history, dating back to college, of embracing left-wing causes, and his current professional position was an administrative spot with the Boston branch of the American Civil Liberties Union. He had no hangups whatever about egalitarian standards for men and women. Nancy gambled that he would be receptive to her presentation.

Samuel was incredulous as he listened to Nancy's idea. His reactions vacillated between exhilaration and skepticism. "I just can't believe this could be for real!

How could I possibly sustain a pregnancy? This is bizarre, to say the least."

"But wouldn't you welcome the opportunity to do this for Ellen?"

"Of course, if it were a viable option."

"That's my point exactly. Obviously, you wouldn't want anything to happen to her. And now with her blood pressure problems, it might be a mixed blessing even if she were able to conceive. I've seen some horrendous complications from elevated blood pressure in pregnancy."

Nancy's last sentence had its desired effect on Samuel. The thought of Ellen enduring the physical and emotional burdens of a complicated pregnancy, or worse, losing another baby, presented him with an unbearable image. He decided right then and there that he would do anything he needed to for Ellen's sake.

"All right, Dr. Sanderson, I'm interested. But you'll have to tell me more. I need to hear all the baggage that goes along with this, and I don't want you to hold anything back."

Nancy leaned forward in her chair. "Samuel, I couldn't hold anything back even if I wanted to. Even in routine procedures I'm obligated to break down the risk-benefit analysis to my patients. In this situation I'll have to spend even more time on the risk factors. For one thing, this is not an FDA-approved procedure. In fact, to the best of my knowledge, the bureaucrats don't even know about it. So I'm obligated to protect your interest here, and, to be perfectly honest, I'm worried about covering my tail too. When you see the risk paragraph I have to ask you to sign, you might not be so hot for the idea."

"I hear you, but how about breaking down exactly what the procedure entails, including any surgery and all the costs. If we get past that, then you can read me the 'cover-your-ass' stuff."

"Well, first of all I can tell you that you're thinking clearly, Samuel, and I admire that. To start with the costs, my services will be gratis, although I will have to ask you to pay me for any medications and materials I can't beg or borrow from the hospital. And let me warn you. Some of them will be expensive. Then, if you do manage to get pregnant, the hospital bills will be huge, and I can guarantee you that your insurance company, no matter who they are, will renege on payment because this is an experimental procedure."

"Yeah, I can believe that. Okay, let's get to that later too. For now, just tell me what's involved in actually getting me pregnant." He paused for a moment and shook his head. "I can't believe I just said that! You're really serious about this, right?"

"Yes, I'm serious, Samuel. And if it's not you, it'll be someone else. I only ask that you keep every bit of this in confidence, as you promised you would."

"Yes, of course I will, no matter what I decide. That's clearly understood and you have my word on it. But don't write me off just yet, Nancy. I didn't say I wouldn't do it. It's just in my nature to look before I leap. I want to know everything, no matter how frightening or risky it is."

Nancy launched into a lengthy discourse on what Samuel would have to anticipate and endure if he was to be the first man ever to carry a pregnancy. He listened intently as she described injections, ultrasounds, blood tests, and major abdominal surgery for the delivery. He heard about bleeding, infection, incapacitation, fetal anomalies, even death. But through it all he continued to imagine Ellen's exultation if this experiment should turn out to be successful. The earlier image of her sadness had hooked him initially, and now the prospect of her unbridled joy set that hook to a point from which there was no retreat. When Nancy read this in his eyes she decided to deal what she thought would be the monkey wrench in her scheme. At this point she gambled Samuel would accept it.

"There's one more issue we have to talk about, Samuel. It involves how we get the eggs for the in-vitro fertilization."

"I'm assuming they'll come from Ellen. What other option is there?"

"Yes, they'll come from Ellen. But I don't think we can let her know what we're doing with you. She'll have to think we're doing IVF for her, but some of the fertilized embryos will be injected into your abdomen."

"So what's wrong with telling her what I'm doing?"

"First of all, I doubt that she'll let you take the chance. And secondly, it'll complicate matters for me legally. Another party in this sort of arrangement will undoubtedly lead to a multiplication of problems. So I'm afraid this is a deal-breaker for me. If you're set on informing her, we'll have to call it off."

"All right, let me sleep on it. But don't you talk to anyone else about this either. Just give me a little time. I'll get back to you."

Smiling to herself, Nancy thought of the old real estate ploy of hurrying a client's decision by making them think someone else was waiting in the wings to buy their property. She had her customer right where she wanted him.

"Okay Samuel, just don't take too long on this. My materials are ready to go, so I need to hear from you as soon as possible."

She shook his hand earnestly and looked directly into his eyes. At that moment Samuel felt a small shudder which he wrote off to a rush of adrenaline. His voice shook slightly as he spoke.

"Thank you Nancy. I'll be in touch with you tomorrow."

THIRTY - FIVE

Samuel lay awake that night, his eyes fixed on the ceiling. He listened to Ellen's sleep-breathing and turned his head to look at her, the little girl innocence in her face summoning his deepest love. He decided at that moment to bestow on her the ultimate gift, the baby she prayed for every day. Christmas was coming, the perfect time to make a selfless decision. He fell asleep dreaming of their future happiness.

Nancy got a call from him the next morning. They met behind closed doors at the hospital. "I'm ready to go, Nancy. I'm sure."

"All right, Samuel. Then what we need for our next step is to set up a meeting with Ellen. Please understand that you'll need to be a little deceitful, though. She'll have to think it's because there's been a technical breakthrough that'll make it worthwhile for her to keep going through though IVF attempts."

Samuel looked pensive. "I guess there's also the possibility that she could still get pregnant, right?"

"I suppose so, but the odds against that have to be astronomically high. And with her blood pressure issues, it would make for a more complicated pregnancy."

"Okay, I guess we'll have to trick her into going along so I can take the risk for her."

Nancy was impressed by Samuel's devotion, although she didn't lose sight of her primary goal, the establishment of the first human male pregnancy. "I have to agree, Samuel, but you have to promise me that you'll be strong enough to keep this completely confidential until I decide to divulge what we're doing. Even after you get pregnant, the announcement can't be made until we're sure everything's okay with the baby."

"I understand. Strictly between you and me."

"Good. Now we have to work out the logistics involving Ellen. That should be easy because we've done it before. My concern is that you and I can't be seen together outside the hospital for now. In fact, except for medical appointments, our only conversations should be through private phone lines. I'm assuming you have that sort of setup in your office."

"Yes, that won't be a problem. In fact, there's a way to ring my line directly without going through the receptionist. Normally, I'm the only one who answers it."

"Perfect. I don't have that arrangement at the hospital, but it won't be suspicious for you to occasionally call me there since you and Ellen are in this together. There's one other thing, though. I don't think it would be a good idea to give you my home phone number. My boyfriend's there a lot and I don't plan to tell him about this either."

"Got it. Just tell me when we can get started."

Nancy delayed her answer, making Samuel uncomfortable until she finally spoke.

"Theoretically we can start immediately, but first we've got to return to that sore subject of informed consent and a medical release form. Unfortunately I can't proceed until all of that is cleared up in writing."

"I don't have a problem with that, Nancy. I told you I've considered the potential consequences. I've thought everything out to its worst possible scenario and I'm ready to sign whatever you need."

"I know you've thought about this, but I've got to warn you again. There's stuff in there about bleeding, infection, death, the whole nine yards; so please be prepared for a reality check when it's right in front of you."

Again Samuel was unfazed. "I'm telling you I hear you. I'm sure about this now, and I'll be sure about it when you shove that piece of paper under my nose. I know you have to inform me completely, but none of it's scaring me away."

Nancy nodded. "Okay, Samuel, we have a deal. If you can come to my office tomorrow, we'll get the formalities taken care of and then we can work from there without worrying about the legal hassles."

At this point Nancy held her breath. As soon as she used the word "legal" she regretted it, thinking that Samuel might decide to have an attorney review her document, but he showed no signs of hesitation. They parted on an upbeat note, with Samuel exuding optimism and Nancy imagining her name in lights.

The scheme to delude Ellen worked flawlessly. She had taken the super-ovulation agents without question and was now on an operating table under the influence of intravenous sedation. Nancy prepped Ellen's vaginal walls with an iodine antiseptic and inserted an ultrasound probe which contained a long needle used in retrieving eggs from ovarian follicles.

"You can look to the right if you'd like," she said, referring to the ultrasound picture of Ellen's ovaries. Ellen barely grunted in reply from her drug-induce stupor.

Nancy expertly maneuvered the needle into the follicular fluid and suctioned it cleanly into a specially designed receptacle, repeating this maneuver until all of the follicles were drained. Then she removed the instruments from Ellen's body and supervised while two assistants helped to move her onto a stretcher. Samuel was waiting in an adjoining room, looking slightly embarrassed and holding a freshly collected sperm sample. Nancy formed an "OK" sign with her thumb and forefinger as she took the container from him.

Two days later Nancy called Samuel on his private line. "You know who this is?"

"Yes..."

"Everything's ready, but instead of my office I want you to meet me at the Ritz-Carlton. Room 322. Do you know where that is?"

"Yes, I'll be right there."

Nancy opened the door when she heard Samuel knock. Adopting a professional tone, she said, "This won't take long, Samuel. I hope you understand why I can't take do this into an examination room in my office. The staff will surely want to know what's going on, and we need to keep this our little secret for a while."

Samuel eagerly agreed. "I understand." Following her instructions, he undressed to the waist and laid down on the king size bed, trying to make himself as comfortable as possible. He closed his eyes and considered what he was about to do. Was it insane, or was it medical history? How would his wife react to his pregnancy? His heart raced at the thought.

Nancy had prepared all her paraphernalia. She spread a sterile drape across the bed next to him and placed her instruments in a neat row. Then she reached for her squeeze bottle of ultrasound gel. "This will be cold, Samuel," she warned him. After squirting a glop of the aqua-tinted gel onto his abdomen, she applied the portable ultrasound transducer. In just a few moments she found a suitable spot and marked it by pressing her index fingernail into his skin, leaving a small indentation. A wipe of antiseptic was followed by a sting of novocaine and then the insertion of her needle into Samuel's abdominal cavity. Guided by the ultrasound image, she positioned the needle into a location next to the abdominal aorta, a huge artery where the blood supply would be especially rich. Then, using her thumb, she pressed on the end of the syringe, forcing the physiologic saline solution and three developing embryos through the needle and into the nurturing world of Samuel's abdominal cavity.

The entire process took only moments, but even during the short time that the needle was in Samuel's abdomen, Nancy was mentally processing a future possibility. She had actually harvested five embryos from the couple's sperm and eggs. The other two were currently frozen and would remain available for future use if Nancy needed them. She preferred using fresh biological materials, however, and wouldn't resort to using the frozen stuff unless absolutely necessary. In an instant she made the decision not to tell Samuel about the extra embryos because she didn't want to be constrained in her choice of how to handle this material. In fact, if she had no alternative use for them, such as possibly implanting them in another patient, she planned to perform what was cynically referred to as a "sink test," meaning that the material would be literally discarded down a drain and simply flushed away.

Samuel breathed a sigh of relief as Nancy removed the needle. "Done already?"

"All set. You can go back to work if you want. Just avoid medications and x-rays, plus tobacco and alcohol. And it's probably a good idea to cut down on caffeine. Other than that, you can live normally. I need to see you in a week to draw blood for a pregnancy test."

"That soon?"

"Yes, believe it or not. If one or more of these embryos taps into your blood supply, we'll have our answer in no time. So 'think pregnant' and I'll see you next week."

Precisely seven days later Nancy drew Samuel's blood and sent it to the lab under her "research" category. This enabled her to label it as "Patient X", thus retaining anonymity and allowing the fee to be buried in the department's budget. To Nancy's disappointment the result came back negative for pregnancy. Samuel was disappointed as well, but immediately recovered his optimism and volunteered to go through the procedure again.

"I knew this wouldn't throw you," she said. "Of course it would have been fabulous if we got it right the first time, but that sort of expectation is just unrealistic. Even two perfectly fertile people only conceive at a rate of twenty five percent per cycle."

"I guess I know that," Samuel answered. "I can't tell you I wasn't hoping for quick success, but I'm in this for the long haul, as long as you and my wife are willing to put up with the process. I do have a question for you, though. What happens to the embryos that don't survive?"

"Basically they disintegrate like millions of other cells your body processes every day, but I don't think you have to worry about what they'll do to your internal organs."

"No, I wasn't concerned about anything like that. It's more like what happens to the potential life that's in them. You know, it's funny. I've always been very big on reproductive freedom, and I still feel the same way. But now I'm seeing it from a different perspective. I actually feel a sense of loss about this situation. It must be devastating for women who go through this and then have to deal with the cold reality of having a menstrual period as well."

Nancy realized that she liked this guy, prompting her for a brief moment to rethink her decision to expose him to the considerable risk associated with this procedure. She flashed on Samuel in a death pose, his skin grotesquely blanched from a catastrophic episode of internal bleeding. But almost immediately she purged these thoughts, subjugating them to her ambitious goal of achieving a major scientific breakthrough. She knew that it was her destiny to be a luminary in medical history, and she couldn't allow emotions to get in her way, no matter what the cost. In the final analysis, the end would justify the means and the only thing anyone would remember would be the name of Nancy Sanderson, the brilliant young physician who discovered how to create pregnancies in human males. It would mean fame and fortune, academic recognition, international stature of unimaginable height.

Samuel noticed her distraction.

"Are you feeling all right, Nancy? You seem troubled."

"Yes, I'm fine, Samuel. You just stick with me and we'll make medical history together."

"Making history is fine, Nancy, but I'm in this to get a baby that's biologically mine and Ellen's."

"Yes, of course," Nancy smiled cryptically. "That's what this is all about, isn't it?"

Samuel felt another of his tiny chills, but again wrote it off to adrenaline. He was already planning to tell Ellen that she'd have to go through another cycle of ovulation induction.

THIRTY - SIX

Four weeks later Samuel, Ellen and Nancy went through the same process as the month before. Again, however, the effort failed and Ellen was discouraged. She spoke to her husband one morning as they were both dressing for work.

"I don't know if it's a good idea to try this again, Sam. It's going to end up costing us a fortune and I don't know if I can accept another disappointment."

Samuel was alarmed at this development, but managed to maintain his composure. "I know it's hard for you, Honey. It's starting to get to me too, but I'd like to hang in for another couple of tries if you can tolerate it."

"Do you really think it's worth it, though? Maybe it's time to talk about adoption now."

"I don't think you really mean that, Ellen. Look, we went into this with the idea of trying it a total of four times. If we do that, I'm willing to call it off and then we can talk adoption if you want."

"Okay, but that's really as far as I want to go. I guess I'm starting to get fatalistic about the whole thing. If it isn't meant to be, maybe we shouldn't push it any more."

He kissed her as he finished knotting his tie. "Okay, we're agreed. Two more cycles and that's it. I can live with that."

As it turned out, four cycles were not necessary. One week after the third attempt Nancy called Samuel again on his private line.

"Samuel, this is Nancy!"

"You sound excited. Is it positive?"

"First of all, are you alone? Is your door closed?"

His heart began to pound. "Yes! Tell me!"

"No, it's not 'positive'. It's off the scale! We did it, Samuel! You're pregnant! The first human male pregnancy in history!"

"That's fabulous! I can't believe it! Yeeeow!"

Samuel's office door opened, revealing the concerned face of his secretary. "Is everything okay in here?"

"Yeah, everything's great, Mrs. P. Just some good news. Thank you, though."

Mrs. Prudhome had seen a lot of characters come and go in her long career. She shook her head and closed the door.

"Sorry Nancy." Samuel lowered his voice to a whisper. "My secretary popped in for a moment....So I'm pregnant! I can't believe it! But I don't feel any different. Should I expect any symptoms yet?"

Nancy laughed. "Not quite yet. But I wouldn't be surprised if you experience some nausea over the next few weeks. And maybe some breast tenderness. We'll just have to wait and see."

Samuel's enthusiasm was boundless. "What else? How about a due date? When am I gonna have this kid?"

Nancy laughed again. "Slow down. It's too early to get into that right now. And keep in mind we'll probably have to deliver you early. This kind of pregnancy rarely lasts to term."

"Yeah, but just theoretically. What would the due date be?"

"All right. I can see you're not going to be dissuaded. Let's see, this is mid- February. I guess early November would be 'term', but again, don't count on it to last that long. I'd take a guarantee of seven or eight months right now."

"Right. Okay, that's good. What about vitamins? Do I need to start taking them now or anything?"

Nancy pursed her lips and nodded. "As a matter of fact, that's a good idea. I'll call you in a prescription right now .... No, wait. I'll have to prescribe it in your wife's name and you can pick it up. And just to be safe, it should be at a pharmacy where they don't know either of you, so no one will congratulate Ellen and blow our cover. And one more thing. Don't carry the vitamins in their original container. You'll have to transfer them to some sort of nondescript vial. In fact, I'll make the prescription for a generic brand so no one will recognize them."

"I have to compliment you, Nancy," Samuel gushed. "You're really on top of this. It's nice to know nothing gets past you."

"Thank you, but there's one other detail we have to consider. The plan was to take Ellen through four cycles, and this is only the third. Surely this will fail again, and then she'll expect to go through another cycle. I'm not sure how to handle that, except to put her through a fourth IVF procedure, unless you have any other ideas."

Both of them racked their brains for a logical explanation they could present to Ellen for calling off the fourth attempt, but in the end they drew a blank and decided they would have to go through the motions to maintain credibility.

As the next few weeks passed, Samuel grew increasingly euphoric, despite having to endure the standard pregnancy symptoms predicted by Nancy. He found it difficult to keep his promise to her about not announcing his condition until she approved. And it was especially difficult to resist sharing it with his wife. She was having trouble accepting the fact that they would never have a child of their own, and the temptation to tell her about his pregnancy was almost irresistible. Still, he took his promise seriously. He didn't want to disappoint Nancy and he definitely didn't want Ellen to be crushed in the event this pregnancy didn't end successfully. Nancy had told him that there was a chance for spontaneous miscarriage. She didn't want him to make any kind of announcement until after three months, when the prognosis for the baby's survival would be much better. But she had already been able to visualize the pregnancy by ultrasound and the image of the embryo was miraculous to Samuel. It took every ounce of his willpower to keep from insisting that Ellen be told about it so that she could share his excitement.

Nancy was also fascinated by the ultrasound image. It showed a normally developing embryo but the location concerned her. She had purposely arranged to have it growing near Samuel's large abdominal arteries so that there would be a good chance of establishing an adequate blood supply, but when she scanned the area around the embryo she noted that it was extremely close to the internal iliac vessels. This location carried the risk of invasion by the placenta into one of these large arteries or veins with a potential consequence of disastrous internal bleeding. While adding this observation to her already voluminous notes about Samuel's case, she considered sharing the information with him, but decided against it. What was the point, she reasoned. There was nothing she could do about it anyway. The essential thing was to record it for scientific reasons.

Nine weeks after the conception of Samuel's pregnancy, everything seemed to be going well. He returned from lunch in a happy mood and greeted Mrs. Prudhome with a jaunty rap on her desk as he walked by. She looked up, dismissed him with her usual disdainful sniff, and returned to her work without a word. Half an hour later the phone rang.

"ACLU administrative office, may I help you?"

The caller was an excited Ellen Foster.

"Hello, Mrs. Prudhome. May I speak with Samuel? I have some really thrilling news to tell him." Then, unable to contain her emotions, she blurted out, "I'm pregnant!"

Mrs. Prudhome was happy for her boss and his wife. She knew that they had wanted a child for a very long time. "Oh, that's wonderful! Just a moment and I'll le him know you're on the telephone."

She pushed his intercom button but got no response. Concerned, she walked into his office but stopped in her tracks at what she saw. Samuel was slumped in his chair, his head leaning back and his body tilted sideways, supported by the chair's right arm.

"Mr. Foster?"

He responded by falling forward, his head thudding sickeningly as it hit the desk.

Mrs. Prudhome gasped and brought her hand to her mouth. She froze for a moment but then moved to assist him, noting that the blood vessels in his neck were pulsating. Immediately she grabbed for the phone and dialed for emergency assistance. Then she pushed the button for the line where Ellen Foster was waiting to hear her husband's voice.

"Mrs. Foster," she stuttered, "something has happened to Mr. Foster. I've called 911 and they'll be here momentarily. I'm sorry but I can't talk right now. I'll call you back as soon as I can."

While she waited for the paramedics she cradled his head in her hands and spoke soothingly to him, but Samuel remained unresponsive. His skin felt cold and was turning a mottled purple, but she wouldn't release her cradling grip from his head, even after the emergency crew had arrived. Hovering over him like a mother bird, she insisted that he be handled gently while being transferred to the ambulance.

The emergency room at St. Catherine's hospital had been alerted that a thirty seven-year-old unconscious male would be arriving shortly. The report indicated that he was in shock, with a blood pressure of 70 over 40 and a thready pulse. Via radio communication the ER physician on call had directed that an IV containing lactated Ringer's solution be started and that a 1000 cc bolus be infused as rapidly as possible. As the ambulance pulled under the building's canopy, a waiting crew transferred Samuel's limp body onto a stretcher and moved him inside without delay. After a rapid evaluation revealed that his abdominal muscles were rigid, the working diagnosis was established as some type of intra-abdominal bleeding.

The ER doctor quickly splashed a jigger of antiseptic on the skin of Samuel's distended belly, attached a large-bore needle onto a syringe, and plunged the needle through the muscular wall until it reached the abdominal cavity. Immediately, a gusher of blood returned with such force that it blew the plunger completely out of the syringe's barrel, spraying dark red gore over the doctor's face and clothing.

"Shit!" he cursed. "Get him to the OR right now! Tell the blood bank we'll need at least four units of whole blood, and probably a lot more after that! Call anesthesia and tell 'em this is a real emergency and to get their asses in gear! And page the Dragon! Stat! He's the only one around here with the balls to go in on a case like this without a lot of bullshit! C'mon! Go, dammit!"

The emergency room staff moved with lightning efficiency, transporting Samuel to the operating room within minutes of his arrival at the hospital. Two large bore intracath needles were expertly threaded into his veins, through which huge volumes of fluid were infused in an attempt to restore his blood pressure until the blood became available. The surgeon, Joe Draganoff, arrived as Samuel was being intubated. He listened to a rapid-fire briefing as he scrubbed, nodding calmly while he absorbed the pertinent details from the emergency room physician.

"It sure sounds like he blew out a big vessel somewhere," Dr. Draganoff observed. "Is there a history of trauma? How about a ruptured spleen?"

"No, nothing like that. Apparently the guy came back from lunch and collapsed at his desk. No history of medical problems. Nuthin'!"

"Well, I guess we're about to find out, aren't we?"

After dropping his scrub brush into the sink, Dr. Draganoff entered the operating room by pushing the swinging door with his back. He held his wet hands and arms in front of him to keep them sterile. The scrub technician handed him a dry sterile towel, followed by a scrub gown made of a silky material that was impermeable to blood.

"Size eight gloves, Dr. D?"

"Nope. Seven and a half, same as the last eighteen years," he said, his eyes smiling behind the surgical mask.

"I'm sorry, Doctor. I've been working in the heart room for a while but I should have remembered your glove size anyway."

"No problem. I'm glad to have your help."

Dr. Draganoff was bewildered by the screamers and whiners on the surgical staff, having long since learned that the operating room crew performed much more effectively when they were made to feel calm. Despite everyone's pleasant demeanor, however, there was a definite sense of alarm for this patient, a young, apparently healthy person who had been dropped on their doorstep in frightful condition.

Draganoff looked around. "Do we have a resident to assist?"

"Yes, Doctor, but the senior resident is scrubbed on another case right now and he asked if you would mind working with Betty Carter. She's only second year but has really good hands."

"Fine, but where is she? We need to get going right now."

"Do you mind if I first assist until she arrives?" the scrub tech asked.

"I guess you're gonna have to, hon. This guy just can't wait."

Together, they positioned the drapes over Samuel's abdomen and limbs, leaving an opening over the area of his stomach since a perforated ulcer was a prime possibility.

Dr. Draganoff looked at the anesthesiologist. "Ready?"

"He's asleep, if that's what you mean, but I think we're still behind on fluid and blood volume."

"I understand, but he's probably still hemorrhaging from somewhere and I wanna get moving before he bleeds out completely."

"I guess there's no choice. You'd better go ahead."

Dr. Draganoff held out his right palm. "Knife, please."

The technician passed him a scalpel with a number ten blade. Without hesitation he made a six inch vertical incision just below Samuel's sternum. Moving quickly, he then cut through the layers of the abdominal wall: skin, subcutaneous fat, fascia, and finally peritoneum. The last layer was of a thick cellophane-wrap consistency. Dr. Draganoff noted that is was bulging with old blood.

"I'll need suction right here."

"I've got it for you, Dr. D." The resident had arrived and was moving into the first assistant's spot, freeing the scrub tech to give proper attention to her duties.

"Hiya doin' Betty? This looks like lots of fun, doesn't it?"

"Really! What happened to this guy, anyway? They just pulled me out of clinic to come down here and I haven't heard anything about him."

"Don't know yet, Betty. We're gonna find out soon, though. Get ready to grab this retractor for me, will ya?"

As the peritoneum was opened, he slipped the metal suction cannula into the abdominal cavity and began clearing away as much of the clotted blood as possible. "Jesus, there's a ton of it in here! Do you guys have any more blood available?"

"They tell us they're workin' on it," the anesthesiologist answered. "In the meantime I'll pump in as much fluid as I can."

Doctors Draganoff and Carter worked harmoniously while exploring the abdominal cavity. Their first maneuver after suctioning several units of blood was to explore the area of the stomach and duodenum, where a perforated ulcer would be located. However it was quickly apparent that those organs were normal. Next they inspected the spleen, then the liver, and found that they were also in perfect condition. Within minutes they made the decision to explore the lower abdomen. Dr. Draganoff deftly used the scalpel to curve the incision around the umbilicus and continue downwards, thus expanding the abdominal incision to create the huge exposure they required. Eventually they were able to see the source of bleeding, a bizarre hemorrhagic mass located just below and lateral to the aortic bifurcation. By this time the stream of bleeding had slowed down and they were able to take their time and inspect the odd looking tissue.

"What the hell is that thing?" the resident asked.

"Damned if I know, Betty. I guess we're gonna need to take a piece for frozen section."

As they wedged a nickel-sized slice out of the spongy tumor, an alarming amount of bright red blood welled up immediately. "Aw, shit!" Draganoff called for a sponge. "Hold that on there, Betty. Keep pressure on it for at least a minute. By the clock. Don't let go until I say so."

As it turned out, several minutes of pressure were required to control the bright red flow while they waited for the pathology report. Each time they tried to remove the sponge, fresh blood spurted up. The resident frowned. "This is weird. How're we gonna control this thing? It's too friable to suture."

Dr. Draganoff tried to lighten the moment. "Not to worry, Betty. All bleeding eventually stops."

"Whaddya mean?"

"Think about it. Sooner or later, all bleeding stops."

He waited for the sinister implication to sink in, then smiled as the resident's eyes widened. "Only kidding, Betty. We're not gonna let him bleed out. I hate when that happens. Creates a ton of paper work."

They were sharing a laugh over the black humor when the operating room intercom crackled out a burst of static, followed by the pathologist's gravelly voice.

"Hello, is Dr. Draganoff in there?"

"Yeah, I'm here. Who's that?"

"Hiya, Dragon. This is Ed Bulewich. What're you up to, buddy?"

"Whaddya mean, Ed? What'd you find under your microscope?"

"That's what has me interested. You sent me a piece of placenta! Have you switched specialties or something?"

"Placenta? What the hell're you talkin' about, Ed? I'm operating on a thirty seven year old guy with an acute abdomen. He's bleedin' like stink from some kind of hemorrhagic mass near the aortic bifurcation. What'd you do, mix up your specimens, or what?"

"I don't think so, Dragon. We just got it, and it was delivered by hand directly from your operating room."

"Naaah! Somebody screwed up somewhere. How about if I send you another piece?"

"Fine. Send it over. I'll call you right back."

The result was the same: "Placenta."

For the first time in his surgical career, Joe Draganoff didn't know what to do next. His hand was frozen in position while holding pressure on the oozing tumor mass. The tension became unbearable until the resident finally broke the silence.

"Dr. Draganoff? Are you okay?"

"Yeah, Betty. I'm okay. I just don't know what the hell to do about this. Any ideas?"

The scrub tech spoke up. "I saw Dr. Dunn, the gynecologist, out in the lounge just before we started. Maybe he's still around."

"Hell, yeah. I'll be glad to have his opinion. I've certainly never seen anything like this."

Bill Dunn poked his head through the door. "They tell me you're looking for me, Dragon, but I'm thinking it's some kind of joke. That is a man you're operating on, isn't it?"

"It's no joke, Bill. I've got a hemorrhagic mass here and the pathologist is telling me it's placenta. How about scrubbing and taking a look at this for me?"

"Anything for you, Dragon, but I hope you're not pullin' my leg. I've got a dozen patients waiting for me in the office."

"No, no kiddin' around. Come look and you'll believe me."

After several minutes of inspection, everyone at the operating table agreed on the same course of action. Whatever this spongy mass was, it had to come out to prevent further bleeding. They began to dissect around it in order to reach its primary blood supply. Soon it became apparent that there was an intimate attachment of the vasculature to the internal iliac artery.

"Clamp the base of the tumor, will you, Bill?" Draganoff requested.

Dr. Dunn asked for a Kelly clamp and carefully guided it towards the underside of the mass. Draganoff retracted it to the side so that his associate could see more clearly, but suddenly, before a clamp could be applied, the traction ripped the tumor loose from its primary blood supply. In a flash the operative field was flooded with fresh blood, making it impossible to see anything.

"Suction! Suction!"

Bill Dunn tried to remain calm. He knew it wasn't like the Dragon to get excited. "I am suctioning, Joe, but I can't clear it fast enough. See if you can throw a clamp in there blindly.'"

Draganoff agreed and tried to guide a vascular clamp by feel, but his efforts only intensified the bleeding.

The anesthesiologist became concerned. "I'm losing blood pressure fast up here, and we've used up all our available blood. Can you control that with pressure for now, Dragon?"

"I'm trying that right now but the stuff is coming from five directions! I'm gonna need an aortic clamp. There must be a hole in the iliac and I can't control it any other way."

"Well then, you'd better grab the aorta by hand until the clamp arrives because I've lost his pulse now."

Several heroic and frantic attempts were met with failure until it became apparent that it was useless to go on. Cardiac resuscitation efforts met with no success because of the lack of blood supply and oxygenation. Ultimately, the anesthesiologist delivered the dreaded phrase.

"Pupils are fixed and dilated."

All three surgeons stood transfixed over the body until they looked up and made eye contact with each other. No spoken communication was necessary.

Joe Draganoff broke scrub and left to look for Samuel Foster's family.

THIRTY - SEVEN

On the morning following Samuel Foster's intra-operative death, a buzz of rumor activity began to circulate throughout the hospital. In the coffee shop, one of the pathology technicians was talking to her friend from the hematology lab.

"I'm not kidding. It was placental tissue. And I heard Dr. Bulewich say he found an embryo when he did the autopsy."

At precisely one p.m. Joe Draganoff received a phone call from a television news reporter.

"Hello, Dr. Draganoff. This is Sherman Falk from Channel 4 News. I wonder if you could give me a statement on the 'male pregnancy' story. We're hoping to feature it on our six o'clock newscast. And if you don't mind, we'd like to send a film crew to your office for a personal interview."

Draganoff couldn't believe it. "What in the world are you talking about? What male pregnancy? How did you even hear about this?"

"We've already interviewed Dr. Bulewich and he told us you were the surgeon on the case. So we were hoping to get the story from your angle as well."

The reporter's last sentence was met with silence followed by a loud click. Dr. Draganoff was seeing red. He immediately dialed the pathology department. "Bulewich! I just hung up on a TV reporter who wants to interview me about yesterday's case! He's talking about some kinda cockamamie male pregnancy! And he says he got the information from you! What the hell is going on here?"

"Joe, I couldn't help it. I had barely finished the autopsy when my phone started ringing off the hook and I was getting questions from every news reporter in the city. Someone must have called around after I found the embryo."

"Embryo? What embryo! What the hell are you talking about?"

"Jesus, Joe, I'm sorry. It's been so crazy I didn't realize I hadn't talked to you about this. You were the first one I thought to call but I just couldn't get off the phone from the time I got back to my office.

"Listen. Here's what happened. I did the autopsy on that guy you operated on yesterday. You know, the one where I gave you the 'placenta' reading on frozen section. So anyway, I'm doing the autopsy this morning and I come across the operative site near the iliac artery. After I get the blood cleared away I see this spongy tumor you were talking about and, sure enough, the freakin' thing looks like placenta! So I keep looking, and right there underneath the hypogastric vessels is this sac of tissue with some fluid in it. Then, when I hold it up to the light, I swear there's an embryo inside!"

"You're puttin' me on, Ed!"

"Hang on, Joe. Lemme finish …. I don't know if you can imagine the reaction in there. In no time there are all kinds of people coming into the autopsy room and the story is flying all over the place. God knows who must have called the media and the first thing I know I'm getting blitzed with phone calls and questions a mile a minute. Anyway, that's why you haven't heard from me. I just got overwhelmed and forgot to call you. I'm really sorry. I couldn't control the situation."

"I can't believe this! Are you sure, Ed? There's gotta be some kind of mistake. Maybe this was a dermoid or something?"

"Joe, as God is my witness, that tissue yesterday was placenta, and what I found today was a human embryo. It doesn't make any more sense to me than it does to you, but I'm only telling you what I saw. If you want, come on over here and I'll show you the tissue personally. But in the meantime, you and I are gonna have media types down our throats. Maybe we'd better get in touch with hospital administration and see if an attorney should get involved. I really think we're gonna need a spokesperson. Otherwise we might be sticking our necks out legally and every other way."

"Hell, I guess so. I sure as shit don't know what to do. Damn, what a nightmare, Ed! Out of nowhere this guy shows up in the ER, bleeds to death right under my nose, and it turns out he's pregnant? I still don't believe it!"

THIRTY - EIGHT

While Doctors Bulewich and Draganoff were having their telephone conversation, Nancy Sanderson was occupied in her laboratory, mulling over the potential advantages of a paperless record system. By using computer storage instead of bulky paper charts, she reasoned, a patient's lifetime medical history could be contained on a variety of tiny storage devices, easily duplicated, transported, or e-mailed. The idea appealed to her mostly because of its potential research applications. Data gathering could be accomplished in a fraction of the time it now required. As she toyed with a sample electronic record, her lab assistant returned from lunch, bursting with a nugget of juicy news.

"You won't believe what I heard in the cafeteria just now, Nancy. Honestly, the rumors that fly around this place are worse than the tabloids."

Nancy grunted, listening peripherally as she remained absorbed in the screen in front of her.

"Supposedly they operated on some kind of alien over at St. Catherine's," she laughed. "The word is that they found a pregnancy in the guy. Can you believe the crap that people come up with?" She stopped short as Nancy turned a colorless face to her.

"What? What'd I say?" the assistant asked. "It's only a rumor, for gosh sakes."

Her attention was diverted to Nancy's computer screen which was running off a stream of eeeeeeeeeeeeeeeeee's. "What're you typing there, anyway?"

Nancy looked at the screen and managed to lift her frozen finger from the keyboard.

"Are you okay? "Did I upset you or something?"

"No, no, I'm fine. I thought you said something else." Nancy cleared her throat. "What'd they say? Some guy was pregnant?"

"Yeah. Can you believe that? You'd think people would be embarrassed to repeat something that stupid."

"Really," Nancy's voice trailed off. "Stupid." By sheer determination she willed her stricken hand to delete the offensive eeeeeeeeeeeeeeeeee's, then sat unable to move while trying to appear unfazed.

After a few minutes, while her assistant was occupied with a project of her own, Nancy left the lab and went to her office where she closed and locked the door. She picked up her phone and dialed Samuel Foster's private number. After a dozen rings she tried again, praying she had misdialed. This time a woman's voice came on the line. Nancy slammed down the receiver. Her mind now racing, she reached for her directory and flew through the pages to find the public listing for Samuel's office. Holding her breath, she dialed once more. This time the answer was prompt, but subdued. It was the same woman's voice.

"ACLU. Director's office."

Nancy choked down the bile in her throat

"Hello. Is Mr. Foster in?"

After a paralyzing delay the voice yielded its dreadful response.

"I am afraid Mr. Foster passed away yesterday." Then, after another delay … "Is there something I can help you with?....Hello?.... Hello?"

Despite her visceral reaction, Nancy instinctively fought to gain control. She would have to keep up appearances lest her lab assistant start to suspect something.

The problem was that too many thoughts were swirling through her head at the same time. In desperation she reached for a piece of blank paper and started to write on it.

She created two columns, one headed by a minus sign, the other with a plus. In the first column she wrote down her concerns in stream-of-consciousness frenzy:

Samuel Foster dead / What can I say to Ellen?

Experiment a failure / Might get into trouble

She forced herself to dwell on this list for a full minute before making her entries in the other column:

First ever male pregnancy

I'm protected / he signed release / Experiment technically a success

Don't talk to anyone! Furor will subside, then I'll get credit!

She studied the second list for a long time, then got up from her chair and reviewed it once more. Finally she picked up the piece of paper, methodically tore it into shreds, and carried the fragments to the ladies room where she flushed them down the toilet. Before she got back to the lab she had her inner turmoil under control and breezed in as though nothing had happened.

She had convinced herself that things would turn out for the best.

THIRTY-NINE

By the end of the first week of the murder trial, all predictions of sensationalism had long since been surpassed. The image of a male pregnancy had so caught the public imagination that scores of media reporters from the US and abroad had descended on Boston to get first hand information. Traffic around the courthouse had turned into gridlock. Hordes of security personnel scoured the premises. News helicopters hovered each morning and afternoon, using telephoto lenses to film the comings and goings of the principal players.

Inside the courtroom, District Attorney Burke decided to play one of his trump cards. "Your honor," he announced with a note of fanfare, "as the state's next witness I call the wife of the deceased, Mrs. Samuel Foster."

A clearly pregnant Ellen Foster marched resolutely to the witness stand, was sworn in, and sat at the end of her chair, barely able to wait for the opportunity to malign the woman who killed her husband.

"Thank you for appearing here today, Mrs. Foster," Burke began. "I know this must be difficult for you."

Foster nodded through a clenched jaw.

"If you will, Mrs. Foster," Burke continued, "please describe to the jury what sort of person your husband was."

She took a breath and briefly closed her eyes.

"He was a wonderful man," she began.

"He would never hurt anyone. I only regret that I ever introduced him to Dr. Sanderson." At this point she swallowed hard, already on the verge of breaking down.

"Do you need a moment, Mrs. Foster?" Burke asked tenderly.

"No," she said, blinking back tears. "I want to do this."

"All right. Could you try to describe how Mr. Foster met Dr. Sanderson?"

"I was seeing Dr. Sanderson because I was having trouble getting pregnant," she said.

"My husband came with me for every one of my visits."

"And how did those visits go?"

"They went all right , I guess," she said. "We discussed the testing, what to expect, what our chances were."

"And what did Dr. Sanderson tell you about your chances?"

"That they were so-so, but we should keep trying." "I see," Cross said. "And were you satisfied with the care that you were receiving?"

"At that time I was. She seemed normal then." "And your husband? You say he was with you at every visit?" "Yes, he always supported me." "And did he get along with Dr. Sanderson?"

"Yes, he thought she was very professional, and he believed in her." Ellen Foster's breathing came faster now, her body visibly tensing. "He believed in her. He actually liked her," she said, clenching her fists. "He liked her," she repeated, louder this time, her face turning increasingly red, now spitting her words. "He liked her ... he trusted her ... and she killed him! She killed him! THAT MURDERER KILLED MY HUSBAND! AND NOW MY BABY WILL HAVE NO FATHER!"

The courtroom erupted. Charlie Cross rose to object, then reconsidered and sat back down. The judge banged his gavel and demanded order. When the clamor subsided, he turned to the witness. "Mrs. Foster, I understand that you're upset, but I must ask you to confine your responses to questions from counsel."

She burst into tears. "But she did!" she sobbed, the energy in her voice dissipating as her body sagged. "She killed my husband ... she killed my husband ...."

Franklin Burke quickly offered his designer pocket square so she could dry her tears and wipe her runny nose. When she finished and handed it back to him he placed his comforting hand on hers, and then took care to turn towards the jury so that they could see him replacing the soiled pocket square without regard for his elegant suit jacket.

"Your honor," Burke said, oozing chivalry, "I wonder if we might allow Mrs. Foster a short recess."

An hour later, Ellen Foster was back on the stand, having finished her testimony with attorney Burke. Now it was Charlie Cross's turn.

"Miz Foster," he began soberly, "please allow me to offer my condolences for your loss."

She eyed him suspiciously and barely shook her head.

"And I apologize for having to ask you these questions, because I know some of them might upset you and I'm truly sorry for that."

No response. She sat rigidly and stared at him.

He proceeded pleasantly, as though there was no tension between them. "Miz Foster, may I ask how long you were trying to get pregnant?"

Cross already knew the answer to this question so he wasn't surprised by her response.

"We tried for over three years," she said.

"And if it's not too personal, may I ask if there were any problems that the doctors could identify?"

"Objection!" piped up Burke.

Ellen turned to the judge. "Do I have to answer that?"

"Objection sustained," the judge said. "No, Mrs. Foster, you do not have to answer that question."

"Question withdrawn," Cross said. "I surely apologize, Miz Foster."

She shot Cross a hostile look and then turned again to the judge.

"You know what? I'll answer that question. It's nothing to be ashamed of." "All right," the judge said. "If you wish."

She turned back to face Cross and jutted out her chin.

"Actually, the doctors never found anything wrong with either me or my husband.

We were both in excellent health."

"I see," Cross said, bobbing his head at her answer. "Your husband loved you, didn't he, Mrs. Cross?" "Of course he did." "And you loved him."

"More than I can ever tell you.""And you would do anything for him."

"Yes I would." "And he would do anything for you."

Even in her emotional state, Ellen Foster realized what Charlie Cross was up to. She hesitated, and then responded in a whisper.

"Yes."

"I'm sorry, Miz Foster," Cross said, cupping his ear, "mah hearin's not what it used to be. Would you mind repeatin' that?"

She looked to the judge in mute appeal.

"You must answer, Mrs. Foster," he said.

She sat very still and closed her eyes.

"Yes, anything," she said quietly.

Cross waited until he was sure the jurors had heard her.

"Thank you, Miz Foster," he said gently. "I won't bother you anymore with any more questions at this time."

FORTY

Josh Cantor was overwhelmed with compassion for Ellen Foster as he listened to her moving testimony. He thought about the events that had changed her life so dramatically; events that she had no power to influence. He remembered that day well, because that was the day that he had been drawn directly into this case ....

By mid afternoon on the day of Samuel Foster's death, Dr's. Bulewich and Draganoff were in a meeting with the hospital's CEO, a public relations officer, and a senior attorney from the city's highest powered law firm. But despite their efforts to keep the story under some semblance of control, local newspaper headlines and television newscasts had served it up with all the gusto of a tabloid rag. And before the week was out the majority of the civilized world had heard about it. Ellen Foster had to leave town to take refuge in her sister's home.

Doctors of national stature were asked to proffer their opinions about how this might have happened. One theorized that Mr. Foster's body had somehow reverted to parthenogenesis, a method of asexual reproduction inherent to lower life forms. Many scoffed at the story and labeled it a hoax. But no matter who wrote or said what, the public clamored for more and the media gave it to them. Ultimately, doctors Draganoff and Bulewich flat out refused to give out any more interviews.

Unable to get any work done anyway, both of them decided to take early vacations.

One person who found the Samuel Foster story particularly compelling was Dr. Timothy Collins, the pathologist from the school of veterinary medicine. Dr. Collins couldn't help making an association between this episode and that of Hamlet, the research pig that had died of intra-abdominal hemorrhage. He had been brooding since he was forced

189

by Dr. Farnsworth to retract his original diagnosis of placental tissue and sign out the specimen as a choriocarcinoma.

Meanwhile, another medical professional was perplexed. Josh Cantor lay awake thinking about the similarities between Sarah Moore's case and this crazy story about a pregnancy in a male. Both patients had abdominal pregnancies and both patients died of internal hemorrhage. He decided to investigate the case of Samuel Foster and compare it to that of Sarah Moore. Perhaps by doing so he could discover some factor that would lead to better understanding and management of abdominal pregnancies in the future. The problem was that a male simply could not produce a pregnancy, in his abdomen or anywhere else. Probably it really was a hoax but he wanted to find out for himself.

Dr. Bulewich's secretary wearily answered yet another phone call from someone wanting to ask about the male pregnancy case.

"I'm sorry, but Dr. Bulewich has a great deal of work to catch up on. He gave me strict instructions to refuse any more calls about this case."

Josh decided to stretch the truth in the name of a good cause.

"I can certainly understand that, but I'm calling on behalf of the Massachusetts Maternal Mortality Committee. Would you mind telling Dr. Bulewich that Dr. Joshua Cantor called? I'm in Brookline at 555-8484 and I'll be in my office all afternoon."

She sighed. "All right, Dr. Cantor. I'll give Dr. Bulewich the message."

Before she bothered her boss, the secretary took it upon herself to inquire as to the legitimacy and telephone number of Dr. Joshua Cantor. When his credentials checked out she informed Dr. Bulewich and placed the phone call for him.

Ed Bulewich remembered Joshua Cantor's name from a now legendary episode at the Mass. Maternal Mortality committee. Cantor had gone to the wall for a moonlighting resident who was under fire for the death of a young pregnant woman. The circumstances were extraordinary and Cantor's intervention had saved the kid's ass. Bulewich, among others, admired Cantor for his gallant stand.

"Hello, Dr. Cantor. This is Ed Bulewich. I understand you're investigating the 'maternal' death of Samuel Foster."

Josh chuckled. "I guess you could put it that way. This is a bizarre thing, isn't it? I'm still trying to convince myself it isn't just a big hoax."

"I can't blame you for thinking that way, Dr. Cantor. If I hadn't been there myself I don't think I'd believe it either. But I assure you, there was placental tissue and an embryo in that guy's abdomen."

"All right, assuming that's the case, do you have any theories on how it might have happened? Was this patient anatomically male? I mean was there any history of sex change surgery or anything like that?"

"Not only was his anatomy normal, we actually ran chromosome studies on him. He was male, no question about it."

"All right, then, are there any other leads you can give me. Anything, no matter how remote?"

Dr. Bulewich thought for a moment before he responded. "The only thing I can think of off the top of my head is a strange call I got from a veterinary pathologist who told me a bizarre story about a male pig that died of intra-abdominal hemorrhage. He claimed to have found placental tissue but said he was politically forced to sign the case out as a choriocarcinoma. The guy seemed sincere but he was agitated and I'm not sure if he has any credibility or whether he's just trying to save his job after screwing up a path report. Anyway, if you're interested his name is Timothy Collins and I can tell you where he works."

Doctors Cantor and Collins agreed to meet in person to discuss their mutual concerns. After brief negotiations over the location, they settled on a hotel lobby in Framingham, a point halfway between them on the Mass Pike. Over lunch, Josh listened sympathetically as Collins angrily told his story of being forced to compromise his professional integrity. After venting for fifteen or twenty minutes, Collins felt better and was ready to discuss things in a rational and professional manner.

"So you believe there was definitely placental tissue in this male pig's abdomen. But was there any other evidence of pregnancy? In other words, in the Foster case they actually found an embryo, but I gather that wasn't so with the pig?"

"That's right, but as I think about it, there were some suspicious aspects to it."

"Like what?"

"Like how could there be a placenta without an embryo, and why was the placental tissue so macerated? It just didn't look like it had been presented to me in its natural state."

"So you think someone may have altered the specimen? Who were the people involved in the autopsy?"

"Well, there was Farnsworth, of course. I've really come to hate that bastard. He was the one who forced me to change my diagnosis. He told me, in so many words, that I could look for another job if I didn't do it. The only other one involved was a veterinary student named Philip LeDuc. He helped Farnsworth with the autopsy and was the one who suggested the possibility of choriocarcinoma. I guess he did some reading and found that there were some similarities between that and placental tissue, that chorio could cause a lot of the same findings as a pregnancy, blah-blah-blah. And Farnsworth immediately bought it. He came to me with the idea, and you know the rest. Hmmph! Choriocarcinoma my ass. They even gave LeDuc a big honor at the conference when they presented the case. All kinds of fanfare, the whole bit. It was so hypocritical I thought I was gonna puke."

He paused to breathe.

"I don't know, LeDuc's probably a good kid, but you might get somewhere by talking to him."

Before the day was out, Joshua had tracked down the whereabouts of Philip LeDuc. He reached him by telephone at the veterinary school.

"Hello, Mr. LeDuc. This is Dr. Joshua Cantor."

"Yes?"

"I suppose this will seem strange, but I'm studying the death of a fellow named Samuel Foster. You know the story? The fellow who died in surgery and they claimed he was pregnant?"

"Yes, I know who you mean."

"Well, I recently met with Dr. Timothy Collins. I believe you know him also. He's a pathologist in the school of veterinary medicine."

Philip hesitated, sensing something was wrong. "Yes, I know him."

"Dr. Collins told me you were involved with the case of a male pig that died of abdominal hemorrhage. Is that correct?"

Philip's heart began to race. He wished Nancy were there to help him. Then it dawned on him. Joshua Cantor was the guy Nancy knew from the hospital. They had met once briefly the day he and Nancy were looking at that video of the abdominal pregnancy. Philip prayed she hadn't mentioned his name again. He looked around to assure himself that nobody else was listening. When he answered his voice was shaky. "Yes, I helped Dr. Farnsworth with the autopsy. Why? What's wrong?" He regretted the question as soon as he had asked it.

Josh sensed the anxiety in Philip's voice.

"I don't know, Mr. LeDuc. I'm faced with a complicated puzzle and I'm just looking for pieces that might fit. It just seems a little strange that the case of Samuel Foster and the story Dr. Collins told me about your pig have so much in common. Both were males, both died of abdominal bleeding, and both had pregnancy type tissue in their abdomen. Dr. Collins told me about your choriocarcinoma idea but he says he never bought it and he remains certain the tissue from the pig's abdomen was placenta. What do you think about that?"

Philip's voice rose, and he spoke more rapidly.

"I don't think anything about that. And excuse me, Doctor, but who are you? And why are you grilling me like this? I haven't done anything wrong."

"I never said you did, Mr. LeDuc. But I am wondering why these questions are upsetting you. It makes me think you might have something to hide."

"Look, I don't have to take this! I don't know what you're talking about. You're putting words in my mouth."

"No, you're own words are just fine. That's all I need for now. Thank you for your time, Mr. LeDuc."

"Philip LeDuc, Philip LeDuc..." Josh sat at the dinner table, absentmindedly fiddling with his coffee cup and rolling the name off his tongue while trying to remember where he had heard it. "Must be my imagination."

Aviva Cantor was amused at her husband's preoccupation.

"Talking to somebody?"

"Yeah, but no answers yet."

"What's got you so crazy, anyway? You've been in a fog since you came home."

Josh sat back in his chair with a sigh and drummed his fingers on the table. After a moment he answered her.

"You know this abdominal pregnancy thing I've been talking about? There's this kid named Philip LeDuc. He's a veterinary student who I suspect is involved in some way and I'd like to know more about him."

"And...?"

And I've been doing a little bit of digging, but it's taking up too much time."

"Can't someone else do it?

"You interested?"

"Right. Sherlock Holmes Cantor. That's me."

"Sure," Josh laughed. "Get yourself a cape and a pipe. Maybe you could pull it off."

Aviva affected a comical, mysterious look and shielded her eyes with her hand as though searching for something. She wandered about the room, opening and closing drawers, until she came to the one with the yellow pages. Then she turned serious.

"I've got it, Joshua! Why not hire your own Sherlock Holmes?"

"Whaddya mean? Like a private eye?"

Aviva shrugged her shoulders. "You think it's crazy?"

"No, it's a possibility. Maybe I could even get someone to finance it."

"Like who?"

"I don't know, maybe the Maternal Mortality Committee would allocate some funds for something like this."

"Pfff! Get real, Joshua. After your famous scene there I can't imagine a whole lot of sympathy for any project you propose. If this means a lot to you, why not consider financing it yourself, or maybe through your office somehow. At least you could get some cost estimates. Here. Check it out."

He opened the phone book. Under the heading of private investigators he found a variety of splashy, full-color ads touting hi-tech electronic surveillance, but he was daunted by the fees that would surely come with these packages. Then a simple, one-line ad caught his eye.

Private Investigator Reasonable fees Retired police officer 508-555-3965 Josh recognized the telephone exchange as being from Newburyport, a sleepy resort community on the north shore about 45 minutes from Boston. He chuckled to himself because he had once dealt with an antique dealer there. They had become friendly and the man confided that when business was slow he could perk it up by raising his prices.

He decided to try the number and reached an individual named Richard Phelps.

"Hello, Mr. Phelps. My name is Joshua Cantor. I'm looking for some information about a certain young man and I wonder if you can help me."

"Uh-huh. Does he live in the area?"

"Yes. Grafton, I believe."

"What sort of information ya lookin' for?"

"Nothing too specific, actually. Just some basic data. Daily routine, who his friends are, maybe a little about his background."

"That's it? No underworld stuff or criminal activity? Nothin' like that?"

"There could be something illicit. I'm not sure. It's a complicated story. But the information I just described would be a good start. Can you give me an idea of what this might cost?"

When the response was slightly delayed, Josh recalled his antique-dealer friend and wondered if Phelps followed the same principle with his fees.

"Well, lemme see. What you're talkin' about would only take a few days. I don't use nothin' fancy like the big firms an' I work outta my house so my overhead's low. Prob'ly two or three hunnerd dollars'd cover it, more or less."

Phelps was running a bare bones operation, to be sure, but Josh liked his no-nonsense style. It just felt right. Josh answered a few questions about himself and they quickly struck a tentative agreement.

"Okay, Doc. I'll need t' talk t'ya in person first. If ya still wanna do this, I'll need a down payment then.'"

They met at noon in Josh's office. Phelps was not at all like Josh's preconceived image of a beefy, square-jawed "private eye". Instead he was a little guy, somewhat rough around the edges, with a gray complexion, narrow shoulders, and a paunch. He wore his shiny trousers hiked up high, along with a skimpy windbreaker which made his meager upper body look even smaller. Incongruously, his voice was big, just as Josh remembered it from their phone conversation. As Phelps began to speak he broke into a deep-throated cough. Josh pointed to the cigarette pack in his shirt pocket.

"Have you heard those things are bad for you? There's been some talk about it lately."

"Naah, I can stop anytime I want, Doc. Hell, it's easy to quit. I do it ever' day!" He began to laugh and broke into another hacking spasm, then waved off Josh. "I know, yer right. Th' old lady gives me hell about it alla time, but I tell 'er, 'Hey, I ain't a boozer or a chaser. You coulda done worse!' Am I right, Doc?" He gave Josh a sly wink. "Anyway, I just hadda come here in person so I could be sure yer on th' level.

If ya wanna go ahead, I'll need a hunnerd down and the rest when I bring ya the information yer lookin' for."

"Don't we need some sort of contract?"

"Naah, you look okay ta me. I do this mostly fer kicks, anyway."

Josh had to make a decision. Did he really want to go ahead with this idea? And was this character the one to work with? He took a hard look at Phelps and read honesty in his eyes. Then he reached into his pocket, counted out five twenty-dollar bills, and shook Phelps' hand.

"Good enough, Mr. Phelps. I'll wait to hear from you."

Three days later Phelps was back in Josh's office, reading from a crumpled sheet of notes. He made himself comfortable in a swivel chair, turning side-to-side as he read. "Philip LeDuc goes to the vet'nary school in Grafton. He's twenty-eight years old, grew up on his family's farm in Maine, and graduated from the state university up there. After college he worked at a couple odd jobs, including a stint where he returned to the farm after his father died. Then one o' his brothers took over the family's business an' he began goin' ta the vet'nary school, where he is now. Seems like a decent kid, gets good grades and all, but I couldn't find him at his listed address. He's supposta be livin' inna rat-trap house with three other students but he doesn't spend too much time there. Turns out he's shackin' up inna fancy apartment in Cambridge with some lady doctor name o' Nancy Sanderson."

Josh's stunned expression made him pause.

"Somebody you know, Doc?"

This piece of the puzzle served to convince Joshua Cantor that there was a connection between the stories of Hamlet and Samuel Foster. Somehow these two male creatures, one animal and one human, had developed pregnancy tissue in their abdomens. There had to be a common denominator, and Josh knew it was Nancy Sanderson.

The department chairman, Dr. Landry, was incredulous as he listened to Josh's theory. The presentation was sound and Josh had obviously done his homework, but Landry was skeptical.

"You're telling me Nancy Sanderson is behind all of this."

"That's what I have to assume."

"A man and a male pig both got pregnant and died, and she did it."

"Yes. I think it was Nancy."

"And you didn't have any trouble believing it."

"Leon, I didn't even want to believe it."

"But you do now."

"Right."

Landry leaned back in his chair and looked at Josh.

"So where do you want to go with this?"

"I've already gone there … to you."

"Josh, you know this has some serious legal implications. If it gets out and you can't make it stick, she could slap a lawsuit on you."

At the very mention of the term, Josh had a flashback to the aftermath of Sarah Moore's death, accompanied immediately by a spasm in his chest. He took a moment to catch his breath

"I know that, Leon, and I did a lot of soul searching before I came in here. I'm sorry I had to dump it in your lap, but I thought better you than the police, at least at this stage."

"All right. I'll look into what she's been up to lately and get back to you, but in the meantime maybe you'd better keep this under your hat."

On his way back to the office, Josh mulled over their conversation. He had to take Landry at his word but sensed he wasn't quite convinced. It would require some corroborating information. As he was driving, an idea struck him. He started to reach for his cell phone but decided to use a land line instead. He pulled led into a gas station and parked by a phone booth at the edge of the lot. After pulling the booth's door closed he called information for the number at Cambridge Computerworks.

"Hello, Dr. Cantor. What's up?"

"First of all, Michael, can anyone hear this conversation?"

"No, just us."

"How about the operator?"

"No, there's a privacy feature in our phone system. It's just you and me."

"Good ..."

Josh held his breath for a split second before continuing.

"Mike, I'm onto something, but I've run into a problem that I think you might be able to help me with."

"Sure. Anything."

"Well, before you say yes, I'd better tell you it's not exactly legal."

"Huh? Not legal? You?"

"I'm afraid so.... Mike, do you think we could talk in person about this? There's a good bit to the story and if you don't mind I'd like to get your input."

Michael answered immediately. "After what you've done for me; anytime, anywhere."

"Thank you, Michael. How about my office around 5:30 today?"

"I'll be there."

The office was closed and Bridget had gone home when Michael arrived. Josh opened the door when he heard Michael's knock.

"Thanks for coming over, Michael. Can I offer you something to drink? There's some soda in the refrigerator."

"No thanks, Dr. Cantor. I'm pretty curious about what's on your mind, though."

"Well, first of all maybe it's time for you to start calling me 'Josh', especially when you hear what I'll be asking of you."

Michael laughed nervously. "Okay, but I'm not sure I'll be able to make that transition too easily." He waited while Josh organized his thoughts.

"It's probably obvious that I'm not too comfortable about this, Michael, but I sense I can trust you. It'll also be obvious that this needs to be confidential. As I said on the phone, what I'm proposing isn't exactly legal."

"Yeah, I still can't believe that part, but go ahead. I'll keep it to myself."

"All right, here it is. What I need is access to the computer records at the Boston Lying-In Hospital. Specifically, I'm trying to get some information on a doctor named Nancy Sanderson who might have conducted an unethical experiment, maybe even criminal, and right now I don't have an efficient way of getting the material. I know what I'm looking to do is against the law, but I see the situation as a 'least of evils' thing. Basically, I'm asking you to break their codes and get me a list of all the activities this doctor's been involved with over the past couple of years. If you choose not to do it I'll certainly understand, but I'd appreciate it if you'd consider it."

"And what's the doctor's name again?"

"Nancy Sanderson."

Michael took on a thoughtful expression. "You know, I think that's the doctor who perforated Sarah's uterus that time when she was trying to have an abortion. 'Dr. Nancy Sanderson,' right? Yeah, that's the name!"

"You're certain? She never said anything about that to me."

"I'm certain."

"Well, before I tell you anything else, let me ask you how you feel about what I'm asking you to do."

"I don't need to hear any more, Dr. Cantor ... I mean 'Josh'. Like I said, after what you've done for me, I'm more than happy to offer something in return. You just give me the details and I'll get you the data. I can hack with the best of them."

The next morning, a Saturday, Michael showed up in Josh's office with reams of computer printouts. "This represents Dr. Sanderson's hospital activities since she was appointed to the staff," he said. "It's cross-referenced every which way so there's a ton of stuff here. I just hope it's not overwhelming."

Josh could immediately see that the printouts correlated Nancy's name with several different categories. There were patients' names with their ages, addresses, telephone numbers, names of relatives, medical and personal histories, work information, disease classifications, dates of admission and discharge, laboratory results, HIV testing, treatment outcomes, insurance providers, billing records, credit histories. Josh second guessed himself as he contemplated the amount of privileged information he had accessed.

"I feel like a peepingTom, Michael. As soon as we find the information we need I want to destroy this stuff immediately."

"No problem. That's what paper shredders are for."

Despite the huge volume of data, it took only a few minutes to hone in on the pertinent information. He scanned the list of patients' names in the left hand column. On page three he came to the 'F's. His pulse quickened as he came to a familiar name and read across the printout.

Surname: First name: D.O.B: Spouse: Condition: Operative Procedures:
Felton Katherine 4-4-85 Joseph Pelvic Adhesions Adhesiolysis
Ferris Dierdre 12-2-88 (Single) Amenorrhea None
Foster Ellen 3-28-72 Samuel Endometriosis Laparoscopy, IVF

Michael was startled as Josh jumped out of his chair.

"Ohmigosh! Look at this, Michael! Nancy was treating Samuel Foster's wife!"

He began to pace, thinking out loud. "She must have convinced him to go along with some kind of experiment."

He snapped his fingers as he shifted from one conclusion to the next.

"Of course! Somehow she got that male pig pregnant and carried the idea over to a man!" He looked at Michael, who wore an expression of utter confusion.

"I know, Mike. This doesn't make sense. I can't believe it myself, but I'm about to tell you the damnedest story you've ever heard!" Josh bounded out of his chair.

"Let's get outta here, Michael. I can't sit still while I'm telling you this."

The two men walked briskly to a city park near Josh's office. They came to a duck pond and tramped around its perimeter as Josh, barely able to contain himself, detailed the incredible saga that began with Sarah Moore's abdominal pregnancy and ended with Samuel Foster's death. As he began, Josh forged ahead so fast that Michael had trouble keeping up.

"Hold it a minute. You're losin' me. Back up to that part about the pig again. Nancy did what?"

"All right, I'll try to slow down." Josh forced himself to pick up a few small stones and began to throw them absentmindedly into the water. As the story unfolded, Michael's expression grew more incredulous by the minute.

"Jesus! What kind of monster is this woman? How could she ever be allowed to practice medicine?"

Josh felt an impulse to come to Nancy's defense.

"There's a lot more to it, Michael. Maybe I've made her sound a lot worse than she is."

"You mean there could be a good side to someone who would try an experiment like this?"

"Not on the surface, but when you get to know her she has some positive qualities."

"Like what, if I may ask."

"Well, she's, uh, she's kind of complicated but, uh, …. Nancy's a very talented physician. Probably a genius."

"Right. So was Dr. Frankenstein." Michael looked at Josh, who was clearly uncomfortable. "Why I am I getting vibes here, Dr. Cantor? - sorry, I mean 'Josh' - Do you two have some kind of connection that your wife doesn't know about?" Michael stopped himself and held his hands up.

"Wait a minute. I'm sorry. That was uncalled for."

"No, actually you're at least partly on target, Michael. We did have a close relationship at one time, but it's been years … before I was married. My wife knows about her, and there's absolutely no problem there, but our past is what makes this so complicated for me."

"Michael leaned on a nearby tree. "I don't have anywhere to go."

Josh began walking again and Michael followed him while Josh processed several thoughts in rapid succession. In the past he had been Michael's confessor. Now the tables were turning. He was uncomfortable with this, and simultaneously uncomfortable with the fact the he was uncomfortable. Typical of physicians, he found it easier to give consolation than to accept it. Typical of men, he was reluctant to manifest vulnerability. He debated the matter with himself. He had just entrusted Michael with a piece of very sensitive information, so why shouldn't he discuss his past with Nancy? Normally he would confide in Aviva about a matter as important as this, but certain aspects of previous relationships were better left unexplored, even between the closest spouses.

All of these matters flashed through his mind in a matter of seconds. He took a critical look at Michael. There was character there … and integrity. He stopped walking.

"Michael, I'm going to bare my soul here, so I need your word that this will remain between us."

Michael gave him a small wave. "You have it."

They came to a bench and sat down. Josh hesitated again.

"I'm not even sure how to start, but I'm just going to tell you what there is to tell, and hopefully you'll be able to help me think it through."

He leaned forward and fixed his gaze on the ground while speaking.

"I met Nancy here, in Boston I mean, when she began her residency. She was brand new, right out of medical school, and I was in my last year of training. We weren't on the same service at the time but I knew a little about her history. She wasn't your typical 'Boston resident' because of her southern background. It made her unique, though. You know, with her accent and mannerisms. She took a lot of abuse about it at first, but it wasn't long before she was taken seriously because she was super bright and worked harder than anyone.

"Eventually our work assignments brought us together. Our relationship was pretty much professional at the time, although there was no way to ignore how attractive she was. I was unattached but I made a conscious effort at keeping things at arm's length, partly because I didn't want to be accused of favoritism when it came to handing out assignments. Eventually we moved on to different areas of the hospital, and that's when our relationship changed.

"To my surprise, she was the one to make the first move. One day I got a phone call at home and she asked if I'd like to go out sometime, and that pretty much started us off. We dated for several months and it actually got to the point where we were discussing a serious commitment, but it didn't work out."

Michael had been following every word.

"Why not?"

"Mostly cultural differences, I guess, but we came close to overcoming them. At one point I was more interested in a commitment than she was."

Michael thought of himself and Sarah. It had been much the same with them, but the similarity ended there. Sarah and Nancy were worlds apart. He returned to the conversation.

"And forgive me, but we're talking about the same woman who did this 'evil scientist' thing? Killed a guy by trying to get him pregnant?"

"Yeah, the same woman."

"So how could that be? I mean, like what was there about her - besides her looks, I mean - that you found attractive?"

Josh turned towards him. "Well, she's bright, brilliant I should say, unspoiled, not afraid to work her butt off. Her family situation is strained, though. She's got this thing about proving herself, especially to her father, and that gets out of hand from time to time."

"For example?"

"Well, when she decides on a project, it tends to consume her. The prospect that she might fail, or worse, that she might be embarrassed, is pretty much intolerable to her. I'm sure that's why she never told me about Sarah's abortion attempt, by the way. And if anyone or anything gets in her way, look out. It's like she bought in way too much on the concept that women have to be tough to pursue a career. That was one of the things we had trouble with.

"On the other hand, she had the capacity to surprise me. Like the first time our relationship got physical, or I should say we tried to get physical. I was on call, but it was quiet at the hospital and I was able to get out for a while. We were at her apartment -- it was this tiny little one bedroom in a bad neighborhood -- and things were heating up between us when I got paged for an emergency. I ended up running out of there half dressed without so much as saying goodbye. Then the next day, before I even had the chance to call her, I get these flowers with a card that says 'I'd like to give you something even more beautiful.'"

"So what made you break up?"

Josh considered this question before answering. He looked down and contemplated his thumbnail. Michael waited patiently.

"I guess we pretty much came to an impasse about having a family. I never expected her to be a homebody, but her career commitments went way beyond what I thought I could live with. I mean it was like children were an afterthought at best. She wouldn't even consider the idea until she had reached this long list of academic goals, and when I asked her for a timetable she'd just change the subject." He turned to Michael with an ironic smile. "Devoting her life to infertility research and couldn't care less about having children of her own."

"So that was it, then? Everything else was cool except the family thing?"

Josh shook his head. "No ... She has a dark side ...."

"Go ahead. You're on a roll."

"It's not what you're thinking. She's not sociopathic or anything."

"I didn't say I was thinking that. Why don't you describe what you mean, and I'll draw my own conclusions."

Josh mulled this over, then slowly returned to the subject. "Her intensity could be scary. There were a couple of times when I saw this cold frenzy in her eyes, like when she was talking about an experiment that she was committed to. And once I made the mistake of suggesting that her mathematical research model might be flawed. I'm telling you, she shot me a look that chilled me to my bones. Then she said, 'I'll tell you what, Josh. How about if I do my thing and you just stick to what you know. I'm afraid this is a little out of your league.'"

"Ouch. That's cold, man."

"Yeah , but it wasn't so much what she said, it was more the way she delivered it. Way beyond sarcasm. I mean scary. It was stuff like that that gave me doubts."

"So how did it end?"

"I cared too much about her to start dissecting her character. Basically, we ended it by agreeing that our personal values made us a mismatch. At the time I thought the split had gone smoothly, but the next thing I knew she was transferring her residency across town to the Boston General. She didn't return to the Lying-In until after she had finished all her training and done two extra years of fellowship in infertility. And you know how it is. Once you've had that intense a relationship with someone, it carries over in some way. Up 'til now it hasn't been a problem, but I don't know how I'm going to handle this mess. Half the time I'm mad as hell at her for dragging me into it in the first place."

Michael couldn't resist challenging Josh on this point.

"Dragging you into it? I think you might have trouble defending that description now that you've conducted an illegal computer search."

"But only after I was confronted with a ton of evidence. I couldn't ignore all of that. Still, we have this past that conflicts the hell out of me. Do you see what I mean? How am I going to turn her in under these circumstances?"

Now Michael shook his head. "I'll say this. You're absolutely right. That is the damnedest story I've ever heard."

Again Josh turned to look at him.

"Okay, so where do I go from here?"

Michael leaned back and folded his arms.

"I'd say you have to tell someone. That's a given. The question is, how to do it?"

They sat in silence for a moment. Then Michael picked up the conversation again. He unfolded his arms and held up his index finger.

"Wait a minute. Now let's just get some perspective on this. You're not the one who did this evil experiment. And there's no way that you can keep silent. My take on it is that you have to detach yourself from every aspect of this except the clear fact that something awful happened and you're obligated to report it. I'm not saying you have to go to the newspapers. How about some responsible person, someone authoritative? And if you want to cop out, I could understand that, too. Like maybe letting someone find these printouts on their desk with the key names and information highlighted in magic marker."

Josh looked at Michael thoughtfully.

"You know, I've already approached the department chairman aboutdepartment chairman about Nancy. Somehow, without proof, I didn't have a problem talking to him, but now it's gonna be a lot harder." He rose from the bench with a resolute expression.

"Thank you, Michael. I know what I have to do."

****

FORTY ONE

Josh Cantor jumped as he heard his name being announced.

"The court calls Dr. Joshua Cantor to the stand."

District Attorney Burke dispensed with the usual preliminaries, pouncing the minute Josh finished taking his oath.

"Dr. Cantor, let's first establish that you are currently in the practice of obstetrics and gynecology, and you specialize in infertility- is that correct?"

"Yes, that's correct," Josh answered.

"And you were once were in a personal relationship with Dr. Sanderson, is that also correct?"

"Yes," Josh answered, "that was several years ago, when we were both in our residency training."

"And currently?"

"Currently I'm happily married. Dr. Sanderson and I are professional associates, nothing more."

"So you're prepared to confirm that your testimony will not be affected by anything in your past."

"Yes I am."

"Very good, Doctor. Now can you tell the jury how you reacted when you heard of Dr. Sanderson's involvement in the death of Samuel Foster."

"How I reacted?"

"Yes. How did you feel about what she had done?"

"Well, of course I was shocked by it."

"And what did you think about the ethical element of her behavior?"

"I thought it was out of bounds."

"In fact, you were the one who discovered that Dr. Sanderson had performed this experiment on Mr. Foster, and you reported it to the authorities."

"Yes, that's true."

"Even before you confronted her with it."

"Yes."

"And that's despite the fact that you once had a personal relationship with her." "Yes." "To whom did you first report it?" "To Dr. Leon Landry, our department chairman." "And what was his reaction?"

"At first he had his doubts, but when he confronted her, she acknowledged that she was the one who had attempted to create a pregnancy in Mr. Foster."

"And what was her demeanor when he confronted her?"

"Initially, she was proud of it. She thought it was a milestone that would benefit the hospital."

"She was proud of it?"

"Yes, she felt that it would be a breakthrough in infertility research, and suggested that the hospital should hold a press conference to announce it."

"But that's not the way Dr. Sanderson characterized her reaction during her deposition several weeks ago. Are you sure about how you remember it?"

"Yes, I'm sure."

"And what was Dr. Landry's reaction?"

"Dr. Landry was very upset." "Upset in what way?" "He strongly disapproved of what Dr. Sanderson had done."

"And what action did he take?"

"He dismissed her from the hospital staff."

"Despite the fact that she had obtained a signed consent form from Mr. Foster?" "I'm not sure if he knew that at the time." "Would that have made a difference" Charlie Cross jumped up so fast that he had to grab his pants and hike them over his paunch.

"Objection! Calls for speculation," Cross bellowed.

"Sustained," nodded the judge.

Burke didn't miss a beat. "But you were there when this happened?" "Yes."

"Did she ask you to defend her?" "Not in so many words, but she sort of looked at me for support."

"And then?" "I don't remember what I said, but I do remember shaking my head 'no'."

"Meaning that you disapproved." "Yes, I disapproved."

"So what's the nature of your relationship with Dr. Sanderson as of today, Doctor?"

"Well, I was advised by an attorney to not communicate with her, but even before then there was an awkward distance between us."

"All right, Doctor Cantor, just one more question: Can you tell the jury whether you believe Dr. Sanderson conducted a criminal experiment?"

This time Cross didn't bother to actually voice an objection. Instead he slapped his hand on the table in front of him and raised his hands in a gesture of disbelief.

But Burke had made his point. Even before the judge could admonish him, he turned to the stenographer.

"Sorry. Strike that. Nothing further, Your Honor."

Charlie Cross was already busy jotting down his thoughts on paper. When he didn't rise, the judge addressed him. "Does defense counsel wish to question this witness?"

Distracted, Cross lifted his pen momentarily while answering "No, Y'onnah, no questions at this time," he said, quickly returning to his scribbling.

FORTY TWO

Josh felt weak as he walked back to his seat. He wanted to run out of that courtroom, to get as far away as possible. When he sat down he noticed several members of the jury looking at him. What were they thinking? As he settled into his seat he thought about his testimony. Had he been too harsh? He tried to reconstruct the events that led up to Nancy's dismissal .... Leon Landry had been stunned when Josh Cantor brought him the information to support his theory. "I can't believe it! Where'd you get this stuff?"

"Let's just say I asked some questions and it just sort of turned up."

"Can you give me a source? Someone who led you to it?"

"No, but why don't you ask Nancy about it and see what happens."

"That's it? You can't tell me any more than that?"

"I don't think so, Leon. You know Nancy and I were in a relationship several years ago, so this is awkward for me. Please. Talk to Nancy."

"All right, I understand, Josh, but I'm afraid you're going to have to be more involved than you'd like. The only way I'm willing to handle this is to interview her in your presence."

Josh tried to come up with an alternative to Landry's condition, but he knew instinctively there was no choice. He massaged his left temple before he spoke. "Okay, Leon. I'll be there."

As he prepared to interrogate Nancy Sanderson, Dr. Landry had become increasingly certain that she had played a key role in Samuel Foster's death and he was determined to elicit any and all possible information from her. When Nancy entered she immediately noticed Josh. She looked askance at him but remained calm. "Hello, Dr. Landry. You wanted to see me?"

Nancy listened impassively as Dr. Landry detailed the story and then all but accused her of engineering Samuel Foster's pregnancy. When he finished there was silence. She sat perfectly still, unshaken. Slowly, her features transformed from indifference into a cryptic smile. And then, to their complete surprise, she squared her shoulders and spoke with bursting pride.

"Well, congratulations, you two! It looks like you've solved a complicated puzzle. Yes, I'm the one who masterminded this experiment. I got Samuel Foster pregnant! Can you believe it? The first ever human male pregnancy! And right here at the Boston Lying-In!"

She was gratified at the shock registered on their faces.

"I've been putting a paper together, which was supposed to be a surprise, but you've obviously figured it out already. I guess we'll have to call a press conference. I thought it should be published in a journal first, but maybe the media should have the first crack at it. What do you think?"

Landry and Josh both struggled to digest this remorseless disclosure. As they looked at her beaming face, it slowly dawned on both of them that she didn't have the faintest notion that this would be considered aberrant behavior. Josh was speechless. Landry, however, wasn't. "What do I think, Nancy? I think you're a loose cannon with a license to practice medicine! You've done an atrocious thing in the name of medical research while you were a member of my department. A man is dead as a result of your recklessness, and you're going to have to answer for it!"

"But what about this breakthrough? Think of the publicity for the hospital."

"Publicity? You don't get it, do you? Now listen carefully. We've been through a lot together, and I've overlooked some of your questionable values in the past, but this time you've crossed the line."

He stared at her.

"I'm going to recommend your dismissal from the staff, Nancy. And I'd suggest you get a lawyer." She looked to Josh, who shook his head 'no'. She stood still, unable to fathom the way her announcement was received, then quietly left the room and closed the door behind her.

In the aftermath of her exit, the two men communicated solely by reading each other's eyes. In Josh's, Landry saw disbelief. In Landry's, Josh read non-negotiable resolve. Finally they unlocked their gazes and Josh rose to leave. There was nothing left to say.

FORTY - THREE

As Nancy sat stoically at the defense table her demeanor belied her thoughts. In reality, she had been shocked at the medical establishment's response to her revelation. She had assumed that the world would hail her as an icon of creativity, that her place in history would be assured, that medical schools would be vying for her to join their faculties as a full professor, chairing a division of reproductive technology. Instead, she had found herself the subject of yet another investigation, this time by a pair of homicide detectives who had invited themselves into her office. Until then she had been shaken, especially by Dr. Landry's assertions, but this intrusion was another matter. Now she was annoyed. "Homicide? What are you guys doing here? I was doing medical research with a legitimate volunteer. He knew exactly what he was getting into."

Detective Ralph Seely glared at her. Normally Nancy was on the other end of such a non-verbal exchange, but this man's demeanor was intimidating. It had been a long time since she felt the need to avert another person's gaze. She felt the color draining from her face. Sensing that he would know whether she was being truthful, she decided to tell it straight out, without embellishment.

"Now, look. Samuel Foster was a willing subject in my experiment. He understood the risks. If you have any doubts, I'll be glad to show you his consent form, complete with signature. I even made it clear, in writing, that this was an experiment and that it wasn't approved by the FDA. He knew what he was doing, I assure you." Detective Seely's poker expression remained unchanged.

"I'm afraid our understanding of this situation is different from yours, Doctor. According to our consultants, this represents an unacceptable degree of variation from standard medical practice. What you've done is tantamount to murdering this patient, and that is precisely the charge being considered against you ....'Murder'." When Seely paused to observe Nancy's reaction, he was taken aback. Instead of recoiling in fear, she had regained her defiant attitude and had managed to turn the tables by locking her gaze on him. He took a moment to recoup, clearing his throat before resuming his harangue. "What we're trying to determine now, Doctor, is whether Mr. Foster was fully aware of the repercussions of your 'experiment'." Nancy looked at him like he was crazy. "Are you guys off the wall, or what? I just told you he agreed to this project. It was completely voluntary. I didn't hide anything from him. Can you understand that, or is the concept a little too esoteric for you? And by the way, are you here with a warrant of some sort? Am I obligated to talk to you, or not?" "No, Doctor. No formal charges have been filed against you, but perhaps you'd like to show us your signed document." "It's not here. I have it under lock and key somewhere else in the hospital." "Would you be willing to make us a copy?" She felt a surge of confidence. "Sure. Why not? In fact, if you want to wait I'll prepare it right now, and then maybe you'll get off my case. But maybe I'm assuming too much. You can read, can't you?" Seely looked at his partner and got a shrug of exasperation."All right, Doctor. We'll be happy to wait here while you do that.""Like hell! You can wait out in the hall. I'm not gonna have you two snooping around my office while I'm not here."   The detectives shot each other another glance, after which they shuffled out with Nancy shooing them through the door like a perturbed nanny. When she returned from duplicating her papers, she found the two men leaning against the wall and looking slightly abashed. She handed them the copy with a brisk send off. "Will that be all, gentlemen? Because I have a lot of work to do .... And by the way, don't show up here again without legal papers." As they walked away meekly, Seely muttered. "Feisty broad, huh?"

His partner shook his head.

"I wish my balls were as big as hers."

To the detectives' consternation, the medico-legal form Nancy had prepared was impressive. She had, in fact, drawn up an exhaustive release form and Samuel Foster had signed it, his signature confirmed by handwriting analysis. But it wasn't the open-and-shut case Nancy had anticipated. After extensive legal considerations there was disagreement over whether or not she was liable, and the situation became even murkier when Ellen Foster filed a wrongful death suit on behalf of her late husband. As the charges against her began to pile up, the normally unflappable Nancy became alarmed. For moral support she turned to Philip. "You know what, Nancy? This has gone too far. I'm not gonna let

you take the blame by yourself. It'll go easier on you if I'm involved."
Nancy embraced him."I can't let you do that, Philip. You were against this
from the beginning. I did it on my own.."

"Yeah, but if we tell the whole story, about how this all started in the
animal lab and what we were originally trying to do, I think it'll make a
difference." "No, the price will be too high. We have to be practical. If we
divulge all of that, you'll get the blame for Hamlet and end up getting
kicked out of school, and then maybe neither of us will have a career.
I think we need to play it cool and see what happens. If I get into bad
trouble we'll consider something else, but not this. And don't forget
the 50,000 dollar thing with Hamlet. We'd probably get stuck for that,
too." Again, Philip was amazed at Nancy's capacity to think clearly under
pressure. "All right, but then what's your next move?" "Maybe I'll talk to
Josh Cantor again. He might be able to pull some strings, and, despite
everything, I think he'd be willing to advise me." She tried to read Philip's
face. "What do you think?" "Worth a shot, I guess. I don't see what you
have to lose, unless you'd be upset by rejection." She briefly pondered
the possibility. "I can't worry about that. There's too much at stake."
Sitting in Josh's consultation room, Nancy was overwhelmed by a flood
of memories and emotions. "Josh, I know how you feel about what I did,
but now I need you to advise me as a friend. What am I going to do?" Josh
was in the conflicted position of having turned Nancy in, and now she
was asking him to help get her off the hook. He took a long, hard look at
her, trying to summon up his sympathy.

"All right. Tell me what's happening. What's the case against you?
And have you talked to a lawyer?" "Not yet, but the police are snooping
around and their questions are so accusatory that I'm getting concerned.
Plus, Samuel Foster's wife has filed a wrongful death suit. The thing is, I
have a rock-solid consent form with his signature on it. He understood
the risks and signed accordingly, so I don't know how it can go any
further than that." "On the surface that might make sense, Nancy, but
the problem as I understand it is that a signed consent form may not
protect you, no matter how exhaustive. And I have to tell you, I'm not
sure you understand how far apart we are over this. You used my notes on
abdominal pregnancies to conduct an unethical experiment. How could
you do that when you knew I would never approve?" She put up her hand
in a "stop" gesture. "Can we put that aside for now? I'll go into the details
some other time if you insist." "If I insist? This isn't a minor point, Nancy.
I feel like you were using me to accomplish something unconscionable,
and I can't just ignore it." She responded by rolling her eyes and folding
her arms. After several seconds of waiting to her to speak, he asked,
"Well?" When she failed to answer, he stood up at his desk. "You need

help, Nancy, but you and I are obviously at an impasse. Basically, I agree with Leon Landry. You need to talk to a lawyer."
****

Nancy agreed to meet with Lawrence Bagwell, an experienced malpractice defense attorney who would concentrate on the wrongful death allegation. As for the murder charge, attorney Bagwell referred her to a colleague, Abraham Brodsky, who interviewed her regarding her version of the case. After matter-of-factly collecting the information he told her to expect a written summation within two weeks.

The letter came ten days later.

Shenker, Brodsky P.C., Revere Tower, Boston, Ma.
Personal & Confidential - 6/8/04
Dr. Nancy Sanderson
c/o Boston Lying-In Hospital

Dear Dr. Sanderson: This will summarize the legal principles involved in the defense of the Samuel Foster case. There appears to be no federal or state law or regulation governing a physician's performance of experimental medical procedures, although federal law does govern the use of experimental drugs.

One significant issue in your particular situation is 'assumption of risk'. This will not protect a physician from criminal liability from homicide in Massachusetts because, although assumption of risk is a traditional defense in civil negligence, it does not apply similarly in criminal situations. In addition, 'consent' is not a defense to criminal prosecution for homicide. It would appear that the traditional techniques employed to protect one from civil liability --- i.e., assumption of risk, covenant not to sue, and general releases --- do not provide a protection for the more stringent protections afforded persons with respect to criminal liability.

However, considering the thoroughness of your release form with Mr. Sondheim, i.e., the specific mention of certain possibilities including bleeding and death, spelled out in great and specific detail, should carry considerable weight. Also, the fact that Mr. Foster was an intelligent person, and was familiar by virtue of his work with legal terminology and procedure, would normally be taken into consideration, although this opinion does not presume to predict the outcome of criminal court proceedings .

I will be in touch in the near future to arrange a followup appointment. In the meantime, please feel free to contact me for any questions.

Sincerely,

Abraham Brodsky, Esq.

Nancy threw down the latter in disgust and placed a call to Brodsky's office. She demanded an immediate appointment, her angry tone intimidating the receptionist into carving out a fifteen minute slot that very afternoon. Still fuming when she arrived, she was ushered into a small conference room where Brodsky purposely kept her waiting a few minutes longer than necessary. Having heard about Nancy's mood he decided he'd have to clearly define his ground right then and there. When he entered the office her greeted her with business-like formality. "Hello, Dr. Sanderson. How can I help you? I assume you got my letter?" "Yeah, I got your letter," she answered snidely. "And you can help me by explaining this situation in plain English. Just put aside the lawyer bit and tell me where me stand."

Brodsky's expression remained unchanged.

"All right, Doctor, but first we need to talk about how we're going to treat each other. This isn't going anywhere until you drop your hostile attitude."

"Of course I'm hostile! If I talked to my patients in such technical language, I assure you they'd find some other doctor. I don't need you to impress me with legal vocabulary, Mr. Brodsky."

"Well, Doctor, the first thing you're going to have to understand is that this is a complicated case. The legal precedents are far from black and white so I'm going to have my hands full. And frankly, I'm the best you're going to get. But if you don't like my style, then get another lawyer. And make up your mind right now. I don't want to waste your time, and I don't want you to waste mine." Nancy was impressed with Brodsky's response. If this guy could talk to her that way, he could stand up to anyone.

"Okay, we'll do it your way. But as long as I'm here, at least give me the short version." "Fine. Here it is. The core of this is what amount of weight the court places on Samuel Foster's release form. As I indicated in the letter, his level of intelligence would indicate that he clearly understood what he was signing. The question is whether that relieves you of responsibility for the outcome. That's where the brunt of my argument has to be directed. I don't believe we have any other reasonable strategy."

"Good," Nancy said. "I get it. Now give me your best guess on how it will go." "I'd describe my sense as cautiously optimistic, mostly because of practical considerations. It would cost the state a lot of money to conduct a full-fledged trial, especially in a case as sensational as this, so they might not even proceed with formal charges. But this is the kind of case that will attract media attention, and the DA might have to respond to that kind of pressure, even if it means a costly trial. The other possibility is that you may need to consider a compromise where they'll allow you to plead to a lesser charge. Specifically, I'm thinking about involuntary manslaugter." Nancy nearly jumped out of her chair. "No! No way! I'm not accepting any kind of a charge!" She pointed an aggressive finger at Brodsky. "He agreed to this procedure. He knew the risks. I know he did. I made him listen to them over and over again. Don't you let them con you into accepting some lesser plea. I won't accept it!"

Brodsky allowed Nancy to finish before responding, then waited a little longer to be sure she was done. "Dr. Sanderson, I am going to do everything I can to exonerate you. It's my duty as an attorney and I wouldn't have accepted your case if I didn't have reasonable faith in you and in the system. But if they offer you an involuntary manslaughter plea and you reject it, the DA will almost certainly consider whether he can make a murder charge stick. So please understand, one of my duties is to help you look at things objectively, and right now you are definitely not doing that. "Yeah, yeah. 'Whoever represents themselves has a fool for a client'. But don't forget this, Mr. Brodsky. This may not be your ordinary case, but I'm not your ordinary client either. I want frequent updates. In clear language. And I won't change my mind about the manslaughter idea, so forget about trying to talk me into that, or any other admission of guilt."

She rose to leave, tossing her hair and turning her head to face him on her way out.

"And don't even think of treating me like some moron who doesn't know what's up."

****

Nancy's case took several weeks of consideration, but in time the strength of public outcry prevailed. The state attorney general, acting on behalf of the People of Massachusetts, announced that there would be a jury trial to determine whether Dr. Sanderson had broken the law and was guilty of murder. In the meantime, Ellen Foster's attorney had been keeping close watch on these developments. The state's decision to prosecute encouraged him regarding the potential for success in their wrongful death suit, but he remained cautious.

He met her in his office. "Ellen, I asked you here to advise you on the status of our litigation. Since the state has chosen to pursue criminal charges, our chances for a civil settlement have improved, but it's far from a sure thing." "I don't care!" Ellen cried. "She killed my husband! I want to go ahead with it no matter what the chances are!" "I can understand that, but there are some practical considerations at this point. "Like what?" "Like my fee, to name one. I couldn't convince my partners to let me work on a contingency basis, so I need to know if you're willing to invest your own money." "What will it cost me to continue?" The attorney leaned forward on his desk and folded his hands. "We'll need a retainer of ten thousand dollars to start, and I'm sure it's going to get much more expensive than that. Conservatively, this could easily cost you in excess of thirty or forty thousand before you know it. And her attorney isn't likely to settle." Ellen's eyes misted over, fists clenched in rage.

"You know I can't afford that! This just isn't fair! She killed Samuel and now she's going to walk away!"

"I know, Ellen. If it's any consolation, she's in danger of losing her medical license. You might want to write to the Board of Registration in Medicine while they're reviewing her case."

Ellen stood up abruptly and grabbed her coat.

"Fine!" she snapped. "Just give me their address!"

FORTY - FOUR

While awaiting her hearing, Nancy had accepted Philip's moral support but pointedly declined any advice on how to conduct herself. Even Brodsky, her attorney, was useless, she decided. He was nothing but a legal egghead, and she would take pleasure in firing him.

Because she had made the effort to anticipate their questions and rehearse her answers, Nancy was unshaken by the stony expressions she encountered from the Board reviewers. After perfunctory introductions the chairperson wasted no time in asking her to describe her perspective on what had happened in the case of Samuel Foster. Because she was so well prepared, Nancy had to stifle a smile. When they heard her objective analysis, she thought, they would understand. She held her head high as she began her remarks. "First of all I'd like to establish that Samuel Foster entered into this agreement of his own free will and having signed a release form that he understood the risks. I made it very clear to him that this procedure had never been attempted before and that there were no guarantees. He understood that he might never become pregnant despite considerable cost, and that even if he were to conceive there were no guarantees on the outcome of the pregnancy or on his welfare. I assure you that I reviewed all of this with him repeatedly and there was no element of deception on my part." No one interrupted Nancy as she went on to describe the procedure, proudly detailing the technical aspects and ultrasound findings. Her confidence began to wane, however, when the committee members' expressions didn't change. By this point she had imagined that their scientific curiosity would quicken their interest, but there wasn't a single remark or question about any of it. Finally, when she concluded, one person addressed her.

"Dr. Sanderson, how do you imagine Samuel Foster's family feels about this?" "Well, I'm sure they're upset, but I would want them to understand that this complication was an accident of nature and not the result of negligence on my part. I had been in close contact with him and he hadn't experienced any symptoms that indicated this might happen. Perhaps if they were to review the release form and my progress notes it might help them understand how badly he wanted to do this, especially for his wife." Another member asked her:

"Can you tell us what you would do differently in the future?" "I'm not sure. I've thought of few measures that might prevent this type of internal bleeding, but to be fair I couldn't absolutely guarantee it wouldn't happen again." After the panel members exchanged glances, the chairman asked if there were any further questions. When there were none, he turned to Nancy.

"Dr. Sanderson, is there anything else you'd like to say before we consider our decision?"

Nancy wasn't sure where she stood. She decided she'd better leave them with something to think about. "I'd only ask all of you to try to take the broadest possible view. I've been accused of a lot of things in this case, including unethical behavior. But I would appeal to your sense of history. In the past our profession has made the error of blindly following certain established principles without challenge and it resulted in years, even centuries, of arrested progress until certain luminaries uncovered fallacies that allowed us to move forward. Other physicians have been criticized by their peers, only to be exonerated by historical perspective. So what I'm asking of you now is to recognize that we have been constrained by a primitive code of ethics in human experimentation. I'm certainly not advocating mandatory cooperation on anyone's part, even criminals in prison, but if a well informed individual wants to take his or her chances, I don't think we should stand in the way." The room remained quiet for several seconds until Nancy turned to the chairman. "That's all I have to say."

While the committee considered their decision, Nancy sat alone on a long bench outside the conference room, her imagination racing. She had considered asking Philip to accompany her, and she knew he would have consented, but she worried that his presence might implicate him so when it came right down to it she concluded that it wouldn't be fair to have him there. She was second guessing herself, however, when the conference room door opened to reveal the chairman still wearing his bleak expression. Oh shit, she thought, this isn't gonna be good. "Come in, Dr. Sanderson." Entering the room to an ominous silence, she looked at the panel members. None of their eyes met hers. The chairman came right to the point. "Dr. Sanderson, this committee has the task of determining whether you are culpable for your actions and, if so, what the appropriate disciplinary action would be." He shifted in his chair. Two of the participants cleared their throats. "While we recognize your research talents, it is our opinion that you displayed a complete disregard for ethical considerations. Additionally, you don't seem to fully appreciate the implications of your behavior and have shown no signs of remorse at this hearing." Nancy held her breath while he paused as though to reflect on the decision. Finally he delivered the committee's verdict.

"We have voted unanimously to revoke your medical license for a period of two years." Nancy gasped and began to protest, but he would not be interrupted. "In addition, we are recommending that you attend at least twenty hours of conferences dealing with the topic of medical ethics, as well as undergoing personality profile testing to determine that you are not, in fact, sociopathic. If you meet those conditions satisfactorily, you may apply after twenty four months for this board to consider reinstatement of your license. Do you have any questions?" Nancy shot a hostile look at him.

"Questions?" she asked rhetorically, meanwhile mentally processing the calamity that had befallen her. Instead of attaining recognition for her landmark achievement, she was being vilified, expelled from the ranks of her colleagues, her name trashed. It was incomprehensible. All her work. The endless education. Nine backbreaking years since graduating college and now all of that was being taken from her by a group of bureaucrats whose collective intelligence didn't begin to match hers. She despised these shortsighted little men with their primitive code of ethics. And she'd be damned if she'd undergo personality profile examination. It wasn't her fault if she was ahead of her time and they didn't have the vision to appreciate what she had done.

"Questions?" she repeated, continuing to smolder. "No, Doctor, I don't have any questions."

FORTY - FIVE

Nancy had accomplished her goal of being recognized for her work, but not in the way she imagined. Instead of fame she had achieved infamy, her image portrayed as that of a mad scientist who had conducted an unconscionable experiment. Comparisons were made to the shocking human experimentation conducted by the Nazis. This development had a much heavier effect on her than the reaction of organized medicine. In the case of the medical board's decision, she was able to convince herself that they were motivated by jealousy and a narrow-minded perspective. But when she saw herself being depicted in the media as some kind of deviant monster she reacted by retreating into a protective shell, communicating only with Philip, and even then only rarely. She felt a kinship with Ignaz Semmelweis, the physician who discovered the cause of childbed fever in nineteenth century Vienna. Had his work been accepted, countless lives would have been saved, but his peers failed to appreciate him as well, and he died penniless and insane, only to be recognized posthumously for his titanic discovery. Perhaps that was also destined to be her fate, but she would not accept it lying down. She would show them, and in her lifetime. Dr. Nancy Sanderson was a name that would be recognized and revered in the annals of medical history.

Just a month after her license had been revoked, Nancy stood at a laboratory table, numbed by the boredom of waiting while a centrifuge hummed at 2800 rpm's. As the machine whined down to a blurry halt, she flipped open the lid and removed a vial of human blood that had been separated into red cells and serum. Next she transferred the serum fraction into a small test tube which was marked with a bar code, and then placed this into an auto-analyzer which would do the rest. Soon a digital readout would be printed off and she would dutifully forward it to some doctor she never heard of.

Idiot work, she thought. Per diem, night shift, thirty hours a week max. Eleven-fifty an hour without benefits. If and when they needed her.

The other lab workers, her "supervisors" who were years younger and with a fraction of her medical training, were on break. She looked around the room. Familiar surroundings. She pictured her life before all of his had happened. In her own research lab. An assistant doing the scut work—the kind she was doing now.

She reached into her lab coat pocket and pulled out a different vial. Pig serum. A look at the clock. Twenty minutes before the others would return. Time enough for a quick antibody titer. All the equipment she needed. She considered her current circumstances and smiled.

Soon all of this would change.

****

The way Nancy saw it, the medical establishment had stolen her thunder. The male pregnancy concept was her brainchild, a stunning scientific breakthrough.

And now, motivated by jealousy, they were labeling her an outlier. A criminal! But she had a plan. A plan that would turn the world upside down.

An essential ingredient to Nancy's scheme was a fertilized human egg, and she knew exactly where to get it, but having become an outcast in the medical community, it would require every ounce of her considerable audacity to do so.

That afternoon she walked into a thrift store where she bought two articles, a short blond wig and a pair of fake tortoise-shell glasses. She hid these, along with a white lab coat, in an oversized handbag. Then, after dinner, having announced to Philip that she was going out to do some shopping, she nonchalantly slung the handbag over her shoulder, blew him a kiss from the door, and drove to the Boston Lying-In Hospital.

A quiet side street provided a convenient temporary parking spot. Nancy pulled up next to the curb and surveyed the neighborhood. When she was assured of privacy, she found the wig in her bag and fitted it over her own tresses, taking care to cover every dark strand. She viewed her face in the rearview mirror, applied a quick smear of scarlet blush and lipstick, slipped on the glasses, and assured herself that she was unrecognizable. After driving around to the front of the hospital, she parked in the adjacent lot and checked her watch. Seven-fifty. Ten minutes before the end of visiting hours.

Steeling her resolve, she marched to the main entrance where the hospital's liberal visitation policy was posted for all to see:

BOSTON LYING-IN HOSPITAL
VISITING HOURS 8 AM TO 8 PM

Knowing that the only airtight security protocols in the building were applied to the potential abduction of newborns, Nancy walked through the revolving door, proceeded without incident to the freight elevator at the rear of the building, and pushed the down button. As was the case in most hospitals, safety measures were generally haphazard, security personnel in evidence only when called, and then usually for an unruly or intoxicated visitor. One exception to this laxity was the egg lab, where a modest safeguarding effort was made via a deadbolt lock, a coded security alarm, and a remote location within the building.

When she reached the sub-basement level, she took the white lab coat out of her bag, put it on, and placed a stethoscope in the side pocket, allowing it to hang conspicuously over the edge. Next she walked down the dimly-lit subterranean passage, immediately noticing a clicking echo which reverberated through the empty hallway. Unaccustomed to wearing high heels in the hospital, she tried changing her gait to an awkward toe-first technique, but this effort resulted in an even more conspicuous click preceded by a hissing shuffle. Finally she took both shoes off and walked noiselessly in her stocking feet. When she got to the door she took a pair of latex gloves out of the lab coat pocket, pulled them on, and reached into her bag, her fingers searching for and finding the duplicate key she had made before surrendering the original. Guided by her steady hand, the key slid smoothly into the lock, followed by the reassuring thunk of a bolt release. After entering and closing the door behind her, she turned on the lights in the windowless room and punched in a four digit code on the alarm panel. Only when the red alarm light turned silently to green did she permit herself a sigh of relief.

She moved to a familiar incubator, inside of which were several petri dishes of human embryos. Without hesitation she helped herself to the container closest to the back wall, covered it tightly, and rearranged the others to make it less obvious that one was missing.

Now she prepared to execute the rest of her strategy; to get out of the building as easily as she had gotten in. After organizing her materials, she waited for the familiar evening announcement over the hospital's PA system. "Attention, please. Visiting hours are now over. All guests are requested to leave promptly."

Beginning her circuitous exit route, she walked back to the elevator and re-entered it. As soon as the doors had closed she pushed the stop button, took off the lab coat, and folded it carefully before returning it to her bag. Next she directed the elevator to the second floor and exited in her original visitor disguise. The stairway brought her to the ground floor where she began to move through a different hall towards the front of the building, keeping her head down so as to avoid eye contact with passersby.

Just then she heard footsteps again. This time they were not hers, their sound more muffled than her own heel clicking. They were moving towards her, she sensed, and she lifted her eyes just enough to see matte-black shoes with thick crepe soles. Another quick glance revealed a male figure who was looking straight at her. She dropped her eyes again as the footsteps slowed down, then came to a halt.

"Excuse me, miss."

She looked up to see a large middle-aged man in a dark suit. He wore close-cropped hair and a quizzical expression on his broad features. There was no security ID tag on either lapel but on the left side she thought she saw a subtle bulge, possibly housing a shoulder weapon. She clutched her bag as her breath came faster.

"Yes?" she said, trying to control her trembling hand.

His smiled, revealing a sinister gap between his front teeth.

"You seem to be familiar with the hospital," he observed.

She fought the urge to run.

"What do you mean?"

The smile disappeared.

"I hope I haven't frightened you," he apologized, suddenly aware of Nancy's apprehension, "but I must have taken a wrong turn. Can you direct me to the lobby?"

His gruff features melted into an embarrassed teddy-bear grin.

Nancy exhaled. "Sure. I'm heading there myself."

As they walked side by side, negotiating the halls and chatting amiably, he took a thick wallet out of his left breast pocket, extracted a picture, and proceeded to crow about his brand new, ten-pound granddaughter. Eventually surrounded by a stream of visitors, they passed through the lobby where a stack of tri-fold pamphlets caught Nancy's eye. She read the title:

"IF YOU ARE VISITING THE HOSPITAL AFTER 8 PM ...."

Without breaking stride she picked one up, read it, and smiled at this futile attempt at maintaining building security. She checked her watch again. Less than fifteen minutes after parking her car she re-entered it, the white lab coat in her handbag serving to keep three human embryos warm until they reached their next destination.

FORTY-SIX

There was an elephant in the room, and Josh knew that they would have to deal with it sooner or later. He chose a cozy evening when they were reading and cuddled on the sofa. Several minutes passed without conversation. Aviva was leaning back on Josh. Her breathing had become quiet and regular.

"Viv?"

"Umm-hmm."

"You awake?"

"Umm, yeah."

"Can we talk about something?"

She cleared her throat. "Sure. What?"

"You sure you're awake?"

"Uh-huh. Go ahead."

"We need to talk about adoption, Viv."

Her body stiffened in his arms. There was no reply at first.

"You okay?"

Another delay, then "I know, Joshua. I know we have to. But when?"

"Whenever you're ready."

"Are you?" she asked.

He held her tighter, sensing that she was teary. "Yeah, Viv, I am. I'd like to try to move on. I think it'll help to be proactive instead of sitting back and allowing things to roll over us."

"Do you want to do it right away?"

"I think it'd be better if we did, Viv."

He waited a long moment for her response. She answered in her bravest voice. "Okay, I'll make an appointment."

Two weeks later they sat in an adoption agency office, undergoing their initial interview. After a lengthy conversation the interviewer put down her pen and pushed her chair back from the desk.

"I hope you won't mind if I'm frank with you," she said to them. "On the surface you're an ideal couple for adoption. Your marriage is stable, you've certainly exhausted every imaginable effort at trying for pregnancy, and I'm sure you'll get through our home study. But if you don't mind my saying so, I'm picking up on something else here."

"Like what?" Josh asked.

"I don't know, somehow I'm not sure you're ready for this right now."

"Well, let me assure you you've gotten the wrong impression," Josh answered defensively. "There just aren't any other choices. Of course we're ready."

"Maybe we should ask Mrs. Cantor."

Josh turned to look at Aviva, who was shifting uncomfortably in her chair.

"What's wrong, Viv? Is she right?"

"No ... I mean, I don't know," she tried to compose herself. "No! That's wrong. I'm ready," she stuck out her chin. " I want to go ahead with this now."

"Are you sure, Mrs. Cantor? Perhaps in a few months ..."

At this suggestion, Aviva dissolved into tears and turned to Josh.

"I'm sorry, Joshua. I don't know what's wrong with me. I know we've both been through enough. I want to do this, but ..."

Josh took her hand. "That's okay, Viv, that's okay. I had no idea. I should've seen this."

He turned to the interviewer as he helped Aviva out of her chair. "Sorry. I think we'd better go."

"I understand," the interviewer said gently. "Maybe in a few months ..."

FORTY - SEVEN

Dressed in a tasteful gray suit, simple white blouse, no makeup and low heels, Nancy Sanderson was the essence of the wholesome 'girl next door'. As she walked to the witness stand all eyes followed her, wondering how this beautiful, poised young woman could possibly have been involved in such a horrendous medical experiment. She took the oath and seated herself demurely, folding her hands across her lap as she had been instructed by her lawyer. As District Attorney Burke approached, her heart quickened in a surge of hostility, but she quickly reminded herself of the advice that Charlie Cross had hammered into her:

"Doctor, when you get on that stand, that DA is gonna do his best to rattle you. And I know you got a temper, but no matter what he says or does, you be polite, you hear me? Even your body language has to be respectful. You just sit there with your hands folded on your lap like you're in church. Lean forward a little. Act like he's the smartest guy in the world and you can't wait to hear the next thing he has to say. You gotta convince that jury that you're not some hard ass lady doctor. You got your looks goin' for ya; that's a real good thing. But if you start coppin' an attitude, like foldin' your arms in front of your chest, or if there's an edge to your voice, you're gonna blow it. And if that happens, darlin', it doesn't matter how good job I do, cause you'll be goin' to prison for a long, long time."

"Dr. Sanderson," Burke began, "for the record, please state your name and profession."

"Yes, sir," Nancy answered respectfully. "My name is Nancy Sanderson.

I am a physician and I specialize in infertility problems."

"And where are you employed, Doctor?"

"Until this trial is completed, I am temporarily unemployed."

"Temporarily unemployed?" "Yes, sir."

It was immediately apparent to Burke that Nancy was well rehearsed, but he had done his homework and he knew she could be volatile. He decided to go for the jugular before she could ingratiate herself to the jury.

"In fact, you were fired from your position at the Boston Lying In, weren't you, Doctor?"

"I was dismissed. Yes."

"And then a medical review board yanked your license for two years. Isn't that also right, Doctor? ... And by the way, I should still call you 'Doctor' shouldn't I, even though you're not allowed to practice medicine?"

Charlie Cross's antennae went up but Nancy's composed answer kept him in his seat.

"Yes, I still have an M.D. degree, and I look forward to the day when I can return to serving my patients." "'Serving your patients.' Is that how you would characterize what you did to Samuel Foster? The man died, and you would call that 'serving' him?"

Nancy bit her lip. Her hands tightened. "I am terribly sorry for what happened to Mr. Foster," she said evenly. "Even though we both knew that he was taking a chance." "Uh-huh," Burke scoffed. "That's quite a chance, risking your life when your doctor led you down a garden path."

Nancy shook her head. "I would beg to disagree, Sir. Mr. Foster wanted to do this very badly. He loved his wife, and he wanted desperately to give her the baby she yearned for. I actually tried very hard to discourage him by telling him again and again that .... " Burke cut her off.

"Yes, Doctor. I'm sure you had to practically push him out the door so he couldn't force you to do this to him. But you did do it, didn't you? You implanted a fertilized egg in his abdomen, and you knew that this kind of abnormal pregnancy in women is terribly dangerous and often ends in disaster. But you did it anyhow, because no matter what happened to Mr. Foster, as long as that pregnancy took hold and began to grow, you thought it would advance your career, and that was the overriding consideration. Not his happiness. Not his wife's happiness. Not his safety. Just your cold, greedy ambition." Nancy didn't answer. At this point she was so furious that she couldn't utter a word, but to the jury it appeared as though she was ready to cry. When it became apparent that she wasn't going to respond, Charlie Cross exhaled in relief. "Good girl," he said under his breath.

But Burke didn't let up. "So let me ask you this: How can a responsible physician do what you have done; to risk a human life for the sake of promoting your career?"

This time, Cross piped up immediately. "Objection, your honor."

"Sustained," the judge answered. "Mr. Burke, you will not be permitted to ask questions and pass judgment at the same time. Either rephrase what you are asking or move on."

Burke acknowledged the bench. "Understood, Your Honor." Then he faced Nancy again. "Doctor, I understand that you got a written consent from Mr. Foster before implanting a human embryo in his abdomen."

"That's right," Nancy answered. "He understood completely, and he was totally on board with it. I made it very clear to him that he was risking his life by undertaking this procedure."

"But surely you also know that even written consent is not a legitimate document when a patient is subjected to something that's illegal."

"But I did not knowingly do something illegal," Nancy answered. "Mr. Foster was a willing participant every step of the way. He wanted very badly to do this for his wife, but I wouldn't consider doing it without his full consent and understanding of the risks involved. There was nothing at all misleading on my part."

"So now you have a piece of paper with his name on it, and Mrs. Foster has a dead husband. And the fact remains that his signed consent is not admissible in a court of law. And I want that to be clear," he said, turning to the jury. "It is not admissible. It holds no credibility."

He turned back to face Nancy, but after failing to provoke her with a hostile stare, he thought better of continuing. He flicked out his hand in a dismissive gesture. "No further questions," he said while walking back to his chair.

Charlie Cross was pleased with Nancy's performance, but he welcomed the chance to clean up any minor wounds inflicted by the DA. Predictably, he began by offering softballs. "Just a few questions, Doctor," he said, smiling warmly. "But first, would you mind tellin' us your education history?"

"All right," Nancy answered. "Where would you like me to start?"

"How 'bout college. If I understand correctly, you had an academic scholarship, is that right?" "Yes, for four years at Duke University." "And what was your major there?" "A double major, actually, in Biology and Chemistry." "Whew!" Cross exclaimed. "That's a pretty good load. So how'd you do gradewise?" "It went well," Nancy answered. "I was inducted into Phi Beta Kappa." "Phi Beta Kappa! Now that's impressive. So how 'bout after that?" "I was accepted at several medical schools, but since I was already at Duke I decided to attend there."

"Highly rated medical school, as I understand it."

"Nancy nodded. "Yes, it is."

"And after that?"

"Internship and residency at the Boston Lying In."

"And that's a prestigious institution as well."

"Very. Probably the most competitive residency program in the country."

The DA had had enough.

"Objection, Your Honor, I'm sure we're all impressed with how the defendant did in school, but what does that have to do with the charges against her."

"I'm going to allow it," the judge replied.

"But it's immaterial, Your Honor. The defense is simply trying to ..."

"I'm going to allow it, Mr. Burke."

While the frustrated Burke sat down, Charlie Cross affected an air of innocence. "May I continue, Your Honor?"

The judge nodded.

Cross turned back to Nancy. "Sorry, Doctor. Where were we? Oh yes," he caught himself, "the Boston Lying In hospital. And how long was that period of training?"

"Total of four years."

"And then?"

"Another two years of fellowship in infertility and endocrinology, which I finished last year."

"Mah goodness!" Cross exclaimed. "If I'm figurin' correctly, you were just about thirty years old before you were finished with all that education."

"Thirty-two, actually."

"Well, I sure take my hat off t' you, Doctor. Lots o' young people are too busy havin' fun to study and work hard, but you sure have put in an awful lot o' time in order to serve your patients."

While Burke rolled his eyes conspicuously, Cross took a moment to walk to his desk.

He knew exactly what he was going to say next, but he made a show of shuffling some papers, allowing Nancy's impressive credentials to hang over the jurors. Then, with perfect timing, he reapproached the witness stand. "And I believe you met the Fosters while you were in your fellowship years."

"Yes, I followed them for over eighteen months."

"And they both went through a lot of testing and treatment without any success."

"Yes, that's correct."

"So after all that time had passed, would you describe your motivation for treating Mr. Foster?"

Cross had carefully trained Nancy on how to answer this question. As he had directed, she sat thoughtfully for a moment before answering.

"Mr. Foster was the type of man who had no hangups about gender. After all those years of disappointment and heartbreak, he wanted desperately to do this for his wife.

He was so enthusiastic that I had to calm him down. Believe me, I read him the riot act about the dangers involved."

"And what about the accusation that you were doin' this to advance your career?"

"That's just not true," Nancy protested evenly. "This was done for his benefit, not mine. That's why I was so careful to inform him of the risks."

Cross shook his head approvingly. "Doctor, I know this must be difficult for you, but would you describe how you felt when you discovered that Mr. Foster had died?"

As rehearsed, Nancy hesitated and lowered her head. Her answer was barely audible.

"I was devastated," she said. "It was a terrible shock."

"And did you contact Mrs. Foster about it?"

"I tried to, but she wouldn't accept my calls." "And last question, Doctor. Would you consider trying this with another man?" "I couldn't possibly do that," she said. "I'm too upset to even think about it."

"Of course," Cross said sympathetically. "I'm sorry to have asked you that question."

He reached forward to pat her hand.

"Thank you, Doctor," he said.

"Nothing further ,Your Honor."

FORTY - EIGHT

Before dawn on a still Sunday morning, Philip was gently awakened to the stirring of Nancy moving furtively about the bedroom. Feigning sleep, he squinted as she pulled on her denim jacket, then tucked her hair under her baseball cap. His mind began to race. This was another clandestine foray. Finally, an opportunity to discover what she had been up to.

The moment she left the apartment he flew out of bed and threw on a pair of jeans and a sweatshirt, grabbing his keys on the way out. He watched as her convertible pulled out of the parking lot, top up. Noting its direction, he waited until it was out of sight and then ran to his own car and followed her, leaving his headlights turned off.

Soon it became apparent that she was headed for the animal research lab. Now he pulled back, turning his lights on while following her at a discreet distance. Upon arriving at the research facility she parked and calmly walked to the front entrance and unlocked the door. While Philip watched from behind a grove of evergreens, he could tell she had done this before. Undoubtedly she had made duplicates from his set of keys. Also she must have known that no one would be in the research facility at that hour.

Philip parked his car along the hidden side of the building and quietly entered through a side door. The alarm had been turned off. He skulked through the building's interior until he saw her. She was kneeling next to a large sow and speaking to the animal in a soothing voice, rubbing its ear with her free hand while examining the abdomen with an ultrasound transducer.

"That's a good girl. You're gonna grow me a nice baby, aren't you, Sweetheart?

Such a nice pig, such a good girl...hold on now...we'll be done in just a minute...that's it...that's good....Okay, all done now...."

Nancy finished the examination and gathered up her equipment. Then she wheeled the ultrasound machine back to its storage area and removed the video of the study she had just completed. She wore a curious smile as she carried the plastic case to a remote corner and hid it behind a book cabinet. After looking around to be sure she had left nothing behind, she walked to the door, set the alarm and exited, locking the door behind her.

Philip dropped to the floor, fearing he would trip one of the light beam alarms as he moved around the building's interior. Remaining prone, he crawled to the nearest exit and defused the security system. Then he walked to Nancy's secret book cabinet and reached behind it where his fingers found the familiar square shape of a plastic DVD case. Next he moved to the ultrasound machine, plugged it in, and inserted the recording. As it began to roll, he watched in fascination as the image moved around the abdomen, but became distracted by a rhythmic motion behind the bowel. A sense of deja vu came over him. The field of view moved a little higher. He looked closely but saw only blurry shadows.

Suddenly something flashed across the screen. An embryo emerged from the shadows but it lacked the familiar snout of the piglet. The image began to clarify into what looked like a hand puppet. Then the puppet turned and showed its profile, waving its limbs ....

FORTY - NINE

Joshua Cantor heard a commotion in the hall. Bridget Walsh was clucking furiously at somebody.

"No, I'm sorry sir, but you can't see him right now. Sir! Please!"

Josh excused himself to the patient sitting across his desk and opened the door.

Bulling his way down the hall was a determined young man who was holding a small plastic case in his right hand. Bridget followed tenaciously.

"What's going on, Bridget?"

"I'm sorry, Dr. Cantor. He forced his way in and I couldn't ..."

The intruder interrupted her.

"Dr. Cantor, I'm Philip LeDuc. I have to talk to you- RIGHT NOW!"

It took a moment for Josh to place the name and face. Then it dawned on him.

This was Nancy Sanderson's boyfriend.

"What is it, Mr. LeDuc? I'm in the middle of office hours here."

Bridget stood by, waiting.

Philip answered.

"I know this isn't a good time. But I'm sorry, this can't wait."

The frenzy in Philip's eyes convinced Josh he'd better humor him.

"All right, wait here." He went back to apologize to his patient, after which Bridget escorted her back to the waiting area. Josh then led Philip into his consultation room and closed the door.

Philip waved off an invitation to sit down and he held up the disc.

"You've got to look at this." He looked around the room. "Do you have a DVD player in here anywhere?"

"In another room, but what's this about? And first you need to calm down."

"I can't, Dr. Cantor. I've been debating all morning about what to do about this and I don't have anywhere else to turn. Please, just look at this video."

Josh decided to comply. They moved to an examination room where a mobile cart held a DVD machine and several patient instruction discs. Philip reached for the on button but Josh stopped him by covering the front of the machine with his hand.

"Hold it a minute. First tell me what's going on."

Philip tried to control his frustration.

"Dr. Cantor, if I tell you what's on this disc, you won't believe it. But I will tell you it involves Nancy Sanderson."

"Nancy? Why didn't she bring it to me herself?"

"You'll see why. The recording's only two minutes long. Then we'll talk."

"All right, but I can't spend a lot of time with you right now. I have several patients in my waiting room."

"I understand. After you've looked I'll leave right away if you want."

"All right. Play it," Josh sighed.

Philip inserted the disc and stepped back.

As it began to play, Josh saw what appeared to be an abdomen with multiple loops of bowel. Then the image focused in on the outline of an embryo. From its size he estimated it to be in the early second trimester, but when he looked for the uterine walls there were none.

"What are you showing me? An abdominal pregnancy? Is this Cameron Gallagher's recording?"

"No, Doctor Cantor. It's not that."

"What, then? Don't tell me there's another patient with this condition."

"No. Just keep looking. There's more."

The image moved away from the pregnancy at this point and swung downwards towards the pelvis. Josh waited impatiently for the normal female anatomy to appear but instead he saw a large organ, much longer than a normal uterus, divided into two curved horns and containing an unusually long cervix.

"What the heck is that? Does this patient have some sort of reproductive tract anomaly?"

"No, there's no anomaly. That's the normal appearance of a pig's uterus."

Josh looked at Philip and then back at the screen. He hit the rewind button until he came to the embryo's image. As he studied it he turned pale and turned again to Philip.

"That's a human embryo .... you can't mean .... I don't believe this!"

Philip sat down heavily. "That's what I've been trying to tell you. She's been acting weird lately so I followed her one day and found this recording." He shook his head. "What am I going to do, Dr. Cantor? I don't think I even allowed myself to believe it until now."

"Why would she do this? What was she thinking? What could possibly possess her to do something like this?"

Philip hung his head when he spoke, barely a whisper.

"You know her, Dr. Cantor.

"She believes her research ideas were stolen. Now she's trying to prove something."

"I still can't believe it. Where's the animal that's in this recording?"

"At the veterinary school's research lab. You can't tell a thing by looking at her, though. She weighs at least six hundred pounds."

Josh's thoughts turned clinical. "But how can this pregnancy be surviving?" he asked. "There'd be tissue rejection by now. Is there something different about a pig's immune system?"

"Not that I know of, but come to think of it, I did see her picking up a couple of syringes when she finished the ultrasound. Maybe she's using some kind of immunosuppressive agent."

"That's even worse! If that stuff doesn't kill the baby it'll cause birth defects that are unthinkable!"

Philip stood mute.

"Where's Nancy now?" Josh asked.

"Probably in our apartment. We're living in Allston."

Josh took in the pained expression on Philip's face.

"You've been going through a lot, haven't you?"

Philip nodded. "The thing is, I don't know what to do about this."

Josh sat thoughtfully for a moment. Then he startled Philip by jumping up out of his chair.

"Philip, I want you to take me there right now. Is she at home?"

"Yeah, I think so, but what're you thinking?"

"I'm going to confront her. She can't go on with this."

"No! I mean, she doesn't know I've discovered this yet. She'll flip out if we just barge in on her with it."

"I don't care what she does. This is over the edge and it has to be stopped right now."

"I don't know, Dr. Cantor. I just don't know what to do."

Josh hardened his voice. "Well, I know what to do. What's her address?"

Philip answered numbly and stood frozen as Josh grabbed his car keys and stormed out, looking straight ahead as he passed by the reception desk.

"Bridget, you'll have to reschedule everyone. I won't be back until this afternoon."

Nancy answered her apartment intercom. Her voice came over the lobby speaker.

"Who is it?"

"Nancy, it's Josh Cantor. I have to speak to you."

Her voice became guarded. "Josh? What are you doing here?"

"I have something to talk to you about. Let me in, please."

"Why? I mean, what do you want to talk about?"

Suddenly she brightened up, excitement rising in her voice.

"Did they finally change their mind about me? They couldn't be feeling guilty after all this time, could they?"

Josh made a split-second decision. It would take a lie to gain her confidence.

"Yeah, it's sort of about that. I'd like to speak to you in person if I could." The door buzzed and unlocked.

"All right, c'mon up."

By the time Josh arrived, Nancy's curiosity had overtaken her suspicion but she was still on guard. She restrained herself for a moment until she just couldn't wait any longer.

"They've decided to recognize my contribution, haven't they? It's about time! What took them so long?"

When he didn't answer immediately, Nancy's face darkened.

"What is it? Am I wrong?"

"Well, this is about what you're doing, but not what you think."

Her eyes narrowed. "What are you trying to say, Josh?

Josh steeled himself and blurted it out. "I know about your new experiment, Nancy, and it's absolutely unacceptable! You can't do this!"

She pushed her chair back. "Do what? What are you talking about?"

"You know what I'm talking about. The experiment at the veterinary research lab. I can't believe you've been doing this while you're on trial for murder!"

He produced the disc. "I have your video. For God's sake, Nancy, what's wrong with you! You can't grow human babies in pigs!"

She jumped up. "How'd you get that! It's private property, dammit!"

"Philip LeDuc came to me with it. He followed you to the lab and saw everything. At least he has the good sense to be frantic about it. But you! You're over the edge, Nancy! I'm sure you must be using some kind of immunosuppressive agent, and who knows what kind of monstrous anomalies you're going to produce. You're playing with human embryos, for God's sake!"

She was pacing now.

"First of all, what makes you think I'm using immuno- suppressives?"

"Because you have to be, and Philip told me he saw you using syringes on the pig."

"Well, if you must know, the syringes were for hormone injections. They had nothing to do with immunosuppressives."

"Then how are you avoiding an immune response?"

Finding it irresistible to gloat, Nancy stopped pacing and broke into a derisive grin. She tapped her forehead. "Just think about it, Josh. Haven't you heard about using animals for organ donations? Like liver transplants, for example?"

"Of course, but ..."

"Well, there's been some work with injecting human genes into pig embryos, so when the pigs reach maturity their organs won't be rejected by human recipients."

Josh was stunned. Nancy continued, enjoying his reaction.

"What I've been doing is a modification of that. I began by injecting human blood and skin cell cultures into fetal pigs while they were still in utero. The great thing about pigs is that they only take a few months to reach adult size so I picked a female to use for my research and so far there's no sign of rejection going on with the human fetus." She let out as sinister giggle. "Just wait till the press gets hold of this!

And I'm really dying to hear the reaction from those idiots who took away my license!"

"But this can't be about personal recognition, Nancy. Try to get some perspective. What you're doing is unethical."

"Oh, really! And why is that? What's wrong with using an animal to give someone a chance of having their own biological child? Think about it, Josh. Is this really a matter of ethics? You know, I get the distinct feeling there's a gender thing at work here. What's the problem? Can't stand it that a woman's done something extraordinary?" She started to walk towards the door, then wheeled around abruptly.

"And maybe it's not just the other guys on the committee. You never could stand competing with me. That's why we broke up in the first place. Come to think of it, you've been sabotaging my career ever since I came back to the Lying-In." She started to tick off the examples on her fingers. "You wouldn't help with my pig experiment; you snooped around and turned me in on the Samuel Foster case; and you wouldn't defend me when I was kicked off the hospital staff. You know what, Josh?

It's finally dawning on me. You're jealous!"

Josh's mouth fell open. "Jealous! You know, you really are over the edge, Nancy! When have you ever seen me do anything that could justify that kind of statement? You know I've never been interested in research. And besides, you're hardly in a position to be jealous of right now."

"Oh, really? That's great, Josh. Kick me while I'm down, you jerk! Dredge up all the old shit. I should've seen this coming. You've just been looking for an excuse to let go of your feelings for me. And don't think I can't see through your little 'reluctant' charade, claiming to be disinterested in research. I don't care what you say about treating patients as individuals. You know damn well you'd rather treat an interesting case than something routine. This whole thing started with your grand rounds presentation on abdominal pregnancy. And in case you've forgotten, I was there to congratulate you that day, and now you're sabotaging my work again!"

"What! What the hell's with you, Nancy? You know what? I take it back. You're not just over the edge. You're completely out of touch! And my 'feelings' for you are strictly platonic, by the way. I've tried to help you out of a sense of friendship and now you're twisting things around like everything was my fault."

Nancy's features turned even more sinister.

"Right," she said disdainfully,'

" 'Platonic.' The virtuous golden boy. Well, I've seen the way you look at me, Josh, so don't give me that platonic crap. And not only that! You sold me out! And you can't see a medical breakthrough when it's staring you in the face!" She glared at him briefly. "You know what? I want you to leave!" She stormed to her front door and flung it open. "Now, Josh! I want you out of here. Right now!"

Before he could react she turned on him and struck him in the chest with both hands.

"GET OUT, I SAID! GET OUT OF MY APARTMENT!"

FIFTY

After three weeks of legal maneuvering, posturing, and showmanship; three weeks of testimony and counter testimony; three weeks of media hype and chaos, the murder trial of Dr. Nancy Sanderson was finally nearing its end. The long awaited concluding arguments were at hand.

As per legal protocol, the prosecution went first. District Attorney Burke rose from his chair, briefly leaned over to listen to something his assistant whispered to him, and then walked slowly, deliberately to his position before the jury box. Before he spoke, he scanned both rows of jurors, managing in a very few seconds to make eye contact with each of them. Then, without further preliminaries, he launched into his argument.

"'Murder,' ladies and gentlemen, is a harsh word. It's not a word, or a term, that we should take lightly, and it's certainly not a charge that anyone should make against anyone else without some very strong evidence. When we hear that term, 'murder', what comes to mind is a crime of passion, that there's a weapon involved, that hatred or greed or theft is part of the picture, that the perpetrator is either sociopathic or mentally imbalanced. But I submit to you that murder can take many forms, and one of those forms is knowingly and recklessly putting someone else's life in danger, especially when doing so will result in some form of personal achievement by the perpetrator. And that is exactly what we're dealing with here. Dr. Sanderson maintains that Mr. Foster pleaded with her to perform this experiment on him, to implant a pregnancy in his abdomen. But he was not a doctor, or a scientist. Surely he didn't dream up this idea on his own. So then, where did this bizarre notion come from? You know the answer to that. It came from Dr. Sanderson. She recognized a decent man who was emotionally vulnerable, she took advantage of him, and she led him like a lamb to the slaughter. Now there are elements in this story that were not permitted to be introduced in this trial. But what I can tell you for certain is that Mr. Foster had the misfortune of being in the wrong place, at the wrong time, and with the wrong doctor; a doctor who was an ambitious, glory seeking researcher who knowingly, recklessly, and intentionally disregarded the rules for experimentation.

There are protocols for research methodology. They are overseen, monitored and enforced by organizations such as the FDA, the Food and Drug Administration. This process is designed to protect the public from poorly designed medical trials, from products that haven't been investigated properly, and from ambitious, self-promoting researchers who are so intent on making a name for themselves that they skirt around the rules and don't bother to get the approval of an overseeing agency. And when that happens, the perpetrator surrenders any protection that the system provides. They are outliers. They are out-laws! They are breaking the law, and that makes them criminals.

And that's what happened in this case. Dr. Sanderson intentionally ignored due process. She was so intent on making a name for herself that she led this innocent, decent man to his death. For personal aggrandizement! When she was on the witness stand you heard her say that she was devastated by what happened. But then, Dr. Cantor, a physician himself, and with a spotless reputation, testified that when Dr. Sanderson was confronted with what she had done, she was proud of it. She actually suggested that the hospital where she worked should arrange a press conference to announce the achievement of creating a pregnancy in a man. Never mind that he died.

Never mind that his wife was heartbroken. What was important to her was that she would be recognized for a groundbreaking experiment. An experiment! On a human being who unwittingly signed his own death warrant!

So don't be confused by any preconceived images of a murderer. They're not all hit men, or thugs, or robbers, or convicts who have been in and out of prisons for half of their lives. Sometimes they're brilliant. Sometimes they have stunning academic credentials. Sometimes they're young and beautiful. But your responsibility - your very weighty responsibility - is to make a decision on the evidence, with no regard for those other attributes.

Nancy Sanderson killed Samuel Foster just as sure as if she had given him poison, or put a gun to his head and pulled the trigger. She murdered him, ladies and gentlemen, and she's guilty. Guilty of murder. You must do your duty to serve justice, and to serve your fellow citizens, by bringing back the only verdict that fits this crime. Guilty. Guilty as charged".

At first the only sound in the courtroom was the sound of the DA's heels clicking on the marble floor as he returned to his chair. Once he was seated, however, a soft murmuring began, followed by a gradual crescendo until the room was filled with animated debate. But as defense attorney Charlie Cross approached the jury box, the buzz abruptly ceased as though someone had thrown a switch. Cross began with a deep sigh.

"Ladies and Gentlemen of the jury," he drawled, "I want to thank each and ever' one o' you. It's been a long time, and y'all have made a real contribution here. You've put your life on hold, your jobs, your families, and I just want you to know that it's very much appreciated. You're makin' a real contribution to society, and I believe that's what our civilization's all about, don't you agree?

In this case, y'all have a grave responsibility. You're holdin' the future of a very special human being in your hands, a brilliant doctor who has so much to contribute to the world, if only she'll be allowed to do it."

He paused for a moment, paced, and thumbed his oversized suspenders.

"Now, let's

"Now, let's think about it. What are we decidin' here? Well, it's actually pretty straightforward.

"What it comes down to is whether it's considered murder when a patient dies after a doctor does something that's never been done before, even if that patient knew what the doctor was doin'. Even if that patient wanted to have it done. Even if he pleaded to have it done. Even if he did it because he loved his wife so much that he would risk his life for her. You heard Mrs. Foster's own words, ladies and gentlemen. When I asked her if she loved her husband, she said she couldn't even begin to tell me how much.

And when I asked her if she would do anything for him, she didn't hesitate. She said yes. And then when I asked her if he would do anything for her, she gave the same answer. Because it was true. Samuel Foster would do anything for Ellen, his wife who desperately wanted a baby of her own, even though Dr. Sanderson informed him, again and again, that what he was asking her to do was a terribly risky procedure, one that had never been done before.

"Now let's talk about that for a minute. 'A procedure that's never been done before.'

Have y'all ever heard o' heart transplants? Sure ya have. They been around for a while now. In fact, as I look at the faces in the jury box, it occurs to me that some of you might not have been alive when they did the first one. Well, now, there was a first one.

And I was around to witness what was happenin' back then. A doctor in South Africa did it. And of course his patient knew there was a terrible risk, that he might die. And ladies and gentlemen, that first patient did die. But did anyone come around and start accusin' the doctor of murder? Of course not, because the patient knew the risks and the doctor did his homework.

Now multiply that story many, many times, because every operation or medical procedure that's ever been done had to start somewhere, didn't it? Someone had to be the first patient to take the risk. And of course that's what happened here. And not to someone who was misled or duped into it. Mr. Foster was a willing patient. He knew his risks. He knew what he was doing. It was his choice, clear and simple.

Now lemme give y'all another example. What about our brave astronauts? Some o' them aren't around to tell you about what is was like to be part of that effort, and you all know why: because some of them died as a result of accidents or complications, even though there was a tremendous effort put forth for their safety. So what happened after they lost their lives? Was there sadness? Sure there was. Was there grief? Were their families upset? Of course they were. Who wouldn't be? Did anyone criticize NASA? You bet they did. Ever'body jumped all over 'em. They called for their jobs.

They called for an end to space exploration. But did anyone accuse them of murder, even though they were the ones who had engineered those projects? No sir, and no, ma'am, they did not. Because those astronauts knew the risks. And they believed those risks were worth taking.

Now you can nitpik and argue that those examples are different from what happened here. And yes, they're not exactly the same. But folks, there is one fundamental, common factor. None of these people who died were doing something against their will. And when you talk about murder, that's a fundamental element. It is done against the victim's will. And of course that's not what happened here. So even if you doubt Dr. Sanderson's motives, even if you think she was blinded by ambition, there's one thing you cannot, and must not, overlook. By the meaning of the term, Samuel Foster was not the victim of murder, because nothing was done to him against his will. And so there is no choice here. Your decision is whether Dr. Nancy Sanderson is guilty of murder. You are not being asked if you approve of what she did. You are not being asked if you think it's against the laws of nature for a man to carry a pregnancy. What you are being asked is whether she committed murder, and therefore you must return a verdict of not guilty. Not guilty, ladies and gentlemen. Not guilty.

And one more thing, folks. I don't know what y'all think of me, but I'm not a fool. I know Boston's a big, sophisticated city, and I know I don't look like I belong here.

I dress different. I talk different. I know folks make fun o' me. But I know the law, and I know my client, Dr. Sanderson. And I know that this brilliant young woman burns with a passion to make a contribution to the welfare of her patients, and the thousands, the millions, who are not able to have children of their own. And so I ask you, please, even though you might not like what you see when you look at me, or my accent that sounds so strange in this part of our country, or some of the things they say about me in the newspapers; please, please, do not let that carry over onto Dr. Sanderson.

Whatever you think of me, just remember what I said about the definition of murder, that it has to be done against someone's will. If you do that, I know you'll do the right thing. You will find Dr. Sanderson not guilty. I thank you.

Cross said no more. He played it straight. No fawning gestures, no humble pie. When he finished he simply turned, walked to his chair and sat down.

FIFTY-ONE

After Charlie Cross finished his closing remarks, the judge turned to the jury.

"At his point I would normally address you on how you are to proceed, and then you would be led to a private room to deliberate. However, I'm aware that this has been an arduous day, and it is now nearly 3:30, so I'd like to know if you want to break for the day, or if you are prepared to receive my instructions right now and begin deliberations this evening. Show of hands, please. First option: stop the proceedings until tomorrow."

Twelve hands went up. Everyone wanted a break.

"Very well," the judge said. "We will reconvene here at nine AM. But in the meantime you will continue to not discuss this case with each other or anyone else. And that applies to everyone, including your families, no matter how close you are to any individual. Is that clearly understood?"

Again the response was unanimous. "Yes, Your Honor."

Josh Cantor exited the courtroom with the other spectators and headed to his office.

While there he dealt with a few messages, then leaned back in his chair and began to reflect on Nancy Sanderson and her outrageous pig experiment. The situation troubled Josh greatly, but he wasn't quite sure what to do about it. Having already turned in Nancy for the Samuel Foster case, should he go to some authority about this as well?

And if so, to whom?

He began to compile a list of people who could help him think clearly.

The first person he crossed off was Aviva. It would have to be someone who could be dispassionate, and she definitely wasn't there right now. There was Michael Wilson, a clear thinker whom he could trust implicitly, but Michael's background wasn't in the biological sciences, nor was he uninvolved emotionally. How about the department chairman, Leon Landry? Solid guy, but considering how he felt about Nancy, he'd surely go ballistic over something like this.

The logical choice, he decided, was his colleague, Howard Greenwald. Howard could be blunt, but Josh knew he'd get an objective opinion. He called the perinatal department and found him there.

"Howard, I need to talk to you."

"Yeah? What's wrong? Something with Aviva?"

"No, but I need to meet with you privately."

"All right, c'mon over. I'll be finished in half an hour."

"Perfect. I'll be there."

Greenwald was immediately caught up in the story, barely managing to wait for Josh to finish. "In a pig?! And you really think she's hit on a way to avoid an immune response?"

"I don't know, Howard, but if this doesn't work it'll lead to the blatant wastage of a mature human fetus. And knowing Nancy, she'll keep trying."

"Yeah," Greenwald responded, "but if does work it's gonna turn the world upside down. You know, Josh, I used to believe there really wasn't anything new under the sun, but then Nancy pulled her stunt with that Foster guy, and now there's a human embryo growing in a pig! …. Hell, I don't know what to tell you. I can't think of any precedent for this."

"Neither can I, Howard. My only question is how to force Nancy to divulge it, because if she won't I'll have to go public with it myself."

"Oh, I think she'll go public with it soon enough. She wants the recognition. You can bet your ass on that."

"But how can I put a stop to it? She actually wants to continue this craziness."

"I didn't say I think she needs to stop it. It's a wild idea, but I think maybe she's hit on something extraordinary."

"You can't be serious, Howard! A human baby from a pig? It's against the laws of nature. It's repugnant. It's … immoral!"

"Immoral?" Greenwald raised his eyebrows. Now you're getting into some fuzzy stuff, Josh. If you ask me, morality's just a function of necessity.

Whose morality are we talking about, anyway?"

"What do you mean, 'whose morality'? You think the rules change for every different situation?"

"Absolutely, Greenwald said. "When needs are pressing enough, definitions adapt. Like in China. There's no big debate about abortion over there 'cause they just don't like girl babies and they already have a billion people to feed. Hell, they pretty much force women to abort when they're gonna have a second kid." He turned up his palms. "Like I said, morality's a function of necessity."

"I'm not sure I can buy that, Howard. You can't turn that stuff on and off like a switch. And besides, how's that apply to growing a human baby in a pig's abdomen?"

"Well, let's think about it. Just try putting yourself in someone else's shoes. Consider how desperate your infertility patients are. Ask them how they'd feel about incubating their baby in an animal's body. Hell, ask your own wife, for God's sake! Don't you think she'd accept this idea if it could really give her a baby and she wouldn't have to worry about some surrogate changing her mind at the last minute? You know damn well what she'd say.

She'd say 'let's go for it!' Then ask yourself whether your 'immorality' argument still applies."

Josh was stunned, but he could see that Greenwald had more on his mind. "Go ahead, Howard. Whatever it is, just say it."

"Look, Josh. I have to admit I was ready to fry Nancy after that guy died, but this is another matter. She might be a wacko, or she just might be light years ahead of the rest of us."

They looked at each other before Greenwald continued. "And what about this? Maybe her motives are commendable, or maybe they're not.

Let's just put that aside for now. Maybe the fact that she's not bound by ethical considerations gives her an advantage. Maybe it allows her to explore research areas that would be unthinkable to someone else. In fact, maybe that's the ideal personality makeup for a researcher. And you know, Josh, it even strikes me that one of the reasons you haven't wanted to get so involved in research is that your designs are too restricted by your own ethical standards." He paused before delivering a final speculation.

"And one last thing: What if she turns out to be right?"

Josh was speechless.

"So?" Greenwald prompted.

"I don't know, Howard. I just don't know ..."

The next morning saw Joshua Cantor arriving at his office as usual.

As usual he took stock of the articles on his desk, and as usual he smiled and blessed Aviva's picture. But this day was not a usual day. On this day he was deep in self examination about his place in the world. He was stunned to think that someone he respected as much as Howard Greenwald could take such a perspective on Nancy Sanderson's work. Was he being narrow minded by balking at this?

He shook his head in exasperation. How had he gotten so involved in all of this anyway? All he wanted was for him and Aviva to have a family like everyone else.

Now the question was whether to tell Aviva about Nancy's experiment. So far he had kept it from her but he knew she had picked up on his strained behavior yesterday. He worried about the impression he had given her. Perhaps his distance made her think he was angry. Even so, up until now he believed he was doing the right thing by not divulging this new option. This morning, however, she had wished him good-bye with a worried face, so now he wasn't so sure.

He wrestled with himself, falling deeper into introspection, trying to see it from an objective critic's point of view. He recalled a particular teaching from the ancient Jewish sage Hillel, one often quoted by Josh's father: "If I am not for myself, who will be for me? But if I am only for myself, then what am I? And if not now, when?"

His attention shifted to the wall which held a framed prayer formulated by the twelfth century philosopher/physician Moses Maimonides. Josh had received it as a gift for medical school graduation and he disciplined himself to read it every morning. Titled "The Daily Prayer of the Physician", it encapsulated what medical practitioners should strive for. His eyes fell on the middle portion:

"Should more learned physicians wish to teach me wisdom, grant me the will to learn" ... and, later in the text ... "Grant that truth be my only guide ..." Through his reverie he heard his name being called ...

"Doctor Cantor? ... Doctor? ...."

The voice became clearer...

"Doctor?... Are you all right, Doctor?"

He turned to see a familiar silhouette emerging through his fog, the image slowly focusing into the shape of Bridget Walsh. "I'm sorry to disturb you, Doctor. You were far away for a minute there. Mrs. Cantor's on the phone, and it sounds like she's crying."

Josh picked up his receiver. "Are you okay, Viv?"

"Please don't be mad at me, Joshua," she sobbed. "You've done so much and I know I'm being selfish. I'll go back to the adoption agency if you want. Just tell me what you want me to do."

Josh felt his heart breaking. His eyes drifted to her smiling photograph.

"I'm not mad, Viv. I'm sorry I gave you that impression."

"Are you sure?"

"Yes, honey, I'm sure. And Viv?"

"Yes?"

"I think we need to talk. There might be another option ...."

EPILOGUE

After two full days of deliberation, the jury requested that portions of testimony be read back to them. Then, just before noon on the third day, the foreman asked to speak to the judge.

"Your Honor, we can't come to an agreement. I'm afraid we're deadlocked."

The judge was not pleased. "That's not what I want to hear," he scowled. "First of all, I need to know how your votes are divided," he said. "How many on one side and how many on the other." "It's ten to two, Your Honor," the foreman said. "And the two dissenters aren't budging."

"Well, I'm not about to declare a mistrial," he said sharply. "That's simply not acceptable. This is too soon to give up. I want you to continue your deliberations, and I want all of you to keep an open mind. All of you," he repeated. "Not just the dissenters.

Those of you in the majority are to listen to the minority members just as attentively as they are expected to listen to you. So right now I would suggest you take a break for lunch, but then you are to return to the jury room. And when you are back in there I want you to apply yourselves with every ounce of energy you can summon. And I would also suggest that you change seats, because a different physical perspective might give you a fresh mental viewpoint as well."

The jurors groaned, but did as they were told. And to everyone's surprise, just after noon the next day they sent word that they had reached a verdict.

Bridgette Walsh informed Dr. Cantor that CNN had announced a news flash.

He joined her in the office break room and waited impatiently as the camera panned from the judge, to the attorneys, to the empty jury box.

The CNN reporter spoke in an urgent whisper while closed captioning scrolled across the bottom of the screen.

"After months of anticipation, and days of waiting for the jury to deliberate, we are finally to receive a verdict in the bizarre case of Dr. Nancy Sanderson. As you have surely heard by now, Dr. Sanderson is the physician who conducted an unauthorized experiment by implanting a pregnancy in the abdomen of a human male, Mr. Samuel Foster, and Mr. Foster died from complications of that pregnancy. And now, at last, we are to have closure. Is Dr. Sanderson guilty of murder, or will Mr. Foster's signed consent prove to be the document that exonerates her? Here now is the moment we have been waiting for ....

The courtroom was stone silent as the jurors filed in, each of them looking as though they'd rather be somewhere else, every face a mask of fatigue.

The judge waited for them to settle, then asked the long awaited question.

"Mr. Foreman, have you reached a verdict?"

The foreman stood, appearing shaky and pale. He steadied himself by grasping the rail in front of him.

"Are you all right, sir?" the judge inquired.

"Yes, Your Honor," came the subdued reply.

"And have you reached a verdict?"

"Yes, Your Honor."

"Very well. What say you?"

The foreman brought his fist to his mouth to cover a nervous cough, then drew a breath and exhaled through pursed lips.

Finally he opened his mouth to speak ....

END

LaVergne, TN USA
14 April 2010
179158LV00004B/22/P